HUMAN RITES

JJ MARSH

TRISKELE BOOKS

Cover design: JD Smith
Original artwork: James Lane

Printed in the United Kingdom by Lightning Source.

Published by Prewett Publishing.
All enquiries to admin@beatrice-stubbs.com

First printing, 2015
ISBN 978-3-9524258-6-2

For Aine Kiely and Jo Rowling
Confidantes, conspirators and *tosta mista* sisters

Chapter 1

A controversial decision, placing a forty-five quid bottle of German Syrah at the top of the tree, but in Adrian's opinion it was justified. He tied a glass golden star to the neck with red ribbon and angled the spotlight to hit it directly in the middle. Warm and luxurious was what he was aiming for, to create desire in passers-by. He clambered out of the window display with great care, put the spare decorations on the counter and went outside to assess his handiwork.

"Oh yes," he murmured. Tapering tiers of wine bottles sparkled dark green under the lights, the claret and emerald baubles spoke of sophistication and the gold star caught the eye as if to say *here's what you've been looking for*. He waited till a black cab had rattled past and crossed the street to get another perspective. The bottle tree looked beautiful and enticing and seasonal without being tacky. Not an easy feat. Thankfully the garish street lights depicting cartoon reindeer were limited to Shoreditch High Street so nothing detracted from his display.

He folded his arms against the chill and pretended he was a weary office worker, trudging home in the dark. It was ten to four but dusk had already fallen, and Harvey's Wine Emporium stood out in the gloomy grey of Bethnal Green Road, a glittering temptation. Shivering but satisfied, Adrian crossed over and checked the alignment of the labels. One pinot noir could be shifted a millimetre to the left, but other than that, it was precision stacking.

As he came through the door, Judy Garland's voice warbled from the speakers. One of the many things Adrian detested about the festive season was the bombardment of truly dreadful Christmas songs from every outlet, but on this occasion, Judy wishing him a merry little one seemed entirely appropriate. He sang along as he adjusted the pinot noir then nipped back outside to be certain of absolute perfection.

Damp air penetrated his sweater, but the window looked exactly as he'd pictured it. He rubbed his upper arms as he smiled at the rows of hand-picked reds and congratulated himself. That was when he sensed he was being watched. He adjusted his focus. Reflected in the glass was a nun, standing on the opposite pavement, gazing at his shop window. Adrian turned to face her with every intention of fishing for compliments but she'd already begun walking away, her face averted. Embarrassed to be coveting forbidden fruit, no doubt. He returned to Judy, delighted his seasonal arrangement was already having an effect.

At five o'clock, Catinca arrived for her shift and they worked together for an hour to cover the evening rush. Adrian advised an older couple on dessert wines and directed a stressed suit towards the Date Night selection, while Catinca chirped and cackled at the till. No matter what age or gender, she got a smile or a laugh from every single customer. Adrian suspected some regulars delayed their purchases until after five, so they could enjoy the added bonus of her irrepressible good humour and personal transformations. This evening, the electric blue hair and indigo jumpsuit were no more than a memory. Now she resembled Marlene Dietrich with her dinner jacket, white shirt and a blue-black Mary Quant bob. The only constants were her Converse trainers and Bow Bells-meets-Bucharest accent.

"Get out of it! You worry about calories? Rubbish! Look at you. And wine is grapes so part of five a day. Cheers mate, here is change."

"You like it? Ta very much. No more purple. Is colour of

bishops and suicide. Kettle chips go well with cava, want to try new flavour?"

"Adrian! This lady wants port wine. Tony, not Ruby. Go over and see him, darling, one in stripey jumper."

When the activity died down, Adrian fetched his coat from the office and prepared to leave.

"Catinca, I'm off. Any problems, give me a call. I'm at home tonight. And book a cab to take you home, OK? Just remember to get a receipt."

"Yeah, yeah. I never forget. Your window looks cool."

"Do you think so? It took me most of the afternoon but it's certainly turning heads. Hey, do you know whether nuns are allowed to drink?"

Catinca thought about it. "Yeah, must be. Is a wine called Blue Nun, innit?"

"True. Right, have a good evening and I'll see you tomorrow."

"Cheers, mate. Laters. Don't forget Christmas card."

"Thanks. First one I've had this year."

The Christmas card situation occupied his thoughts the bus journey home. It wasn't the first one he'd had, but most of the cards on his mantelpiece were from suppliers, colleagues and the occasional client of the Wine Emporium, all delivered to the shop. In previous years he'd had to clear the windowsills and use the top of the TV to house his collection of robins, snowmen and glittery greetings. But it was mid-December and he'd not even received one from his mum. In fact, he wasn't sure when he'd last had any post at all.

When he got home to Boot Street, he immediately checked his mailbox in the communal hall. Empty. Not even any junk. He pushed open the slot bearing the name B. Stubbs. Stuffed to overflowing. He tried S. Fasman. Empty. What was it with the ground floor? He rang Saul's bell.

The door opened to a smell of frying onions and Saul wiping his hands on his customary grey jogging suit. Adrian reflected for a second on the irony of the name. Saul was no more likely to jog than Adrian was to take up cage-fighting.

"Hello Adrian. All right?"

"Hi Saul. Sorry to disturb you. Just wondered if you've had any problems with the post? Has your mail been getting though?"

"Yeah. I've had all the usual crap, mostly bills and pizza flyers. You waiting for something important?"

"Not really, it's just weird there's been nothing at all for days."

"Days? Nah, you had a delivery yesterday. Or was it this morning? I had to buzz the postie in. Package for you. I knew you weren't home so I said to leave it in the hallway."

"When was this?"

Saul lifted his chin and scratched his rust-coloured beard. "Must have been today, 'cos I was busting a gut to meet my Friday lunchtime deadline. Someone buzzing at the door was the last thing I needed."

"But there's no package out here. No post for me at all. I've just checked."

"That is weird. Maybe Beatrice picked it up for you?"

Adrian shook his head. "She's not home yet. She hasn't picked up her own mail. He didn't ask you to sign for it, did he?"

"Who?"

"The postie."

"No, no, I just pressed the buzzer and let her in."

Adrian thanked him and went back to his own flat, planning to call his mother to ask if she'd already sent her cards. He switched on the light and as he closed the door, he noticed a piece of paper on the mat.

At first he thought it was blank, but when he flipped it over, there was something typed in the middle of the page.

Romans 6:23

He frowned. Was that a TV schedule, a football score or a bible reference? None would make any sense to him. Without even taking off his coat, he took the paper into his study, opened his laptop and typed the word and numbers into a search engine.

He clicked on the first search result for The King James Bible and there in big red letters was the verse.

For the wages of sin is death
but the gift of God is eternal life
through Jesus Christ our Lord.

Chapter 2

Beatrice buried her nose deeper into her scarf as she trudged down Dacre Street, needle-sharp raindrops assailing her forehead. The Cayman Islands would be nice. Some gentle little money-laundering scam to investigate, then fly home once the crocuses come out. Perhaps she should ask Hamilton for a transfer.

"Sir, since we've agreed I can take early retirement by the end of next year, could you assign me to something relaxing in the Caribbean for a few months?"

Even in the dreary gloom of her Monday morning commute, the thought of provoking Hamilton's apoplexy raised a smile. Until she remembered the meeting. Operation Horseshoe and zero hopes of escaping a London winter. She stopped off for a bucket of caffeinated milk and entered the office with a nutty croissant and a scowl.

"Morning, Beatrice! Don't forget it's Secret Santa today! You got your pressie all wrapped?" Melanie sat behind the reception desk, an elf hat perched on top of her headset, waggling long false nails encrusted with crystals.

"Morning, Melanie. Yes, it's in my bag. When are we doing this?"

Melanie let out a bubble of laughter. "When do you think!? Christmas lunch, just before the pudding. You'll never guess what..."

"No, I won't because I cannot be arsed. It's Monday bloody morning, I'm wet and cold and I have a meeting with Hamilton in ten minutes. What?"

Melanie's face drooped into a sympathetic pout as she tilted her head to one side. "Awww. Bless. You do look a bit parky. Anyway, Hamilton's in hospital, so that's one thing off your plate. The meeting's still on for nine though, with Ranga as Acting Superintendent."

"Hospital? What's the matter?"

"Dunno. Got a message this morning." She clicked the mouse and read from her screen. *"Unexpected hospital attendance required. Updates as and when. DCI Jalan please take helm."* She looked at Beatrice, her artfully painted eyes huge. "You reckon it's his teeth again?"

Ranga spent several minutes of the team meeting on small talk, asking Dawn Whittaker about her house move, joking with Russell Cooper about his latest rugby injury, soliciting Beatrice's opinion on cheeseboards and enquiring after Joe Bryant's new puppy. The atmosphere grew warmer, softer, and every face around the table relaxed. Beatrice knew he would be such a perfect boss and wondered if there was a way to persuade him not to retire. If so, maybe she'd follow suit.

"Now then, down to business. I am not exactly sure what is wrong with Superintendent Hamilton or when he is likely to return to work. I have asked Melanie to send flowers and I will call the hospital later to find out more. Nevertheless, we have to move on in his absence. We need to make staffing decisions regarding Operation Horseshoe. Next Monday, I have a meeting with three out of four of the religious leaders involved. I would like to introduce them to whoever will eventually take over.

"Relationships with the community are the cornerstone of this op. This team is especially trained to be culturally sensitive in order to communicate with a broad range of ages and backgrounds. Given the long-term nature of public liaison, we're looking for a capable manager to develop this unit in the future. Beatrice, I know Hamilton wanted you for this one, but given your own plans to retire next year, my view is that it could be counter-productive to switch the senior detective in twelve months' time."

Beatrice nodded. "That's exactly what I said. To me, it makes far more sense for Dawn to head this op. She's got a great track record of forming alliances and proved her mettle in the knife crime operation. Plus, unlike me, Dawn's just reaching her prime."

Dawn laughed and a faint blush tinted her cheeks. But rather than speak, she opened her palms to her colleagues to offer their opinions. An offer Russell Cooper could not refuse.

"No-brainer as far as I'm concerned. Dawn's perfect for it. She was solid gold on knife crime and can talk to anyone, young or old, black or white, vic or perp and even if she does lack management experience, six months working alongside you will sort that out. What do you reckon, Joe?"

In contrast to Russell's trombone tones, Joe Bryant's softly accented Cornish speech was a tin whistle.

"Yeah, if Beatrice really is going to retire..."

"I am."

"Damn shame, but we've had that discussion. It's logical to assign someone who'll take it on for longer. I'll stick my hand up and vote for Dawn. Does that mean we can have Beatrice for the trafficking enquiry?"

Ranga smiled. "One second, Joe. We've heard from everyone but Dawn herself. How do you feel, DI Whittaker?"

Beatrice watched her friend's face. She was glowing like a like a child presented with a birthday cake. "On condition my apprenticeship satisfies Ranga and the other community leaders, if I achieve all the targets set during the training period, as long as my colleagues and the Super approve and Beatrice doesn't see me as a cuckoo then yes, I'd love to join Operation Horseshoe."

Beatrice could tell from Ranga's beam that her decision was

what he wanted. She watched Dawn laugh and enjoyed a huge swell of vicarious joy. After years of unhappiness following public betrayal, humiliation, loneliness, grief, and bitter resentment, Dawn was rebuilding her private life. Plus her dogged hard work was proving a success at the Met. Not that she or any of her colleagues would comment publicly, but this year had been a turning point.

"I guess we have to wait for Hamilton's green light first?" Dawn asked.

Ranga shook his head. "I'm DCI and currently Acting Superintendent, so the decision is mine. Plus we have no idea when he will be back. DI Whittaker is assigned to Operation Horseshoe. As of now."

The team burst into a brief round of applause before Russell Cooper's voice drowned it out.

"Good on you, Dawnie! You've had a shitty few years with the divorce and kids and everything. But look at you now! New bloke, new flat and taking over a major op!" He stuck his hand across the table. "And I tell you what, that haircut takes years off you. Put it there, mate!"

Ranga, Beatrice and Joe stared at Russell in disbelief. But Dawn crumpled into laughter and took Russell's hand.

"Good luck in the Diplomatic Corps, Cooper. Thanks everyone. I really appreciate the vote of confidence."

Ranga gave a satisfied sigh and turned to Beatrice. "How do you fancy something relaxing with a bit of travel, DI Stubbs?"

Beatrice stared at him. "Acting Superintendent Rangarajan Jalan, you couldn't have made me happier unless you included a slice of Christmas cake."

"Would *Stollen* suffice?"

"Ah. When you said a bit of travel, I pictured the Caribbean. But as it happens, I'm extremely partial to *Stollen* and Germany's lovely at this time of year. What's going on?"

"Art theft. An incident in Richmond last week may have a connection to two similar robberies. One in Hamburg, another in Amsterdam. I'd like you to follow up and report your findings to the Interpol Cultural Protection Task Force. I have a file prepared for you and meetings already lined up. Interview the victim, take detailed notes on the circumstances, hop over to Germany, compare notes and spend the weekend visiting Christmas markets. We get Brownie points for cross-border collaboration and the insurance company here will be satisfied. How does that sound?"

"Like a piece of cake."

Chapter 3

Monday was Adrian's day off. When he started his business, he'd worked twelve hour shifts, six days a week. Now he could afford to employ Catinca for the evenings and they both worked Saturdays. In order to give himself a proper break he closed the shop on Mondays. He loved the freedom of having half his weekend while everyone else was at work. It was also an opportunity to indulge his latest hobby: gourmet cooking.

His upstairs neighbour's loathing of Mondays was well-known, so he'd fallen into the habit of creating something extravagant or adventurous for Monday evening and inviting Beatrice to pass judgement. She said it made starting the week bearable. Today's menu was Salmon Wellington with asparagus and Swiss chard. In the oven, his concoction changed colours. The sliver of fish visible between the pastry edges turned from raw and grey to golden pink, matching the evening sky. A South African Chenin Blanc chilled in the fridge and the table bore a Nordic theme, as close to festive as he could bear.

He'd just begun preparing the vegetables when he heard the external door slam shut. All his calm and positive thinking dissolved in a second. He dropped the knife, rinsed his hands and hurried to the hallway, drying his hands on his apron. On tiptoes, he crept up to his apartment door and looked through the peephole but the vestibule was pitch dark; whoever was out there hadn't switched on the hall light. Adrian waited, straining to hear over his own pulsing heartbeat. Silence. It occurred to him that the door may have indicated an exit rather than an entrance. He switched off the living-room lamp and rushed to the window. Purposeful figures strode along the pavements, wrapped up against the weather, intent on getting out of the cold.

He began to relax. People were allowed to enter and leave the building. One disturbing note should not make him this jittery. His post had arrived as normal over the weekend and his mantelpiece was now crowded with cards. A Royal Mail hiccup and someone's idea of a joke would not affect his equilibrium. And he had asparagus to blanch. He turned back towards the kitchen, inhaling the scent of fish, pastry and dill. He was just reaching for the lamp when he glanced out of the side window and froze.

Under the street light on Coronet Street stood a nun, looking straight at his window. Totally still, hands clasped to her chest, her eyes were fixed on his apartment. Adrian stepped closer to the glass and saw she was not completely immobile. Her lips moved rapidly as if she were reciting a litany. He leaned forwards once again and the orange sodium glow hit his face. She registered the movement and ducked away behind next door's wheelie bins and into the shadows. At that precise moment, the doorbell rang and Adrian jumped like a hare.

He checked the peephole and opened the door. "Beatrice!"

"Yes. The person you invited for dinner."

"Of course, I'm just... you're early."

Beatrice checked her watch. "Ten minutes late, actually. But even if I were, you look like you've just seen Lord Lucan wheeled in by Elvis. Whatever's wrong?"

"Nothing! Nothing at all. Just a little bit behind with my preparations. Come in, sit down and tell me about your day."

Beatrice perched on a breakfast stool, opened the wine and chattered about the big religious unity police thing while Adrian boiled the water and chopped the chard, all the while acting attentive. Every time he passed the window, he checked. The nun had gone.

"Ooh, the smell! I'm positively drooling. Thank you for cooking for me."

"You're most welcome. Tuck in. Why are you in such a good mood on a Monday?"

"I've just been telling you. The outcome of today is that everyone's a winner. Ranga's got his replacement, it's a feather in Dawn's hat and I'm assigned to something cushy involving European art galleries. Berlin on Wednesday, then Amsterdam and on to Hamburg. After that I'm going to stay for the weekend."

An unexpected surge of disappointment mixed with envy rose in Adrian's chest. They'd planned a Tate Night on Friday and he didn't want to go alone.

"Lucky you! Can I come?" he asked, not entirely joking.

"This is absolutely delicious! The pastry is superb. Is this spinach?"

"Swiss chard. Thank you. There's hollandaise to go with the asparagus in the gravy boat."

"Such extravagance for a school night. I wish you could come with me, actually. You'd be the ideal companion for poking around galleries and markets. Pity you have to work on Saturday."

As Beatrice poured the custard-coloured sauce in a zigzag over her spears, Adrian had an idea.

"Will Matthew be joining you over the weekend?"

Beatrice, mouth full, shook her head.

"Tell me if this is a stupid idea, but what if I left Catinca to mind the shop on Saturday and flew over to join you? That's exactly why I hired her, to give myself more freedom. I fancy a mini-break somewhere different. We could visit galleries, pick up some unusual gifts in the markets, drink mulled wine and if we're in Hamburg, we could say hello to Holger."

Beatrice swallowed, her eyes bright. "Quite the opposite of

a stupid idea. That would be the cherry on the cake! Matthew can't come as he's got two university Christmas soirées to attend, so your company would be most welcome. Shall I check which hotel they've booked me into and we can stay in the same place?"

Adrian's first bubbles of excitement surfaced at the thought of a spontaneous getaway and a change of scene. "Yes, do. And I'll call Catinca and Holger to make arrangements tomorrow. This could be fun!"

"You should ask Holger for some restaurant tips. How is he? Have you two been in touch?"

"We chat every once in a while, send each other silly postcards, that sort of thing. Just because the relationship didn't work out, it doesn't change the fact he's a really nice guy."

"He is. It would be lovely to see..."

Adrian straightened at the sound of the building's door buzzer, raised a finger to hush Beatrice and went to the peephole. A pizza delivery driver entered the hallway with a cardboard box. Adrian watched until Saul had opened his apartment door and only then returned to his seat.

"Sorry, just wanted to check who was coming in. Saul's having a takeaway. Not quite to the standard of our meal, I'm afraid." He refilled their glasses, aware of Beatrice's gaze.

"I can't imagine many takeaways reaching these heights. It's beautifully cooked and the vegetables go with it so well. I'm going to treat you to a couple of indulgent meals while we're in Germany to say thanks for these Monday marvels."

"There's no need. I told you I like having someone to enjoy it with. Then again, I never say no to an indulgent eating experience."

They ate in near silence for a few minutes; the only sounds the odd murmur of appreciation.

"By the way, did you hear anything else about the disappearing post?" asked Beatrice, adding another blob of hollandaise.

"No, nothing. Deliveries have been completely normal since Friday. The mystery package hasn't turned up yet and no one in the building knows anything about it. So it seems your theory was correct."

"Perhaps, perhaps not. Though I will say it tends to happen a lot in the run up to Christmas. Someone rings a random bell and claims they've got a connection with another person in the building. Other occupants will often press the buzzer out of trust, laziness or lack of thought. The stranger then scopes the place and checks for opportunities such as keys under doormats."

"Or packages sitting in the hallway."

"Or packages sitting in the hallway. But I didn't mean to unnerve you. If you like, I can get some police-approved wording for a security leaflet. We could stick one in everyone's letterbox."

"Might be an idea. We could all do with being a bit more careful."

Beatrice scooped up the last of the pastry and placed her knife and fork together. "That meal, in my opinion, trumps the savoury choux puffs. Exactly what a body needs on a December night, but not too heavy. A triumph!"

"Thank you. It was certainly tasty and pretty to look at." He prodded the remains of his food and decided to finish it later.

"Adrian, is everything all right? You seem awfully on edge. I've bent your ear often enough with my problems, so if something's bothering you...? Tell me to mind my own business if you like."

Adrian smiled. Beatrice was a great listener and had always taken him seriously. The trouble was, he didn't even take himself seriously. His imagination was sometimes his worst enemy.

"The only thing bothering me is how to plan for a German mini-break in only four days. I'll need to check the weather and plan my wardrobe. I'm thinking wool and tailoring. And as I intend to bring back presents, should I put the expandable suitcase in the hold, or limit myself to hand luggage only and use my travel-sized toiletries? There's so much to consider. Not least what to eat. Is there a Hamburg speciality, apart from the obvious?"

"Fish, I expect. It's a port, so we'll have seafood coming out of our ears."

"Wonderful. Fish, art, markets and a good companion. I am so looking forward to this!"

Chapter 4

Richmond's Roedean Crescent was a far cry from Boot Street. This was where money lived. The police Vauxhall Insignia eased along the road, offering Beatrice glimpses of gated detached properties shielded by neat hedges or strategically planted trees. Most driveways were empty, but occasionally she spotted a Mercedes, a Range Rover or a Jaguar.

DS Pearce continued his briefing without taking his eyes off the road. It was unnecessary, because Beatrice had familiarised herself with the file, but she chose to listen to Pearce's version. He might have picked up something she'd overlooked, and anyway it was better than making laboured small talk. Pearce was not known for his sense of humour.

"You can see for yourself, plenty of space in the driveways and lots of cars on the street. Easy enough to park up and watch the household's routine. It's pretty regular. A driver arrives to take him into the City at seven every morning. He's a senior asset manager with an investment bank. She takes the kid to school in the Volvo just after half past eight. She's home by nine, and two days a week she lets the cleaning company in. Then she hits the gym, goes shopping and has lunch with a friend. Always back here before the cleaners leave at half-one."

"Is it always the same people from the cleaning company?"

Pearce indicated right and reversed into a space in front of some impressive white gates. "No. Depends on the rota. The two

Filipinas are the most regular, but they're not always available." He turned off the engine. "Ma'am, I'm expecting a hostile reception. This bloke's already given a statement twice and he's got a serious attitude problem. If he starts getting arsey, I'll do the same. Leave you to do the charm stuff."

Beatrice raised her eyebrows. "Thanks, Pearce. I'll do my best."

The door was open by the time they'd crunched across the gravel. No butler, no underling, just the master of the house. Chet Waring stood in the portico, wearing a navy suit and a smile fit for Santa Claus. Against his tanned face, his teeth were startlingly white. Beatrice marched up the steps, ID in her left hand with her right outstretched.

"Mr Waring, my name is DI Stubbs. Thank you for making the time to see us. My colleague DS Pearce I believe you already know."

"It's my pleasure. Really. Knowing you guys are taking this seriously is such a relief for me. Yes indeed, DS Pearce has been a rock during this investigation and I couldn't be more appreciative of his thorough approach."

A cool, firm handshake and a warm smile of welcome. Pearce gave no reaction. After many years of practice, he had perfected the neutral mask. But Beatrice was curious. What attitude problem? They followed him into a magnificent hallway, half filled by a gargantuan Nordic pine that almost obscured the grand piano nestling under the stairs. Waring took their coats and ushered them into a large living space full of expensive paintings, arty knick-knacks and a choice of sofas. Knitted socks hung from the mantelpiece, each with a nametag, while Bing Crosby crooned from hidden speakers.

As soon as they were seated, a young man entered with a tray bearing a coffee pot, jug of milk and a selection of pastries. Waring took it and placed it on the table in front of them. A whiff of nutmeg wafted past Beatrice's nose. Spices, carols, stockings, a pine tree... A Child's Christmas of Clichés.

"Thanks Simon, that's all for now. Coffee, DI Stubbs, DS Pearce? Please help yourself to muffins or whatever. Don't know about you guys but I can't work until I've had my morning sugar fix. The amount I've contributed to Caffè Nero's profits this year? I shoulda bought shares."

"Thank you. I'll have mine with milk, no sugar and perhaps one of those mini Danish affairs. As for business, Mr Waring, we're not here to go over old ground. I'd just like a few more details about the painting itself so we can make comparisons to other art thefts around the world. I must stress this is part of a larger operation and may not be of material use in your particular case. However, all reports of art theft have a wider benefit when reported accurately."

Waring poured coffee for Beatrice and Pearce, listening and nodding with such intensity that Beatrice was tempted to laugh. Instead she bit into her sugar-glazed cake.

"Too right. Cultural artefact databases are the collector's best friends. I already reported this to the Art Loss Register. How can I help?"

"Tell us how you acquired the piece. And why."

"Sure. The painting was in my possession for just over three years. I bought it at auction in New York and paid one million, one hundred fifty thousand dollars for it. Today, that's around three-quarters of a million in sterling. I bought it as an investment, obviously, but also because it's an amazing piece. It packs a real punch. Not everyone likes it as much as I do, of course, but they all notice it. That's why I'm so desperate to get it back. It's the centrepiece of my collection."

"Has anyone else ever offered to purchase it from you?"

"Not that I can recall," Waring replied. "Anyhow, I'd never sell."

"You're insured for the full amount, I assume?"

"Yep. Every artwork I own is covered at the professionally assessed value. I'm pretty risk-averse. I guess that's the norm with people in my line of work."

Pearce spoke. "Why do you think the thieves only took this one painting? As you say, you've got plenty to choose from." He looked around the room, his eyes narrowing. "I'd say those horse figurines on the mantelpiece are Lalique. Not only worth a fair bit but easy to carry. Or these little snuffboxes. Russian, aren't they? Major market for these and not as hard to shift as an original Otto Dix."

Waring's grey eyes widened and his face expanded into a broad smile. "You know your stuff, Detective Pearce! The horses are Lalique. And the snuffboxes, mostly Russian, are worth between three hundred and eight thousand dollars each. But let me assure you, I did a careful inventory, as did my wife, and nothing else is missing. My theory is the thieves were stealing to order. Some wealthy oligarch is amassing German Expressionist art from the 1920s and needed a Dix for his collection. The depressing fact is that if I'm right, I'll never see the painting again."

The smallest twinge of sympathy touched Beatrice at the pain in his voice. Rarely had she grown so attached to an inanimate object that its loss would have caused her grief. Yet she recalled the silver bracelet Matthew had given her on her promotion to Detective Inspector. It was an antique, with tiny golden ivy leaves embossed on the surface. During some rather enthusiastic participation in a New Year's Eve ceilidh, it had come adrift, never to be seen again. It wasn't the bracelet so much as its talismanic significance imbued by emotion.

"Do you have a photograph of the painting, Mr Waring?"

He seemed to bring himself back from an unfocussed emptiness and reignited his smile.

"I have a file with all the documentation regarding provenance and the original catalogue, plus various images of the whole picture, detail and frame. Help yourself to more coffee. I'll just be a moment."

The door closed behind him and Pearce got up to examine one of the other large canvases on the wall between the windows.

Beatrice leaned back to see what had attracted his attention. Roseate flesh and entwined limbs writhing on a chequerboard floor. Exaggerated features and a lack of restraint spilling out across the rigid geometry. It somehow made her think of Liza Minnelli. Pearce wrote something in his notebook as Waring returned.

"What do you think, Detective Pearce? Quite a talent, wouldn't you say?"

"I take it you're a fan of the Expressionist school?"

"Darn right. Are you?"

Pearce sat beside Beatrice and nodded once. "I find certain aspects of the movement have a powerful impact. The social commentary after World War One in German art and British poetry is excoriating."

Beatrice tried not to stare. She knew Pearce specialised in culturally-related crimes, but had never spoken to him on the subject.

Waring's eyes lit up. "My thoughts exactly! You know what, you'll totally get why I miss this painting. Someone with such an appreciation of art is going to understand. This is *The Salon II*."

He opened a glossy catalogue and indicated an A4 print of the original on the right hand page. Beatrice took the brochure and shared it with Pearce. The painting depicted a room, shell pink, with ruby velvet curtains parted to allow the viewer access. Six prostitutes in various states of undress sat around a table. Breasts spilled, stockings slipped, curls escaped pins, lipstick smudged, cigarettes drooped and stains marked the cloth. At the head of the table, a sun blasted out black, grey, puce and golden rays, the light reflecting off each weary woman's face.

The most shocking thing about the piece was the women's eyes. Each face was turned to the viewer, as if they had been surprised. Some eyes were fearful, some glittering, some suspicious, some hopeful, some vacant and resigned. The image made the viewer the object of attention and asked a simple question. *What do you want?* The more you stared, the more complicit you became.

Beatrice pushed the catalogue back to Pearce and stood up. "I see what you mean about it packing a punch. May we keep this file?"

"Sure."

"DS Pearce will continue to handle the robbery line of enquiry, whereas I will pursue the art theft connection. Thank you for your time, Mr Waring. One more thing. Your cleaners – I understand one was hurt. How is she?"

"She's recovering. A bunch of stitches but no permanent damage, thank God. I paid to have her treated privately. Here's my personal card, DI Stubbs. Please feel free to call me whenever you need. Thanks so much for your help."

Back at Scotland Yard, an odd electricity charged the air. Melanie was on the phone and merely pushed a plastic folder towards Beatrice. It contained the details of her flights and accommodation in Germany. Pearce trudged off into the main office to photocopy Waring's documents. Beatrice was hanging up her coat when behind her someone wrenched open a door.

"Stubbs! In here, now."

Hamilton's face, pale and lined, was tight with tension.

"Hello sir. I didn't realise you were back. How are you?"

His only reply was to walk back into his office. Beatrice followed. He winced as he lowered himself into his chair and gestured for her to close the door.

"Bloody furious is how I am. Sit down. You knew perfectly well I wanted you on Operation Horseshoe. I fully expect my team to follow orders whether I'm here or not. Then I find that after being out of action for twenty-four hours, I've been undermined by you, Whittaker and Jalan. What the hell were you thinking? I said, sit down!"

Given the intensity of his anger, Beatrice sat. "Sir, there was no intention to undermine you or anyone else. We simply discussed what was best for the operation itself. Ranga said he wanted someone on board for the longer term and seeing as I will be leaving..."

"You seem very sure of that. I do not recall agreeing to your proposal, Stubbs. I said I would think about it, so please do not make assumptions."

The injustice of his remark stung. "Sir, I had your assurance..."

"And I had yours that you would step up to support Jalan in Operation Horseshoe. Now I find you've forgotten that obligation entirely to flit off on another European investigation."

The heat suffusing her face could have been just the effects of coming in from the cold and nothing at all to do with her rising temper.

She took a deep breath and exhaled with some force. "Your detective inspectors collectively agreed that the best allocation of resources would be for DI Whittaker to assist DCI Jalan. She's looking for a longer career with the Met and taking her experience into account, she is the perfect fit. This art theft collaboration with Interpol can be wound up within a week. But if you'd prefer to reassign me to something else, sir, that is your prerogative."

"You were supposed to be assigned to Horseshoe! I believe I made that clear. Why do you always want the jobs that'll get you out of the country, Stubbs?"

"Out of the country? I accept whatever cases I am given, sir. But in light of my intention to retire..."

"In light of your intention to retire, yes indeed. What are you going to do then? Without the job to provide you with opportunities to escape, how long will it take before domestic bliss loses its allure?"

Beatrice took two deep breaths and stood up. Hamilton's grey features seemed twisted and ugly, like those of a gargoyle.

"Thank you for your concern, sir, but I don't believe my private life is any of your business. For the record, whether or not you agree to my departure is immaterial. If you don't grant me early retirement, I will resign. One way or another, I will be leaving at the end of next year. As for allocation of duties, Melanie has booked me a flight to Berlin for tomorrow. Should I tell her to cancel it?"

Hamilton looked down at his desk. Beatrice clenched her fists. He shook his head. "No. Go to bloody Germany and get out of my sight."

She stalked out of the room and made straight for the ladies' toilet.

Five minutes later, Dawn Whittaker poked her head with exaggerated timidity round the bathroom door. Beatrice leant against the wall, her arms folded. She met Dawn's eyes in the mirror. She didn't smile.

"Can I come in?" Dawn asked.

Beatrice nodded.

Dawn closed the door behind her and hoisted herself up to sit between the sinks. "Two hours ago, I was doing exactly that, in exactly the same spot."

"The miserable old bastard had a go at you as well?"

"Ranga got the worst of it. But yes, he had a go at me too. He questioned my competence, accused me of elbowing you out of the way to further my career and stated I was the last person he would have selected for this op. That said, he's decided not to change anything. I think he's just reminding us he's still in charge."

Beatrice shook her head. "I can understand him having the hump because we didn't do things his way. It's just the personal nastiness I find so offensive. What the hell has got into him?"

"The question on everyone's mind. Ranga called the hospital this morning to check on his progress only to find he'd discharged himself last night. The doctors were very concerned and want him readmitted as soon as possible. Obviously they're not giving out any medical details, but they said if he came to work, we were to ask him to return to hospital."

"I pity the poor sod who delivered that message," Beatrice said and ran the taps to wash her face.

"Ranga. Who else but the reigning monarch of diplomacy? I don't know what was said but Ranga came out of there looking more shaken than the time we raided that basement flat in Bermondsey."

"Poor Ranga." Beatrice patted her face dry with paper towels, her outrage deflating as she began to realise Hamilton's anger wasn't just directed at her. "So we still don't know what's wrong with him, apart from being a vicious old git?"

Dawn shrugged. "One thing I know. He's in pain. He's hunched over and tense and he's having problems walking. He really should be in hospital."

"Definitely. At least he couldn't take out his foul temper on us from there. But if he won't listen to Ranga, neither of us has a rat's chance in hell of persuading him."

"No. Let's just get on with the job." Dawn jumped down and checked her hair in the mirror. "Did your art theft victim give you much?"

"Not really. Although I think his stolen painting will give me nightmares. Listen, I'm off to Berlin in the morning. Fancy a drink tonight?"

"On a Tuesday? Too right I do."

When Dawn suggested La Cave at London Bridge, Beatrice knew there must be gossip. One of the pubs local to the office would have been their usual haunt. Dawn's casual rationale for her choice was that the Northern Line was handy for both of them. Beatrice north to Old Street, Dawn south to Clapham.

Beatrice wasn't fooled but the choice of venue made no difference to her. The place served wine and that was all that mattered. Comfortably settled at a window table with two glasses of Rose de Syrah and view of the river, they toasted Dawn's new role.

"So when's the flat-warming?" Beatrice asked.

"After Christmas. But I want you to come round for lunch one weekend. So I can show off the flat and introduce you to Derek."

"Ooh, yes please. I'm dying to meet him. Is he still fabulous?"

Dawn put a hand to her heart in a mock-swoon. "He just gets better. You know what? He actually offered to drive all the way down to Southampton to collect Finley for Christmas. Not that the ungrateful little shit will appreciate it."

"I was just going to ask about the kids. Any improvements?"

"Don't let's spoil a nice after-work drink." Dawn surveyed the Thames, rather festive with its reflections of Christmas lights glinting off choppy waters. "Better views than The Speaker or the Blue Boar, don't you think?"

"Not to mention more private. Come on, whatever it is, cough it up. I know we're not here to discuss the view."

"You're like a truffle pig, you are. If it's there, you'll root it out." She sipped at her wine, drawing out the moment. "I had lunch with Ian today."

"Ex-husband Ian?"

"The same. We meet up about once a month, talk about our horrible children, coordinate strategy and all that. And share any office gossip. The thing is, he knows a lot more about the Met's internal politics than me. Apparently," she glanced around for eavesdroppers, "the board are seeking a replacement for Hamilton."

Beatrice put down her glass. "No! Why? He's always been the golden boy. Half the board are alumni of his old school. Or university."

"I don't know why, but it goes some way to explaining this morning's shit-storm."

"It certainly does. If they want him out and he doesn't want to go, he'll be like a boar with a sore head. What else did Ian tell you?"

Dawn's expression was that of a poker player revealing a royal flush. "He told me that both you and Ranga are slated for the post."

Beatrice burst out laughing. "Perhaps the board should do a bit more research. I'm only a DI and Ranga wants to take early retirement. Pity. I was only thinking today he would have made a great Superintendent."

"Their thinking is that if either of you were offered the role of Super, you'd change your minds. Less field work, more management, comfy chair..."

Beatrice swallowed a large glug of wine. "Ranga might."

"Operation Horseshoe is not quite what we thought it was." Dawn leaned in, holding Beatrice's eyes. "It's a testing ground for a trainee Superintendent because it's all about management skills. No wonder Hamilton was so keen for you to take over from Ranga. He must have blown a gasket when he heard it was me."

"Don't be ridiculous. Hamilton would rather gouge out his own eyes than see me as Superintendent! Or even DCI. He thinks I'm a loose cannon."

"Not according to Ian. Hamilton was the one who put your name forward."

"He must be mistaken. No, Ranga is the obvious choice and to be honest he's the only one I'd vote for. The board should approach him now, and when he hands over Horseshoe to you, he can get the comfy chair. He'd be brilliant. I might even..."

Dawn pounced. "You'd stay if Ranga was Super? Are you serious?"

"I didn't say that."

Like synchronised swimmers, they both reached for their glasses and drank, gazing out at the rolling river and the glitter of new London's money lights twinkling from its surface like a shower of silver coins. Finally Dawn tilted her head, her expression inquisitive.

"Whatever Hamilton's opinion on the matter, the decision is up to the board. If they promoted you to DCI and offered you Super in a year's time, would you stay?"

The greedy hog of Beatrice's ego immediately played a slide show of her as DCI, firm yet kind and as well-loved as Ranga. She saw herself making a speech on Ranga's retirement and making a joke about filling his shoes as Superintendent. Office hours and no personal risk, meetings with the suits upstairs, press interviews, a talented, well-managed group of detectives. Awards, accolades, an increase in salary and status.

She would hate it.

And what of Matthew? What of their plans to cease battling the daily grind; hers the criminal world, his the semi-literate levels of bottom-rung academia. Their dreams of peace, pottering and enjoying the fruits of their labours. Together.

Beatrice watched a Christmas party pleasure cruiser sail past. Enticing warm fairy lights, laughter, music and dancing. The reality, she knew, would horrify her if she were actually aboard. The music at threshold of pain levels a volume that hurt her ears, the flimsy clothing, risky and risqué behaviour of the celebrants, the face-ache of forced jollity. She was too old for all that. Too old for everything.

"No, I wouldn't. If the board selected me as Superintendent, I'd have serious doubts about their judgement. I've scraped by so far and all I want now is a quiet life. I've had enough, Dawn. And if that information finds its way back to the board, I shouldn't mind at all."

Chapter 5

Sphenisciphobia: the fear of nuns or penguins. Adrian didn't believe it for a second. Who on earth could be afraid of penguins? It would be like having a fear of teddy bears. No way. It had to be a made-up word.

He'd been having nightmares again. Last night's involved the pursuit of a monochrome woman through the rain-blurred colours of Soho. She kept disappearing and reappearing in impossible places until he caught her by the neck and beat her head against a parking meter. Violence. Blood. Neon. Hitchcock meets Polanski. Perhaps he should pitch the idea to a film studio. The thought cheered him and he drained his tea, closed the browsing window listing phobias and went back to researching the top ten attractions of Hamburg.

The sleigh bells Catinca had insisted on attaching to the door tinkled as a customer entered. Adrian looked up with a welcoming smile. The shop had been especially slow, even for a wintry afternoon. Every week, The Square and Compass pub next door had a beer delivery around two o'clock on a Wednesday, requiring a huge dray to be parked on the pavement for at least an hour, hazard lights flashing while barrels and crates were unloaded. Adrian's shop was hidden from the casual passer-by, and in the unlikely event that customers made the trip especially, they would have to dodge the delivery men, ramps and open trapdoor leading to the pub's pungent cellar. Few were up to the obstacle course and those who chanced it didn't linger.

The lorry had blocked out daylight till three pm, when ominous clouds took over, filling the narrow strip of sky visible above the street. So this customer was a pleasant distraction. On second glance, more than pleasant. Tall, balding, neat facial hair, tight jeans, a suggestion of musculature around the upper body and a knowing smile.

"Can I help you or would you prefer to browse in peace?" asked Adrian.

The smile grew broader. "Both. I also want to buy some wine."

Adrian blinked, a sense of unease flickering. "In which case, you're in luck. I'm sure we have the odd bottle knocking about somewhere. What sort of wine are you looking for?"

"Red. Full bodied. Maybe South American." His unsubtle tone tipped from flirtatious into leering.

"You'll find some robust Chilean reds over there or I can recommend the Argentinean Shiraz you see on special offer by the door. Check them out." He gave a brittle smile and returned to the screen, aware of the man's movements in his peripheral vision. Clearly not a serious customer, he sloped around the displays with an absence of focus, casting meaningful looks in Adrian's direction before grabbing a bottle at random and approaching the counter.

"Would you recommend this one?" He thrust it by the neck, like a piece of game he'd just shot.

Adrian placed one hand under the bottle's base and cradled the back, with as much tenderness as if regarding a newborn. "There's not a wine in this room I would not recommend. This is a very drinkable Chilean Pinot Noir. Plenty of depth, competitively priced and it goes with everything. Not to mention a stunning label. Is it for a special occasion?"

"Nope. Unless you're free tonight?" The man rested a hand on the counter and loomed over Adrian.

"I'm afraid not. I have to prepare for a weekend away with my partner." He began wrapping the bottle in tissue paper. "That'll be eight pounds ninety nine. Thank you. I hope you enjoy the wine."

The transaction was completed with no further eye contact. Without saying thanks, goodbye or even 'Have a nice day', the man took his bottle and left. He stopped just outside for a moment and Adrian thought he might come back in. But after a second staring at the window display, the man shook his head and walked away. Harvey's Wine Emporium's only customer in two hours hadn't got what he wanted. Outside it was almost dark and rain began to spatter the window. Adrian switched on the outside lights. Raindrops could be miserable drizzles of water or excellent reflectors of rainbows. It was all a state of mind.

He was in the middle of preparing a Christmas selection hamper when the door opened with such force the sleigh bells hit the floor. Catinca, dressed as a Tartar princess in a soggy faux fur parka and ornamented boots, opened her palms and lifted her shoulders so high she appeared to have no neck.

"What the hell! This shit? Wrong on every level. You crazy? Where this leave me? What you thinking, mate?"

She'd left the door wide open. A wintry draught circled the shop and street noise overpowered the subtle sounds of Chet Baker. She pointed a gloved finger at the window in an accusatory gesture. With an uncomfortable sense of dread, Adrian walked past his irate employee to look at the shop from the street.

On the bottom third of the window, illuminated by internal and external lights, ugly red graffiti drew attention from his bottle tree. The scrawled message read:

HERE SODOMY

He stared in confusion and disbelief, clapped one hand to his mouth and shook his head. Catinca yanked him back into the shop.

"First time you seen it?" She held him by the shoulders.

Adrian nodded, unable to speak.

"You here all day?"

He nodded again.

"Arseholes!" she yelled and slammed out the door. The connection between her curse and the graffiti burst a bubble and a snort of high-pitched laughter escaped him. The confusion drained from his mind and he assessed the day in a selection of stills.

Arriving in the morning and taking a moment to admire the pristine façade. Locking up for twenty minutes while he went to Pret-a-Manger for a soup and a sandwich. Sitting in the gloomy shadow of the brewery dray looking up the word for a fear of nuns. The interminable afternoon. The unsubtle customer.

He picked up the sleigh bells and reattached them to the door. Then he went back to sit behind the counter, unable to act, his thoughts as slow as treacle. It was impossible. No one could have sprayed the shop without him noticing. Although when he was sitting at the counter, the wooden dresser in the centre of the room obscured most of the window. Surely someone must have seen who did it? And what was HERE SODOMY supposed to mean? He'd had homophobic reactions more times than he cared to count when he was younger, but never via the shop. Where had Catinca gone? He stood up, wondering what on earth to do.

Two older women came in, looking for something Italian to go with their book club choice. Adrian recommended a Pinot Grigio. He had just finished advising an endearing young couple on vinho verde when Catinca burst back in, breathing heavily and carrying a clear plastic bottle. The couple departed with their purchases, regarding Catinca with some apprehension. Once the door had tinkled shut behind them, she began.

"No one seen nothing! You call police and get CCTV. John over the road gave me this for to clean. White spirit. I'm gonna start. Call police."

Adrian did as he was told and was passed to a Community

Support Officer who asked a series of questions to ascertain if it was a one-off or regular occurrence. He sounded as puzzled as Adrian by the message itself. Since the cleaning had already begun, he told Adrian to photograph the damage and report to him if there were any future incidents.

He put on his jacket to take over from Catinca. She shouldn't have to kneel on a wet pavement scrubbing at red spray paint. But when he got outside, she was pacing around, talking to someone on her mobile, her cloth and bottle of white spirit abandoned. The paint seemed untouched. He took several photographs, his mind muddled.

"OK. See you then, mate." She ended her call and pointed at the bottle. "That shit don't work. Can't get it off, so we gonna hide it, right?"

"Hide it? I suppose we could tape some cardboard to the outside until I can get a professional cleaner here tomorrow. Downstairs I've got boxes for recycling..."

"No. Not cardboard. Not cool. It's organised already. Mates coming. Artists. We gonna graffiti over it, innit?"

Rain dripped down Adrian's neck. His elegant, subtle display with its hints of taste and expense was to be covered in graffiti. Maybe he should just shut the shop, pull down the metal grille and get a glazier in on Monday.

"Catinca, I'm not sure..."

"Adrian?" Across the street, John from the art café called out from his doorway. "Can I do anything?"

Before Adrian could open his mouth, Catinca replied. "We got it sorted, mate. Gonna cover it up. But you know what?"

The phone inside the shop was ringing. Adrian went inside to answer and give this week's order to the wholesaler. By the time he'd finished and served two more customers, he could see considerable activity outside. He followed the last customer into the street.

Catinca was giving orders to three young men with identical haircuts. A variant on the short back and sides, this was more no back nor sides, leaving just a thick black thatch on the top. John was setting up three of his cafe umbrellas to protect the foursome from the rain. Catinca jerked a thumb at Adrian and said something to her three friends. They nodded at him and one gave the thumbs-up. Adrian responded in kind, a deep weariness overcoming him.

"John, thanks for the loan of these. Catinca, exactly what are you going to do to the window?"

"Me? Nothin'. The crew gonna fix it up. Don't worry. It'll be tasty."

"Tasty?"

"Posh, innit? I know what you like. Don't worry, chief, we gonna do it right for the shop. I reckon you wanna keep it after you see. Go inside. Customers."

He shrugged his shoulders, feeling helpless, and went to attend the evening rush. John came over with coffees for the 'crew' and a cinnamon latte for Adrian. The steady clientele kept Adrian occupied but their curiosity about all the activity under the umbrellas drew his attention time and again to the door. At least he could answer honestly each time someone asked him what was going on.

"I have no idea. Catinca has a plan."

The many exaggerated expressions of concern did nothing to reassure him. He chose to keep his head down and manage the ebb and flow of customers as he tried not to think about it. Around half past eight, things quietened down and the temptation to look around the dresser increased like an itch. Instead, Adrian selected a bottle of wine for each of Catinca's helpers. He wrapped them in tissue paper and added ribbons, feeling a little lost. What did young graffiti artists drink these days?

With a tinkle of sleigh bells, the door opened and Catinca came in, her nose red and her cheeks shining. She took off her gloves, stood behind Adrian and put her cold hands over his eyes. He didn't resist. She guided him out of the door, across the street and turned him to face the shop.

"Ta-da!" she said and took her hands away. Adrian's mouth opened. Forming a festive circle to frame his bottle tree was a graffiti wreath of holly leaves, berries, mistletoe and glinting lights. The original message had been completely obliterated, replaced by an urban ring of red, green, gold, silver and white. The corners of the window were untouched, allowing the warm glow from the interior to spill out while the spotlights on the bottle tree drew the eye to the centrepiece of the display. The effect was magical. He clasped his hands in front of him, mesmerised.

"It's beautiful," he said, and meant it.

Catinca pulled down her fist in a gesture of triumph while the graffitists exchanged some sort of complex handshake. John shook his head, grinned and nodded, in a mixture of disbelief and awe. Adrian thanked everyone at least three times before returning to the shop to fetch their gifts. Catinca followed.

"Mate, you gonna give them twenty quid bottles of wine? You know what, just twenty quid will do."

Adrian took her advice and pulled sixty pounds from the till. It seemed to please them and they left after taking several shots of their handiwork on their phones. Catinca took over the shop while Adrian helped return John's umbrellas and handed him a sublime Moscato grappa. John tried to refuse, emphasising the neighbourly support philosophy but when Adrian mentioned how well it accompanied quality coffee, he accepted with good grace.

Catinca's face was flushed. Whether through achievement or warmth, Adrian couldn't tell. He waited till she'd finished serving a chatty regular and leaned on the counter with a smile.

"You are amazing. That was one hell of a save. I'm not going to insult you with twenty quid or a digestif. But I have to do something to thank you. What would you like? Be honest."

She beamed back at him, her rain-smudged eyeliner softening her feline features. "Make me part of team. Design side. I gotta good eye. You know you can trust me, right? Gimme more responsibility. I could open shop on Mondays for you. Day off for you, more money for me, good for shop. Make me proper assistant, innit?"

He didn't even need to think about it and held out his hand. "Deal. Shall we start after Christmas?"

She shook his hand with a delighted grin. "Why not now? Trade is busy before Christmas, not after. And when is quiet, I can do displays. Next Monday?"

"Why not indeed? Sure, start on Monday. Don't forget I'm away this weekend, so it's good practice for you to handle the shop alone on Saturday."

"I can handle it, mate. Don't worry. Now, you go home. Yeah, yeah, I'll get a cab and keep the receipt. One more look while it's quiet?"

They stood on the pavement, leaning against one another, gazing at the window and grinning like loons.

"You get the CCTV?" she asked.

"No point. The pub had a delivery lorry parked in front this afternoon. Whoever did this had a good hour to act unseen."

"Arseholes."

As he walked down Boot Street, he saw Beatrice's lights were off. Eager to tell her of the evening's triumph, his stomach dipped with frustration until he recalled she was already in Germany. Still, he would be there in two days, eating cake and drinking mulled wine and regaling her with his story. He fumbled in his pocket for his keys and opened the gate, only to see a knot of people in the hallway. Saul looked round as he approached.

"Here he is!" Saul's voice betrayed relief.

The instant the two men in overcoats turned towards him, Adrian knew they were police. His first thought was Beatrice. Plane crash? Kidnapped by German art robbers? High-speed motorway accident on an autobahn?

"Good evening, Mr Harvey, my name is DI Quinn and this is my colleague, DS Marques. Could we have a word?"

A series of images flashed across his mind, both real and imaginary but all equally potent. Two plain-clothes police officers, his post box stuffed with mail, Saul's concern and curiosity, tonight's choir with an empty space in the tenor section, the sheet covering Beatrice's body in a German morgue, a Christmas wreath on a window, the thin wall between him and his own chaise longue.

"Is something wrong?" he asked.

"No, no, we'd just appreciate your assistance with an enquiry. Could we go inside? Thank you for your help, Mr Fasman."

Saul gave Adrian a worried look and retreated inside. Adrian opened his own flat door and led the police in, aware of the smell of last night's garlic. They wouldn't sit.

"Thanks Mr Harvey, but we'd better get on. Would you mind bringing your computer and mobile phone down to the station and answering a few questions? It's nothing more than eliminating people at this stage."

"Eliminating people from what?"

DI Quinn's eyes held his, steady and reassuring. "I'm afraid we have received an anonymous accusation. We're pursuing anyone in possession of images of child pornography in connection with a wider operation. I'm sorry to say your name has come up on two separate occasions and we need to eliminate you from suspicion. It won't take long, sir, and best get it out of the way."

Speechless, Adrian fetched his laptop, put his coat back on and followed the detectives out to their car, conscious of Saul peering out of his front window.

He was released without charges at quarter past twelve. They kept his laptop and smartphone overnight to be subjected to further checks in the morning. He sleepwalked along the street, unaware of the direction he was heading, inhaling the petrichor smell of rain on pigeon shit. Up ahead, a black cab came out of a T junction, its yellow sign glowing. Adrian yelled 'Taxi!' at the top of his voice. The driver's head snapped around and the right indicator blinked.

He bent to the window. "Boot Street, please."

The driver unlocked the doors. Adrian sank into the leather back seat and stared out at the shadowy, rain-lashed streets.

"Horrible night," the taxi driver observed.

Adrian met his eyes in the mirror. "You got that right."

Chapter 6

Frau Professor Doktor Edeltraud Eichhorn. Beatrice tried to envisage the bearer of such a moniker, but failed. The Frau part of the title was useful, as the name Edeltraud gave Beatrice no clue as to gender. The theme from *The Magic Roundabout* danced through her head as she walked along Hardenbergstrasse in the sunshine. The Universität der Künste Berlin stretched along one side of the dual carriageway, a mixture of imposing old architecture and low modern buildings, flanked by trees and flags. Very impressive.

Beatrice checked her watch. Twenty past eleven. Professor Eichhorn's email specified the appointment as eleven thirty and emphasised the importance of punctuality. She passed a row of bikes and entered the main portal. Calling it a door would have been a disservice to the twin columns either side of an ornate sculptured motto held aloft by stone eagles. Inside, the reception looked like any other university hallway. Notice boards, groups of young people chatting, scuffed floors, a reception desk with a glass window and a waiting area whose only occupant was a little old lady. Beatrice approached the receptionist but before she could announce herself, the old lady appeared at her side.

"Detective Inspector Stubbs?"

"Yes."

"You are ten minutes early. However, that is better than being late. My name is Frau Professor Doktor Eichhorn." She held out a hand. Dressed entirely in black, she only came up to Beatrice's shoulder. Her pewter-coloured hair was cut in a sharp geometric style reminiscent of the 1980s, and her features were highlighted dramatically. She wore deep red lipstick and her peony blue eyes were framed by eyeliner and mascara. For a seventy-five year old, she looked cooler and more stylish than Beatrice had ever been in her life.

Beatrice shook her hand with a smile. "I'm very pleased to meet you. Yes, I wanted to arrive a little early in order to find your office. I didn't expect to find you waiting for me."

"We are not going to my office because I don't have one. I retired completely last year and continue my research at home. The reason I asked you to meet me here is that it is a public place and I have to be sure you are who you say you are. You could be dangerous. Can I please see some kind of official identity?"

"Of course." Beatrice reached into her jacket for her badge, rather taken aback. "Have you had much experience with dangerous detective inspectors?"

The woman scrutinised the badge and handed it back. "Sometimes those who profess to protect us can be the most lethal. Since we have established your identity, I suggest we retire to the office where you can ask your questions in privacy. I dislike the main cafeteria here as it is unpleasantly loud."

"I thought you didn't have an office."

"I borrow one when it is necessary. Wait quickly." She spoke in German to the receptionist, who handed over a key.

"This way." Beatrice followed her along the corridor and into a lift. She cursed her very British trait of being uncomfortable with silence.

"This is a lovely building," she said.

"I suppose it is."

"How long have you been a professor here?"

"I'm not a professor. I already told you I retired. I studied with UDK and after a few years' travelling, I came back to lecture here for forty three years."

"Forty three? You must miss it."

"Yes, I suppose I must. Not in a good way. This is our floor."

The image of a university office as cluttered, chaotic and romantic was instantly dispelled as Professor Eichhorn opened the door. The room looked more like a surgery than a seat of learning. Books were filed neatly on shelves, the desk was clean and uncluttered, four discreet paintings hung from the pure white walls.

"Sit, please."

Curious as Beatrice was to take a closer look at the chosen artwork, she obeyed her host, sat on the sofa and took out her notebook. The diminutive ex-professor opened a cupboard and clattered about with something mechanical. An optimist would have guessed it was an espresso machine.

On the coffee table in front of her lay a stack of beautiful Taschen art books. She scanned the titles: Kokoscha, Grosz, Beckmann, Schmidt-Rotluff and most importantly, Dix. Instinct advised her not to touch and she waited until Eichhorn returned with a teapot and two cups. She sat beside Beatrice, folded her hands and looked straight ahead.

"So, Detective Inspector Stubbs, your questions."

"Sorry, but what should I call you? If you're no longer a professor, is it simply Frau Doktor Eichhorn?"

"Frau Eichhorn is sufficient."

"Right. I hoped you could help me formulate my questions. As I said in my email, I have a series of aggravated burglaries to investigate. In every case the target was an example of fine art. The details of all the thefts were in the attachment. My intention is to talk to security experts, victims, insurance companies and art experts such as yourself. I'm a detective so I'm looking for a pattern, for connections. The thefts we associate with violent housebreaking are not limited to a single country, although all of the stolen art originates from Germany."

"That is not strictly true. Tea?"

"Yes please. Milk, no sugar."

"It's peppermint. Milk would be disgusting. The artworks in your file originate from a movement, not a country. Largely a German movement, that much is correct but it encompassed artists across many countries, with western Europe as the locus. All the stolen pieces were created by Expressionist artists. Do I need to start from the beginning or are you aware of the Expressionists?"

She poured the tea and waited for Beatrice to respond.

"I know a little. Artists who worked between the wars and expressed their feelings about their subjects via distorted depiction. I admit I'm more familiar with Expressionist film than fine art, Frau Eichhorn. So maybe you should start at the beginning."

Eichhorn placed the cup on a coaster and looked directly at Beatrice. "Good. To admit ignorance opens the door to intelligence. Can I commence with a question? What do you understand by expressionism?"

The sensation of being back at school, put on the spot with the holes in her knowledge exposed, left Beatrice speechless, her brain scrambling for any kind of association.

"Crudely, I understand the term as meaning a reflection of an individual's subjective experience as opposed to trying to create an objective impression for the viewer."

Eichhorn inclined her head a few millimetres, her eyelids reducing the blue to a mere slit.

"Umm... the artist attempts to convey his own sentiments," Beatrice blustered. "In the most basic terms, it's a question of perspective. If the painter feels oppressed and intimidated by a person, building or even a feeling, he depicts that figure as huge, throwing a shadow across the image. It's an expression of inner thought. And influential across all kinds of media."

"Yes, that is very basic, but we have to start somewhere. Drink your tea and I will show you."

A faint smile softened her face and gave the distinct impression she was looking forward to delivering her first lecture of the year. Beatrice settled back and sipped her milkless, minty tea.

An hour and a half later, she had filled twelve pages of notes. Her mind was full of the stark, exaggerated images of George Grosz's lurid streetscapes, Oskar Kokoschka's troubled eyes, the harsh sketches of Otto Dix, James Ensor's masks, the haunting depravity of Max Beckmann. So many evocative names such as *Die Brücke* and *Der Blaue Reiter* echoed in her ears. Several paintings were familiar but took a new sense of the political with Eichhorn's passionate contextualising. She needed some time to process all this information.

A vague sense of distress tensed her brow and she recognised the signs of over-empathising. Sensitive, intelligent men sent to fight, who experienced extreme brutality and horrors, returned home broken, damaged and ignored. And when they depicted such cruelty with visceral brushstrokes or woodcuts, they met with outrage and disgust. Less than a generation later their artworks, and in some cases livelihoods, were removed by the Nazi regime, labelled subversive.

Beatrice closed her notebook, unable to absorb any more. "Frau Eichhorn..."

"Yes, yes. You must be hungry. I understand. Go and find some food. I also need a rest. We can continue after a break."

"No, that's not what I was going to say. This is all incredibly helpful. I'd like some time to think about it and read some of the material you have given me. Right now, I feel saturated. Would you mind if we stopped here and continued our conversation at a later stage?"

"It depends when. I am free this afternoon but tomorrow and Friday I will be researching. I could meet you on Saturday for a short time. How long do you stay in Berlin?"

Beatrice shook her head. "I have to leave for Hamburg in three hours. Could I call you on Saturday with more specific queries?"

Frau Eichhorn pushed back her metallic grey fringe. "A question for you, first. Do you like these?" She flourished a hand across the open books with all the élan of an Italian traffic cop.

Beatrice looked at the pictures, trying to assemble some kind of cohesive response. Her feelings would not fit into words, so she answered with the clumsy truth.

"I couldn't say I liked them. They are powerful and affecting, certainly. In a strange way, they make me feel a little ashamed or even shocked. It's as if these artists lifted up the rug and showed all the dirt underneath."

"I think they would be pleased to hear such a response. For a police officer, you show some comprehension of what art can do. Yes, you can telephone me on Saturday. Not before, please. Can you find your way out by yourself?"

Beatrice assured Frau Eichhorn she could, expressed her thanks and they shook hands once again. As she turned to wave goodbye at the door, the small figure remained bent over the woodcut prints of EL Kirchner with the intensity of someone reading a love letter.

When she stepped out of the plane in Hamburg, snowflakes tumbled out of the darkness onto her hair, shoulders and face. No one else seemed at all enamoured of this Christmassy spectacle, so Beatrice kept her enthusiasm to herself. She hoped the snow would continue till the weekend. Adrian would love it. The other passengers hurried across the tarmac to the waiting bus, but a man intercepted Beatrice at the bottom of the steps.

"Detective Inspector Stubbs, my name is Herr Jan Stein, detective with the Hamburg police force. We spoke on the telephone."

Beatrice stared at the impossibly handsome man in front of her. Surely jaws as square as his only existed in comic books? She shook his hand.

"Hello Herr Stein. Good to meet you."

"Likewise. You can clear immigration this way. You have hand luggage only?"

"Yes. Just this." She lifted the handle of her wheelie case.

"I take it. Come. It is snowing." He picked up her case and gestured for her to accompany him. Not exactly a smiler. More of the tall, dark and brooding type. His physique made Beatrice think of a word she would normally ridicule. Hunk.

She followed him through the terminal building, showed her passport and police badge to an official and emerged out of a side door once again into a snowy courtyard. An unmarked Mercedes was parked against the wall. Stein unlocked it and indicated she should get in while he stowed her case. He hadn't said a word since they left the aircraft.

She opened the passenger door only to find a steering wheel in the way.

"You want to drive, Detective Inspector?"

"Oh, of course. So sorry." She gave him a look of contrition and was surprised to see him smile.

In the correct seat, she fastened her seatbelt. He started the car and circled away from the terminal building towards the barrier.

"Did you have a pleasant flight?" he asked.

"Yes, thank you. Very short."

"Good. And your meeting in Berlin was successful?"

"Hard to say. I hope it will prove to be. Perhaps when I meet the cultural crime unit, I'll have more of an idea."

"Ah yes. Unfortunately I have bad news. Herr Meyer had to postpone tomorrow's meeting until Friday. I apologise for the short notice."

"Oh. That's disappointing. I'd hoped to meet him before I go to Amsterdam."

Stein glanced at her. "I suggest changing your schedule. We can organise a flight to Amsterdam in the morning so you can complete that part of your investigation. When you come back tomorrow afternoon, you can use a room at the police department here. On Friday, a meeting is scheduled for two-thirty with the BKA."

"Baker-what?"

"Sorry. That was German. Bravo-Kilo-Alpha. *Bundeskriminalamt* or Federal Criminal Investigations in Wiesbaden. DI Stubbs, it's getting late so I can take you directly to your hotel if you wish. Alternatively, I can take you to meet Herr and Frau Köbel. They were the victims of the first theft. It might help provide some context."

Beatrice thought about it. "Not exactly tired, detective, but the professor gave me a crash course in the Expressionist art movement and I'll need a bit of time to get all that straight in my own head. I'm not sure how much more context I can absorb today."

He didn't take his eyes from the road as he indicated left. "This is a different kind of context."

They only stayed for twenty minutes, during which Stein acted as interpreter for Herr Köbel. Stein's translation of his words lent Köbel's story a haunting sense of helpless melancholy, reflecting Beatrice's impressions of the paintings Frau Eichhorn had shown her earlier. Stein's rendition of the old man's story echoed in her ears.

"He met her at school, fifty-two years ago. Both were good students. They fought and argued and competed with each other to get the best grades. He was in love with her, but was too timid to speak. When he returned from military service, she took control. She asked him to marry her. He says he nearly ruined everything by bursting into tears. In his whole life, he was never happier than on their wedding day. She had her own medical practice, he worked for Deutsche Bank. They had three children, a beautiful home and a passion for collecting art. She had exceptional taste and when her father left her fifty thousand Deutschmarks in his will, she bought the Schlichter. It was her most precious possession. They were planning a trip around the top European art galleries for their fortieth wedding anniversary.

"The night of the robbery, he was attending a business awards ceremony. His driver brought him home late. He found her in the hallway."

Köbel clasped his hands together and closed his eyes. Stein filled in the details in English while the elderly man composed himself.

"Forensics established the basic outline of events. The thieves rang the doorbell. When she answered, they attacked her with a blunt object. She suffered severe head trauma, broken ribs and internal bleeding, indicating she had been repeatedly kicked. From the hallway, they went to the painting in the dining room, removed it and left the way they came. No other rooms disturbed, no searching for anything to loot and none of the neighbours saw anything. The house has a security system with alarms and security cameras. Only active while the owners are absent."

Herr Köbel was listening. He gave Stein a nod of gratitude and continued in German. Stein relayed the content to Beatrice.

"He says she spent half a year in hospital. Physically, she made a full recovery. According to the doctors, there's nothing wrong with her brain. He says he is not a doctor but he is an expert on his wife. She is not there. Her personality, her opinions, her spirit are all gone. She eats, sleeps and likes everything. This is a woman who used to throw shoes at politicians on the television and swam naked in the lake. She shouted at him for buying *foie gras*, smoked marijuana in the garden and cried so hard at a sculpture in the Prado that he had to take her outside. He asks me to tell you this: she loved that painting. Whoever took it also took his wife. He knows he'll never get either of them back."

Beatrice swallowed. "Please tell him we'll do everything in our power to bring these people to justice and restore the artworks to their owners."

Before Stein opened his mouth, the old man spoke in English. "I understand. Thank you. But the owner of that painting is gone."

He reached for the hand of the woman next to him on the sofa.

Her eyes left the muted television and she tilted her face to him with a warm smile. She squeezed his hand, nodded at their guests, patted the cat and returned to a quiz show she couldn't hear.

Herr Köbel walked them to the door and stood, frail yet upright, in the cold evening air to wave them off. Beatrice got into the Mercedes, now covered in a gauzy layer of snow, and waved back. Stein drove away in silence, possibly glad of a rest after twenty minutes acting as interpreter. The snowy streets, the streams of brake lights, the festive decorations, traffic signals and shop windows drifted past, making no impression on Beatrice. Her mind was still in that warm little room listening to Herr Köbel's polite, patient repetition of a story he had told countless times while his gentle wife with the sweetest smile watched a silent TV and stroked a tortoiseshell cat. Detective Stein steered the Mercedes into a parking space and turned off the engine. Beatrice brought herself back to the moment.

"Is this the hotel?"

"Yes. It has a very good seafood restaurant I can recommend. I hope you sleep well and a car will collect you at eight in the morning. Do you need anything else?"

"Just my bag."

They exited the car into wet slush. Beatrice buttoned up her coat while Stein fetched her suitcase.

"Thank you. I really appreciate your showing me the context of the robbery."

"It's not easy, I know. But if we don't see the detail, we don't see the big picture. Have a nice evening, DI Stubbs."

She watched him drive away and dragged her case up the hotel steps. An empathetic, good-looking, intelligent detective? He wouldn't last long.

Chapter 7

He dreamt about his hair falling out. Clumps of it on his pillow, bald patches on his scalp. That was a new one. Usually when he was having a nervous or insecure phase, Adrian dreamt he'd lost his teeth. On the plus side, if he was having bad dreams, at least it meant he was getting some sleep.

He woke at six, packed and prepared for the 'ifs'. If the police gave him back his laptop, if Catinca could cover Friday, if he was permitted to leave the country, if he could get a flight to Hamburg tonight... He occupied himself with the practicalities of if to drown out the whine of the who and the why.

There was little he could do without his computer or phone, so when the eight o'clock pips came on the radio, it was time to leave for the shop. Adrian checked all the windows were secure, watered all the plants, turned off the heating, picked up his expandable suitcase and locked the flat. He had written a note for Saul, but as he could hear the sound of breakfast television from inside, he rapped three times on the door.

Saul was in his dressing gown and Tigger slippers, a circle of ginger hair sticking up around his bald patch. His head looked like a gas ring.

"Adrian! Didn't hear you come in last night. Everything all right?"

"Not really. Someone made unfounded allegations. The police won't say who or what exactly. Anyway, as soon as they've finished checking my computer, I'm in the clear. Look, Saul, I hope you know..."

"Hey, I told them you're a decent geezer who wouldn't harm a fly. Don't worry about it. Anything I can do?"

"Yes, if you don't mind. I hope to get away for the weekend, just for a mini-break. Could you keep an eye on my flat? Don't buzz anyone in on my behalf and let me know if you see any..."

He couldn't bring himself to say the word. Nuns. Even to himself he sounded paranoid.

Saul finished his sentence. "Anything out of the ordinary?"

"Exactly. Thanks Saul, you're very kind."

Adrian spent the morning making arrangements with Catinca, Lufthansa and the Hotel Europaeischer, with irritating interruptions from customers. Just before lunch he tried to get hold of Holger, one of the few people on earth without a mobile phone. He called his home and workplace and left messages. He emailed Beatrice to let her know of his potential early arrival and intended to spend his lunch break retrieving his computer from the police station. But just before midday, the police detective from the previous night, DI Quinn, entered the shop carrying a laptop case.

"Morning, Mr Harvey. Brought this back for you. Your mobile's in the front pocket. Apologies for the inconvenience. Do you have a minute?"

"Yes. One sec." Adrian locked the door and turned the wooden sign to 'Closed for lunch'. He faced the detective, his arms folded.

DI Quinn placed the case on the counter with a reassuring smile. "We're not taking this any further. There's no evidence of your involvement in anything to do with illegal images of children."

"Of course there isn't!" Adrian's relief made his voice sound harsh and raw.

The officer's relaxed manner remained unchanged. "Mr

Harvey, we believe you were the target of a classic misassociation and, more than likely, the subject of a random prejudicial attack. We see this more often than we'd like. There's nothing in either accusation to suggest this is personal. Unless you can think of anyone who might want to cause you problems?"

Adrian shook his head.

"No other incidents you think could be connected?"

"Connected to child porn? I get the odd homophobic comment now and then, or aggressive attitudes in the street. We even had graffiti on the shop yesterday. But associating me with paedophilia because I'm gay? That's sick."

"But not unusual. You'd be surprised at the people who know nothing of statistics but are expert at making assumptions. If any other events come to mind, let me know."

Adrian flicked his eyes to the window and the busy street devoid of nuns.

"Mr Harvey? Is there something else you want to say?"

"Yes. Am I allowed to leave the country?"

"Bit extreme, but of course you can. No charges, no criminal record, you're free to go where you want. Lanzarote's not bad at this time of year."

The last if.

Adrian stood and shook the sergeant's hand. "Thanks for returning my laptop. If I think of anything else, I'll let you know."

"Yeah, you do that. Here's my card. While I'm here, I'd better take a decent bottle of red for dinner. That Argentinean Shiraz looks like a bargain."

The police sergeant hadn't even closed the door with his bargain before Adrian was on the phone.

"Beatrice? I'll be there tonight!"

Whether it was the journey, the stress of the previous twenty-four hours or the two gin and tonics he and Beatrice had consumed in the hotel bar last night, Adrian slept better than he had in weeks. His dreams, if he'd had any, did not involve the loss of any body parts or uncharacteristic violence. The Hotel Europaeischer was quiet and restful, despite its position opposite the main train station. He rolled over to check the time. His watch showed twenty to nine, but that was still GMT. Here it was twenty to ten and Holger would be arriving at eleven to take him on a tour of the city. Adrian sprang out of bed, switched on the mini coffee machine and jumped into the shower, where he launched into a lusty version of *Do You Hear The People Sing?* from Les Mis.

True to form, Holger was punctual. Adrian was waiting in the foyer and had just sent Beatrice a *Bon Voyage* text for her trip to Amsterdam when a tall figure approached.

"Holger!" Adrian bounced out of the leather sofa and opened his arms for a hug. With a moment's hesitation, Holger embraced him with slap on the back then stepped away.

"Adrian, it's good to see you. Are you well?"

"I feel better than I have in a long time. Must be the Hamburg air. How are you? How's the instrument-making business?"

Holger put his hands in the pockets and shrugged. The padded jacket made him look even bulkier than he was and a beanie hid his blond hair, but his eyes, the colour of oxidised copper, were warm and familiar.

"For a change, very good. I'm repairing as well as building and working six days a week. I actually have an urgent job to finish today. Is it OK if we have lunch and I leave you to explore? At the weekend, I'm free, but I wasn't expecting you so early."

Adrian smiled. "I know and I'm sorry. Just fancied getting away as soon as I could. Yes, I had no breakfast so I'm starving. Let's have something to eat then just point me in the direction of the cool places. I'll be quite content to amuse myself before Beatrice gets back this evening."

They took the U-Bahn a couple of stops, a short trip during which Holger used Adrian's map to point out where to go and how to get there. When they emerged at Stadthausbrücke, Holger led the way to a bright bar with hefty wooden tables like a school refectory. It was a bit early for the lunchtime rush, but a few customers were perched on stools looking out the window, drinking coffee and working on their laptops. The bar smelled of herbs and coffee beans, making Adrian feel right at home.

Holger spoke in German to the barman who he made a friendly 'help yourself' gesture towards the tables. They took off their coats, settled on a spot in the middle and sat down to pick up the menu. Adrian put it down again, unable to understand a word.

"OK, the lunch deal here is two kinds of pasta, one meat, one veggie, or the house salad. The pasta is homemade, the sauce is freshly cooked and the salad comes with goat's cheese and fig mustard. What I usually do is half and half. Half salad, half pasta. The sauces on offer today are tomato and basil, or lemon chicken."

Adrian, for once, opted to be guided. "Perfect. I'll have half and half too, with the veggie sauce."

While Holger spoke to the waiter, Adrian looked around at the art on the walls, the cool concrete bar and the orange lettering on the window.

"I ordered you a glass of house red. I take water, because I must work this afternoon."

"The perfect accompaniment. Thank you. What does that say?" Adrian pointed to the words on the window, giving up on trying to read an unfamiliar language back-to-front from the inside of the bar.

"*Erste Liebe* is the name of the bar. It means First Love. That sign says *Die Erste Liebe vergisst man nie*, which means..."

"You never forget your first love."

Holger gave a bashful smile. "Yes. I thought it was appropriate."

Adrian reached across and squeezed Holger's arm. "I'm touched. Although it's probably more accurate to say your first experience."

"No. You weren't my first gay experience. I've been in love before and had sex with both genders, but I'd never fallen in love with a man until I met you."

The waiter brought the drinks, giving Adrian a moment to catch up with the sudden intensity of the conversation. He replayed their entire relationship in the time it took for the waiter to pour their drinks. The initial attraction, the sexual compatibility, the sad and relentless chafing of personalities and the bitter taste of defeat. He looked into the pale turquoise eyes of his ex.

"Well, thank you. I feel privileged. And even more so that we managed to stay friends after we split up. I really am very pleased to see you again."

"Likewise. I have a lot to thank you for."

"You can redress the balance this weekend. I shared all my best London tips and hard-won secrets with you and expect a local's guide to Hamburg in return. Beatrice and I are both keen on fish, so where would you recommend?"

"I made a list of places for you. Here. And I invite you both for lunch on Sunday. I'm babysitting my god-daughter, who you must meet. My plan is to cook lunch for us all, then go to the animal park."

"Lovely idea! How old is she?"

"Nearly seven and she speaks English. As well as German and Danish."

"Oh God. Linguistically shamed by a child. Here's the food."

The waiter wished them *Guten Appetit* as he placed the plates before them.

"*Danke.*" Holger ground some pepper onto his pasta. "Yes, but it wasn't tourist tips I wanted to thank you for. It was for letting me be myself."

"Mmm, fresh basil." Adrian's inhalation masked a sigh. He recognised all the signals. Holger had Something To Say. "What do you mean, be yourself?"

Holger's fork hovered over the plate. "Allowing myself to be gay. Before I met you, I believed I was straight and just occasionally experimented with men. Two conversations with you made me realise I wasn't."

"Really? I love these kind of revelations! Come on then, what did I say? Maybe I should start some kind of blog. The Gay Guru." Adrian speared a cherry tomato and popped it into his mouth.

"It wasn't what you said, it was your attitude. You have a sense of... entitlement. You believe that you can have everything you want in life. That being a homosexual is not a minus."

Adrian frowned, the evening spent answering questions at the police station shadowing his thoughts. "Of *course* it's not. In fact, it's completely the opposite. I couldn't have everything I want in life if I wasn't gay." His reply sounded rather sharper than he intended. He softened his tone. "Although I suppose if I wasn't, I wouldn't want that in the first place. But you know what I mean."

"Yes, now I do. It's hard to explain to someone like you."

"Someone like me?" Adrian wished they could just eat their lunch and talk about the weather.

"Someone whose background was very different. My family were not exactly homophobic, mostly left-leaning and liberal, at least for Bavaria. Although they didn't condemn gay people, they taught me a strong sense of pity. They never said it in so many words but their attitude was that homosexuals can't help themselves. We should be kind to them, compassionate and never persecute a person for what he is, but they can never have the social advantages straight people have. It was as if being gay was a kind of disability."

The pasta was going cold. Adrian had stopped eating and Holger hadn't started.

"What on earth do you mean by social advantages?"

"Love, marriage and children. Social acceptability. Equality. All the kinds of things a bourgeois son of a councillor believes are the key to satisfaction. If I am completely truthful, I thought if I ever came out, I'd be throwing myself into a ghetto. You showed me another side to the story. You and Beatrice."

"Beatrice isn't gay. A total commitment-phobe, perhaps, but

definitely straight." He scooped up some goat's cheese with a piece of bread. "Will you eat? I can see you've got something to get off your chest, but that can be done without wasting a lovely meal."

With a half-smile, Holger cut up a chunk of chicken. "You're right."

They ate, appreciating the food.

Adrian took a sip of wine and said it for him. "You want kids."

Holger nodded and shook his head simultaneously, an evasive gesture.

"Don't avoid the question. I know you do. And why not? You live in Germany, in a progressive city where I bet you can marry and adopt and bring up a child in a happy community with bike lanes and crèches and gay parenting support groups."

"In Hamburg, yes that's true. The laws here are progressive and the people have an open mind."

"So your biggest worry is what the parents will say? Holger, you cannot let your upbringing dictate your life. Your family taught you a lot of good things, such as respect and manners and responsibility, but there comes a time when you can teach them something about how the world has changed. One of the worst things you can do is to live the life your parents wished for you, because it will never be your own. Seriously, I know what I'm talking about."

Holger shook his head, this time a definite no. "That is not my biggest worry. My family will accept it or they will not. I will be sad if they don't, but it's up to them. My biggest worry is that I'm thirty-five, I just realised who I am, and I only ever met one man I loved. I want children, yes, desperately. But as myself, in a loving relationship with someone who wants that as much as I do."

Adrian put down his cutlery and dabbed his mouth with a napkin. "I don't suppose we could compromise on a Schnauzer?"

Holger smiled but didn't laugh. "I wasn't suggesting you. We're not right for each other, I know that. I'm just afraid I'll never meet someone who works with his hands, who has a feeling for nature, who takes care of those he loves, who wants to raise a child and is someone I can respect."

"You will. You are a lovely person, not to mention hot as hell. There is someone out there fantasising about their dream man this minute and you tick all the boxes. I promise you'll find him. Believe it and it will happen."

"Thank you. Can you give me some idea of when?"

Adrian closed his eyes and pressed his fingers to his temples. "February the second. That gives you just enough time to join the German equivalent of Grindr, ditch the timewasters and start meeting a whole new bunch of friends. I'll compose a profile for you this afternoon because trying to express one's own fabulousness is impossible. I know because I've tried."

Chapter 8

Geert de Vries was not happy to see Beatrice. He opened the door to his beautiful red-brick home on Apollolaan in Amsterdam's Oud-Zuid district with all the enthusiasm of a dead fish. A small man with a thick steel-grey hair, he asked for ID, examined it and only then shook her hand, a cold, limp gesture. He led her to a morning room at the back of the house overlooking a wide canal.

All the relevant documentation was spread on the table and he pulled out a chair for her to sit down. He offered no refreshments.

"I am afraid your visit here is wasted. I can add nothing to previous statements, which were exhaustive." His voice was tight, rehearsed and passive-aggressive.

"Thank you for making the time to see me. I apologise for the change in schedule."

"I should be at a business meeting in St Petersburg right now. Instead I had to cancel my plans to repeat myself to the police. I have nothing more to say about the loss of that piece."

Beatrice gave him a patient smile. "I'm less interested in the practical elements of the theft, Mr de Vries. I'm working with the BKA to establish any links between a series of art robberies. Could you tell me a little about the painting?"

His eel-like eyes flickered over her. "It was one of my most expensive acquisitions. One point four million Euros. An original

Max Beckmann can go for much more. One sold for twenty million dollars at action in New York. The self-portraits of his exile here in the 1930s are in demand. Those and his nudes."

"What attracted you to the piece?"

"I'm a professional collector. I buy and sell with a view to appreciation in value. Beckmann is one of the most highly prized artists in certain circles. I had intended to sell *Portrait of an Exile* in the next two years."

"I assume you liked it? As it was a picture of Amsterdam as well."

His lip pulled up into a sneer. "I deal in art. I handle many pieces I do not personally like. Collecting artworks because they depict your home town or favourite animal is for old ladies. I am a professional. That said, this piece was a favourite and I hung it in this room. The thieves got in through that window and escaped via the canal. It seems either the intruders disabled the alarm system or the security firm were negligent. However, I was fully insured so I have been financially compensated."

"If the piece surfaced again, would you buy it back?"

De Vries narrowed his eyes. "Why would I do that?"

"You said it was a favourite."

He gave a dismissive shake of his head. "Tastes change. I am now focusing on more contemporary European artists."

Beatrice changed tack. "I notice from your statements you have been burgled before."

"Unfortunately, yes."

"It is odd that on both occasions only one piece was taken, don't you think? I understand you lost a Paula Rego in 2010."

"Which was underinsured. I made a loss and learned my lesson. Do you have many more questions? I have a lunch appointment."

"Just a few, I won't keep you long. That Rego painting, *The Schoolgirl*. Was it stolen from this room too?"

His cool grey gaze didn't waver. "No. That picture hung in my bedroom."

"I see. So the casual visitor would have been unlikely to know it was there."

"The criminal element knows I have an expensive hobby."

"Mmm. Let's just hope the criminal element doesn't do it again, shall we? Otherwise it might look rather like a pattern. Now, can I ask about the provenance of the piece?"

Her hint found its mark and two smudges of colour bloomed on his cheeks. He held out a folder. "It's all here. What more do you need to know?"

Beatrice made a pretence at reading the document for appearances' sake. She already had what she needed to know.

After she left the unpleasant little man, she had a couple of hours to potter around Amsterdam before catching her flight back to Hamburg. She wandered along the canals until she saw a cafe with green-clothed tables and chairs in the sunshine. She stopped for coffee and a waffle, entranced by the spectacle of a young couple taking a small black piglet for a walk. On her way back to the station, she found a patisserie selling alphabet letters made of chocolate. She bought an M for Matthew, though the chances of it surviving the weekend intact were slim.

A melancholy settled on her as she looked into windows of homes decorated for Christmas, gazed at gabled roofs reflected in canals and stepped out of the way of bicycles. When she was younger, everywhere had the potential to be a place she might live one day. Not any longer. Her future was mapped – retirement to the English countryside. It was exactly what she wanted. Yet however well-travelled she might be, she'd never experienced the adventure of becoming a local in another country.

She sighed and stopped on the apex of a bridge. A glass-roofed boat passed beneath and tourists waved up at her. She waved back, wondering if they thought her Dutch. Somehow making a choice was cause for regret in itself. It was the same sensation she often encountered when handing back a menu. Those other dishes, tastes and sensory experiences were no longer an option.

All the things she could have tried, all the places she could have known, all the lives she could have lived. You open one door and a hundred others slam shut behind you.

She dallied at the skating rink behind the Rijksmuseum, where her attention was caught by a Chinese couple. Hopeless skaters, giggling and clutching each other, they spent more time horizontal than vertical. In the couple of minutes she watched them, he fell over four times and took her down with him. Her thin legs skittered about like those of a newborn foal, shooting off in all directions. The man clambered to his feet and held her, standing still as the swirl of skaters passed by and in their own little eye of the storm, they kissed.

A wave of loss hit Beatrice, as forceful a sensation as when one's stomach gets left behind in a dropping lift. She wanted Matthew, here, this minute. Exploring a foreign city was no fun without someone to exclaim and point and take pictures with. This time next year she would be in Devon, adding brandy to her cake mixture, mooching about in markets, hiding presents from him and preparing their very first Christmas as cohabitees. Twelve more months and she would be handing back the menu and enjoying the dish of her choice. She should be happy. So why could she hear the echo of slamming doors?

Her job was done, if not to her satisfaction. By Friday morning she had completed her task in Hamburg's police department and was fully prepared for that afternoon's meeting. She'd checked connections, interviewed victims, sifted evidence and collaborated with local officers, but nothing stood out. That lack of substance niggled at her all morning. She finished typing and sat back to stare at three walls of her borrowed room covered in art prints, documents, photographs and a blown-up map. Where was the connection? She went over it all one last time.

The paintings. Apart from belonging to the same art movement, they were all quite different.

Hamburg. Rudolf Schlichter. *Frau mit Zigarette und Katze.*

1932. White background, smoking woman in green dress, black cat, both gazing at the viewer with absinthe green eyes.

Amsterdam. Max Beckmann. *Portrait of an Exile.* 1939. Man on bridge. A canal in the background, signs of wear and tear on face and clothes. Eyes cast left in fear as locals look on.

London. Otto Dix. *The Salon II.* 1921. The prostitutes at rest, staring at the intruder, breath held, waiting to see which way their fate would go.

The paintings had as little in common as the robberies. Brutal attack leaving woman permanently damaged early evening. Break-in while family on holiday. Mid-morning assault on cleaner. The thieves had done thorough research on the occupants' routine as well as the precise location of the paintings. In each case, nothing else was taken. Not even in the Oud-Zuid incident in the Netherlands, where the security system was disabled and the burglars had all the time in the world.

The owners were all wealthy, but seemed to have varying levels of passion for their acquisitions. Yesterday in Amsterdam, the haddock-faced art dealer saw dollar signs instead of brush-strokes, where Frau Köbel, according to her husband, had loved the painting with the same passion she used to have for many things in life. The American in London, Chet Waring, had given the impression of enjoying the controversial content while fully cognisant of the piece's value.

Beatrice stretched and stood up. Perhaps there were no connections and she should stop trying to invent them. She looked out through the glass wall at the activity in Hamburg's open plan police department office and wondered what to do about lunch. Her mobile buzzed. An incoming message from Adrian with no text but a photograph. A selfie, wide-eyed, jaw dropped and one hand clasped to his cheek, standing underneath a street sign: Reeperbahn. She smiled. So he'd found 'The Sinful Mile'. His mock shock reminded her of Edvard Munch's most famous work. Another Expressionist.

Someone rapped a knuckle on the glass door. Mr Mills and

Boon stood outside waiting for her to beckon him in. In a crew-necked jumper and jeans, Stein looked twice as handsome as when she'd first seen him. She motioned for him to enter with her right hand, smoothing her hair with her left.

"Hello Detective Stein. How are you?"

"Thank you, fine. Is everything in order? Do you have all you need?"

"Absolutely. Just making the final preparations for our meeting, then I'll remove everything from the walls and tidy up before I leave."

"You leave us today?" His jaw, shaded by planes of stubble, jutted forward, making her think of a snowplough.

"I should say so. I've discovered nothing new, so once I've reported back to Herr Meyer, I'll get out of your way."

"You are not in anyone's way. Do you have plans for lunch or would you like to come with me to the police canteen? My team are keen to meet you. The menu on Friday is usually fish."

"Yes please. I'd be delighted to meet your colleagues. As a matter of fact, I love fish and I've eaten it at every meal since I arrived – including breakfast."

She packed up her laptop and cleared away her notes, looking forward not only to some food, but also to sitting opposite Detective Stein. Pleasant scenery guaranteed.

Stein's team were a friendly bunch, if a little reticent to begin with, who soon began asking general questions about Scotland Yard, London and Interpol, gradually getting more specific and related to her current case. She tucked into a fish pie and answered as best she could. Two of the sergeants, Rudi and Kurt, could have been catalogue models, both blond and bland. The youngest of the group was Margrit, a tomboyish young woman with a ready smile and an expression full of curiosity. The remaining members of the team were Berndt, a retired detective, acting as a consultant and Tomas, the IT specialist. Neither of the latter two said much and Beatrice suspected they were uncomfortable speaking English.

Stein worked the table like a professional cocktail party host. DI Stubbs might be interested to know that Rudi (Blond No. 1) had studied in London. Cue conversation on locations and impressions. When it came to languages, Margrit was their star. How many was it, he asked her.

"Five. This is mostly luck of birth, DI Stubbs. My mother is Danish, my father is a Finn and I grew up in Germany. I learned English in school and spent summer camp in Spain. If you have two languages, it just gets easier."

"I'm sure you're right. I do admire people who speak more than one language. I can barely say good morning in any other tongue but English."

The IT expert, Tomas, lifted his head from his plate. "You don't need to. English is the world's second language."

"Yes, that is true. But I imagine Spanish or Chinese would also be useful. Are you multilingual too, Tomas?"

Margrit laughed. "Yes! He speaks German, English and HTML!"

Everyone joined in her laughter although Tomas contributed nothing more than a close-mouthed smile. Beatrice observed him in her peripheral vision while responding to a question about her opinion of Hamburg. He bent his head over his food, clearly listening but reluctant to participate. She watched as he cut off a portion of fish, added a potato cube and a dab of spinach and forked the arrangement into his mouth. His skin had a wan, unhealthy pallor, not helped by the grey jumper and stone-washed jeans.

Beatrice added a comment designed to include everyone. "And I'd appreciate some advice from you locals. One thing I plan to do before I leave the city is visit a Christmas market. I hear you have several."

Margrit, Rudi and Kurt shouted over each other to tell her which was the best, and even Berndt proffered an opinion by nodding his head. Tomas reached into his back pocket for a fold-out map, which he handed to Beatrice. She opened it.

Stein stood up. "Plenty of advice there, DI Stubbs. I need more water. Can I get anything for anyone else?"

They all shook their heads and he glided off across the room with all the grace and strength of a ballet dancer. Beatrice admired his impressive physique over the top of Tomas's map.

"Have a look at the backside."

Beatrice snapped around, mortified, aware of her colour rising. Tomas reached across and turned the map over.

Margrit shrieked with laughter and broke into German. "*Dass war toll! Tomas hat eben gesagt 'Schauen Sie mal am Arsch'!*"

The blonds and Margrit slapped the table in amusement, Berndt chuckled but Tomas had blushed a livid red. Beatrice, excluded from the joke, did not smile.

"Sorry, DI Stubbs," Margrit wiped her eyes. "I was explaining Tomas's mistake. He didn't know that 'backside' has a different meaning in English. He was trying to tell you to look at the back of the map, but you understood 'Look at the arse'! Your face was so funny. I wish I had my Handy."

The honking of the blonds and Margrit began to grate on Beatrice's nerves.

"The mistake was mine. I should have realised. Sorry Tomas."

Stein returned with his water bottle. "What's the joke?"

Tomas pushed his plate away and wiped his hands, preparing to leave.

Beatrice placed her knife and fork together. "Another example of my linguistic incompetence, I'm afraid. But while we're on the subject, Margrit, the correct word for your communications device would be mobile phone. Cell phone in the US. Handy has quite a different meaning in English. Well, that meal was quite delicious. I must say you are lucky to have such an excellent canteen. I can't remember the last time I ate at Scotland Yard. It always smells of frying."

Margrit's grin had disappeared, Tomas's blush returned, the blonds and Berndt looked to each other for some indication of how to react, and Stein picked up his cue with effortless style.

"Good to know, thank you. Our canteen also has a reputation for delicious desserts. Would you like to select one? Then you and I can take a coffee and discuss how we approach this meeting."

"Yes, please. Nice meeting you all and thank you for your hospitality. Have a pleasant afternoon." She bestowed a general smile as they wished her the same and followed the broad shoulders of Detective Stein in the direction of the dessert counter.

Herr Meyer represented the central Federal Criminal Investigations Office, but was also a member of Interpol's Expert Group on Stolen Cultural Property. He listened with silent attention as Beatrice reported her lack of findings. He asked several questions of her and of Stein, courteously using English so everyone could follow. His line of questioning focused on the insurance cover for each painting and he showed scant interest in the background of the artists. He took Beatrice's report and placed it straight into his briefcase.

She reined in her irritation. He had not apologised for postponing their meeting, nor had he attempted to provide her with any guidance. Thus she had been left alone to work her own line of enquiry. Now it seemed she had wasted her time. She aimed for a polite, conciliatory tone.

"I'm far from an expert," she said, "but the only visible element connecting these three thefts is an art movement. My task here is complete, but if I had the chance to continue, I'd want to pursue those links. Or perhaps I'm being naïve? Do you believe this is nothing more than an insurance scam?"

Meyer checked his watch and addressed Stein. "Will you arrange a car for me? My flight is in ninety minutes. Thank you."

Once Stein had left the room, Meyer faced Beatrice with a smile. The same sort of smile a dentist or clinician might wear while delivering a diagnosis.

"I wish you could continue, DI Stubbs. If I had the budget to pay an art expert or committed detective inspector to 'pursue these links', I would. Our problem is that there are two main reasons for art theft. The myth of the ruthless collector is the most glamorous and the least plausible. I'm not saying that discerning, wealthy and amoral collectors do not exist. They do. Unfortunately, so do organised gangs of thieves, fences, lawyers and corrupt white-collar individuals.

"Our experience is that most thefts are in fact 'art-napping'. Thieves steal to order, keep the piece in a safe place for up to three years, then via a third party, offer a ransom to the owner or the insurance company. No insurers admit to paying ransoms, of course. But artworks are frequently returned, their condition generally worse."

Beatrice frowned. "But that makes no sense. Why would an insurance company pay out twice? Surely the owner has already been compensated?"

"Yes, but rarely for the full amount the piece is worth. Few museums and only the richest collectors can afford to insure all their works for their market value. So it's in the interests of the collector or insurer to pay whatever the art-nappers demand, usually ten to fifteen percent of the true value. The owner regains an invaluable artwork, the insurance company writes off the loss, and meanwhile the notoriety of the theft increases the value of the painting substantially, increasing the insurance premium." Meyer smiled again. "A scam with no losers."

Stein returned, spoke in German to Meyer and lifted an eyebrow to Beatrice. She gave him a tiny nod of reassurance.

"That is fascinating, Herr Meyer. I had no idea it was so organised."

"Most lucrative crime is. My investigation so far has been into the insurance companies and the art-nappers. But the increasingly violent nature of these robberies adds considerable pressure. I am very grateful for your input and will study your report with great care. Thank you for your time, DI Stubbs. Herr Stein, *Ihnen auch*."

He shook her hand and Stein escorted him out. Beatrice watched them cross the office towards the lift, a dull grey official beside a comic book hero. She turned back to her temporary quarters and set about removing all items she had stuck on the walls. First, the reprints of the stolen artworks. She laid the three images side by side on the table and studied the harshly rendered features, the fleshy colours, the eyes.

The eyes.

The prostitutes, staring at the viewer with optimism, lust or fear.

The woman and the cat, green-marble orbs with black slits for pupils, their unblinking focus on the observer.

The self-portrait, the man's eyes cast left, looking over his shoulder at the row of Dutch houses, the canal and the open-mouthed gawpers.

Eyes. Was that it?

A rap once again on the glass door. Stein really did take formality to the max.

"Come in. No need to knock," she called, squinting at each painting in turn.

A cough.

Beatrice turned to see the young IT expert standing with his laptop clasped to his chest.

"Hello Tomas. I thought you were Detective Stein."

"Is he gone?"

"Stein? I think he's just escorted Herr Meyer to his car. He'll be back in a minute if you want to wait."

"No. I want to show you something. Can you, before you leave, come to me?"

His intense, hooded stare bothered Beatrice. Under the circumstances, she erred on the side of caution.

"Once I've finished with Detective Stein, perhaps you'd like to come back? I need to clear this room this afternoon. Is that OK with you?"

He glanced over his shoulder at the rows of desks and blue-lit faces. "Maybe. My number is in the directory. Tomas Schäffer. Till later."

Stein helped her detach her material from the walls, making a neat pile beside her briefcase.

"Are you disappointed with Meyer?" he asked, as he unpinned the map.

Beatrice looked up in surprise. "Not at all. He's got the experience and I know when to shut up and listen. I'm just disappointed I can't take this further, as it was about to get interesting, but I know what it's like where funding is concerned."

"So do I. A shame, as you say. It would have been good to keep you for a few more days."

Beatrice turned to the wall to hide her smile. "Thank you."

The clear-up was completed without further conversation and once the room had been restored, Stein held out his hand.

"It was a pleasure working with you, DI Stubbs."

They shook hands and Beatrice experienced a fleeting wish that Germany was one of those countries where people kissed each other all the time, like Spain or France.

"Same to you. Thank you so much for all your help. I wasn't very useful, I'm afraid, but I genuinely enjoyed my experience of Hamburg."

"You were useful. I found your handling of my team over lunch impressive, by the way. Berndt explained to me what happened and how you managed Tomas and Margrit."

"Talking of whom, Tomas came in a few minutes ago. He said he wanted to show me something. He's not the most socially skilled man, so I asked him to come here, mainly because this room has a glass wall."

Stein's eyebrows rose. "You are honoured. Tomas rarely shares his findings. He once asked me to pass them onto Herr Meyer, who I'm sorry to say was dismissive and patronising. Since then, Tomas has not spoken of it to anyone, as far as I know. It's the bigger picture, so to speak. You might find it informative. A word of warning – Tomas lacks social skills but he's certainly no threat. He tends to get very absorbed in his work. He'll talk for hours unless you stop him. Don't let him make you miss your flight."

"Thanks for the tip. I'm not flying till Sunday, so I should be safe enough. Have a good weekend, Herr Stein and I am most grateful for your help."

"Likewise. Goodbye."

She watched him leave and sighed. Never mind Bette Davis eyes, he had Cary Grant eyelashes. She opened the translation app on her phone. *Stein*, she had a feeling, was German for star. Which could not be more appropriate for a man with matinee idol looks. She tapped in the letters and bit her lip as she saw the results. Not star, but stone. Detective Rock. That would do.

When Tomas Schäffer arrived, he set up his laptop without looking at Beatrice or addressing her in any way. Her instincts told her not to attempt chit-chat, so she waited until he was ready.

He sat in front of the machine tapping in commands, and eventually looked up. He tilted the computer slightly to his left and looked at the chair next to him. Beatrice sat down, her attention on the screen.

"This is not a police project. This is something I do in my spare time. Herr Stein found it interesting. Herr Meyer did not. I don't care if you think it is useful or not but it is my duty to share this information."

"Thank you. I appreciate your trust."

His glance darted sideways, as if he suspected sarcasm. "This is a database containing all the information on art thefts in Europe during this year. I have another for the previous year. The data is available in police records but what is different about this is the way I broke it down. Every element of each theft is entered separately. This means the search functionality can find data patterns we might not see. You can search using any combination of criteria. For example, paintings stolen from museums, artworks from 1921, by a particular artist, in the city of Hamburg, worth between one and two million Euros, whatever you want."

His fingers fluttered across the keys and new screens appeared, each with a list of search results.

"That's extremely impressive. Does it work the other way? Could it find any connections between the three thefts I'm investigating?"

"I already ran reports and printed them for you. I don't see anything obvious, but perhaps with your knowledge...?" He handed over a plastic folder. Beatrice took it and studied the papers while he pattered away at the keyboard.

"At first glance, my knowledge seems less than adequate. Can I keep these? There's someone I'd like to talk to whose knowledge is far superior."

"Of course. In respect of this database, all the information is here. It is only a matter of asking the right questions."

Beatrice stared at the mass of data on the screen.

"Tomas, do you think you could spare me an hour tomorrow? I know it's a Saturday, but with your skills and my contact's expertise, we might find a way to exploit this superb resource between us. I just have the feeling something is staring me in the face and I just can't see it."

"Yes. That is exactly how I'm feeling also. I am free tomorrow. When you know what time, call me and we can meet here. I will give you the number of my..." He coughed. "... mobile phone."

His eyes flickered to hers and his lips twitched into the merest hint of a smile before he looked back to the screen.

Chapter 9

Yesterday, a mile of sin. Today, a mile of art. Adrian strolled along the lakeside promenade, hands tucked into coat pockets. The wind whipped across the Binnenalster, shattering the reflections, stinging his cheeks and making his eyes water as he lifted his face to a hazy sun. Maybe Holger was right and all five museums in one day would be too much to take in. Beatrice's attention span hadn't held out for two. But to be fair, her mind was still on her work. For someone normally held rapt by Monet and Cezanne, she'd got all excited about some Expressionist painters at the Hamburger Kunsthalle and scuttled off to the office.

Adrian set off down the lakeside with a heady enthusiasm, intent on seeing the Bucerius Kunst Forum. The combination of good company, art, food and a new city to explore had filled him with energy. He stopped and gazed across the water. Pleasure boats, grand architecture with uniform rows of windows, archways, floating bars, bridges, wide pavements along wider streets, ornate spires and so many expanses of water! Hamburg had a lot of space. Unlike the cramped, narrow backstreets of London, everything was broad and open to the sky. He could breathe here. He could live somewhere like this. Maybe he and Holger should talk about their differences and try again. Weekend markets, art galleries, the sea, all in the company of a beautiful, sensitive man... Adrian could do all that. There was only one thing he couldn't do. Kids.

Daydreaming. He shook his head and retrieved his mobile from inside his coat. The navigator app said the museum was just past the next bridge. Snowflakes began falling, fat and wet, melting on impact with the ground. He held out his gloved hand to catch one and raised his face to the sky, sticking out his tongue. A silent white barrage pelted onto his face, hair, shoulders and shoes, and finally into his mouth. He took a selfie with the lake as a backdrop, pulling a pantomime expression of wonder. He wasn't sure who for. The wind and cold started to seep through his clothes. He shook himself, patting his coat to dislodge the settling flakes and looked behind him to see if anyone had noticed his childish behaviour.

Less than a hundred yards away, on the other side of the street, stood a nun. She was staring directly at him, her arms folded over a black coat, an expression of disgust on her face. Through the snowflakes, like some slow-motion automated mannequin, she shook her head three times. Adrian's breath caught in his throat, the cold going far deeper than his clothes. A huge tourist bus rumbled past, blocking his view and he looked up to see faces pressed against the coach windows, peering down at him as if he were part of the tour. He made a decision. He would not be hounded by some judgemental stalker, whatever her motive. She was the one who should be afraid.

Once the coach had passed, he dodged through the traffic and vaulted over the central reservation. His coat flapping, he splashed through a puddle and tore across two more lanes to confront her. A sudden gust of wind forced snow into his face, making it hard for him to see. He reached the point where she'd been standing. No one, nothing. Not even footprints as the snow was too wet to stick. He ran as far as the corner but there was no sign of her.

In the middle of the tree-lined avenue, snowflakes spinning around his head, he couldn't be sure she'd even been there at all.

His feet were wet and his trousers spattered with mud. He decided to forget the museum for now and get back to the hotel to change. Cold and unsettled, he made his way to the U-Bahn, seeking the comfort of ordinary people.

To Beatrice's relief, Frau Eichhorn had accepted the invitation without hesitation, despite the explicit instructions not to disturb her before Saturday. Yes, she could come to Hamburg. Yes, she'd be glad to help the police explore their data. Yes, she could fly the following morning. Twinges of guilt pierced Beatrice as she left Adrian to his own devices, but her attention would not be drawn from the case. The potential alchemy of mixing these two specialists had such exciting potential that Beatrice had been awake since four in the morning.

She met Tomas at the police station and although a Saturday afternoon was a lot quieter than the previous day, several people were working in the open plan detectives' office. Officially, she did not have permission to enter the building, so she marched through the place with a purposeful air, reoccupied her borrowed room and helped Tomas set up the computer so the results would be visible on the wide screen. A nagging concern bothered her. Before flying an expert witness in to assist, Beatrice should have cleared the expense with Hamilton, or Ranga at least. She hadn't. It would cause ructions on her return, but worse, wilfully going against protocol was often a sign that she was entering one of her mood cycles. The last thing she needed. She added a reminder in her notebook. Mood stabiliser – 11pm.

When Frau Eichhorn's taxi arrived, Beatrice was waiting in the foyer with a visitor's pass. She watched the small woman exit the cab and survey the police station. Today, the ex-professor wore a poppy-red riding coat and black leather boots with flat heels. She looked like something from an up-market perfume advertisement.

Howard Jones. Out of nowhere, the name Beatrice had been trying to remember came to her. Frau Eichhorn's haircut reminded her of Eighties' pop star Howard Jones. She went to greet her with genuine enthusiasm.

"Frau Eichhorn, so nice to see you again. Thank you for coming."

"Detective Inspector Stubbs. You're welcome. It's been many years since I came to this city. I could never live anywhere else than Berlin, but occasionally I like to visit the sea. I brought you a present. My own book on the Expressionist movement and its contemporary ramifications. Even if I say so myself, this is the definitive work on the subject."

Beatrice took the weighty book. "That's an extremely generous thought, thank you. Come this way. I'm very keen for you to meet my colleague and hear about his work."

The first thing Beatrice noticed when they entered the glass-walled room was the smell of coffee. Tomas stood awkwardly to attention and Beatrice made the introductions. She watched them appraise each other as they shook hands.

"I was just going to ask where we could get coffee on a Saturday, but I see you're ahead of me. Thanks Tomas, that's very thoughtful. While I pour, perhaps you could explain the database to Frau Eichhorn?"

He drew out a chair for the professor and seated himself at the computer. Beatrice listened to the German explanation, understanding very little apart from the occasional word such as '*hier*' and '*so*'. The screen filled with various search results and Frau Eichhorn started asking questions. Beatrice placed the coffees on the table and waited as Tomas appeared to try out various combinations at Eichhorn's request.

By the time they concluded their experiments and remembered Beatrice was in the room, she'd finished her coffee and Eichhorn's had gone cold.

Tomas switched to English but didn't look up from the laptop. "Frau Eichhorn suggests adding several new fields to the artwork labelling. This way we can drill down further into the art movement sub-sections. It could take a little time."

The professor nodded her approval. "It's a useful resource and intelligently assembled. But any program can only be as good as the quality of its data. Herr Schäffer's police information, I assume, is perfect. The definitions of stolen artworks need some refinement. I suggest you give us an hour at least, DI Stubbs. Why not go for a walk? But before you do, can I have some more coffee?"

Beatrice had been dismissed.

The U-Bahn 3 went via Mönckebergstrasse, Hamburg's main shopping street. Rather than head straight back to the hotel, Adrian chose to alight there. He was glad he did. A mellow sense of seasonal spirit crept up on him as he emerged from the underground station. Hamburg's Christmas lights were white, delicate and a far cry from England's cartoon reindeers. The still-falling snowflakes, the warmly wrapped shoppers, the festive windows and the smell of roasting chestnuts chased away his jitters and replaced them with a mixture of embarrassment and optimism. So what if a sour old God-botherer had caught him fooling about in the snow and shook her miserable head. It was just one of those things. Nothing to do with the events in London, which were probably unconnected anyway. He really had to get a grip. Germany had nuns too. Look at *The Sound of Music*. Or was that Austria? Whatever. Regardless of what some joyless crone thought, he was on holiday and intended to enjoy himself. He'd been working too hard, and he was feeling a bit run-down and paranoid. Forget it and move on. He had another two hours before meeting Holger, which left him just enough time to see what Hamburg offered in the way of retail therapy.

He dallied in department stores, browsed a few designer outlets, bought a beautiful scarf depicting an old map of the Hanseatic League for Beatrice and a pair of stylish yet tough walking boots for himself. In a café bathroom, he changed into the boots, as his leather loafers were not built for this weather. Dry of foot and internally warmed by caffeine and Kirsch, he stood in shop doorways to take pictures: a spectacular glittering Christmas tree, candlelit street stalls selling Glühwein and fairy-lighted trees with a dusting of snow. At twenty to three, happy and restored, he bought a cornet of roasted chestnuts and set off to meet Holger. He was turning over the problem of a suitable gift for his ex-boyfriend when he heard something which made him stand still in the street.

Voices. Uplifting, beautiful and harmonious male voices. In a pedestrianised street to his left, against a backdrop of a bus stop and a bike rack, stood around twenty men, all wearing dark coats and red scarves, singing 'Hey, Big Spender'. A crowd had gathered to watch in admiration and amusement as the choir entertained them with their comic choreography routine. A tall man with a beard conducted the group whilst another passed out flyers to the watching shoppers. Adrian accepted one of the leaflets with a smile and folded it into his back pocket. He applauded along with the rest of the crowd as they ended the song with a flourish. He stayed where he was and listened with a critical ear. Their star tenor was not up to his own performance standards, although he did have a greater range. By the time the choir had sung and danced their way through 'Super Trouper', he'd finished his chestnuts. His nose, cheeks and knees were frozen. But inside he was warm and fizzing. He'd found the perfect place to start seeking a husband for Holger.

"*Entartete Kunst.* Degenerate art," said Frau Eichhorn, pacing the room as if it were a lecture hall. "From what we have learned from Herr Schäffer's data, I have come to the conclusion that someone is collecting a particular kind of artwork. The police information shows us that a portrait by Kokoschka was stolen earlier this year from a private gallery in Munich. Oskar Kokoschka, like the other artists involved, was labelled a degenerate by the National Socialist regime. The term degenerate was not just an insulting word. Artworks were seized, artists forbidden to paint or even purchase painting materials, and museum directors sacked for exhibiting anything which promoted 'cosmopolitan or Bolshevik' attributes. Many artists escaped to live in exile; Beckmann to the Netherlands and Kokoschka to your own country. Under Culture Minister Frick, art's sole function was to illustrate Nazi ideals and glorify the state. Can you imagine?"

Beatrice couldn't but had no time to reply.

"Goebbels had the idea for the infamous *Entartete Kunst* exhibition in 1937. A kind of public disgracing of such artworks and a hugely successful propaganda exercise. It is worth remembering that many of these pieces, confiscated by the state, were still acknowledged as valuable and later sold abroad or kept by senior officials in their personal collections. It is my view that someone is ordering the theft of such pieces to amass a collection of degenerate art. The fact that it was banned by the Nazi regime has a strange attraction for some people."

Beatrice absorbed the information and Frau Eichhorn's conclusions, a frisson of excitement bubbling in her stomach. "I see. From the criminal perspective, how far does this Munich theft fit our limited pattern?"

Tomas glanced at Beatrice, shrugged and shook his head. "From the criminal perspective, not really. No violence. The painting was stolen at night along with several other items. And because there were no signs of forced entry, suspicions revolved around the security team. The other difference is that the painting was recovered. It was under-insured and the gallery owner paid an undisclosed amount to get it back."

Beatrice watched his expression. He was stating facts, not opinions.

"And what do you think, Tomas? A wealthy collector with a fascination for the forbidden who decided that Kokoschka was not to his taste?"

He didn't look up from his screen. "Herr Meyer said the idea of the wealthy collector is a glamorous fantasy."

"Yes, he said the same to me. As he's a cultural crimes expert I took his opinion on board. I'd like to do the same with yours."

He shrugged again. Beatrice waited. She suspected avoidance rather than evasion, as well as a fear of certain ridicule.

Tomas finally spoke. "My theory is different. I think Frau Doktor Eichhorn is correct. Someone with money and influence is looking for specific pieces to complete a collection. The Kokoschka is not part of it. From the angle of an art movement, it makes sense. From the police records on comparable criminality, not."

A loud buzzing noise startled Beatrice.

Frau Eichhorn took out her telephone. "My alarm. I must leave for the airport. Will you please arrange a taxi? Herr Schäffer, why not run two types of analysis? If the Kokoschka is not part of this, your job becomes easier. Add two other artists to your list – George Grosz and Christian Schad. These were the left-wing 'verists' of the *Neue Sachlichkeit*." She turned to Beatrice. "New Objectivity in English. Check the art registry for where works by these artists are held and who owns them. I'm sure you can operate a kind of protection for potential targets.

"If the collector is picking and choosing from pieces which fell under the umbrella of *Entartete Kunst*, you have a far larger problem. No definitive catalogue exists, the artists come from all over Europe and their works are similarly dispersed. I can give you the name of a curator in Berlin who has written a book on the subject. Thank you for inviting me, it was nice to meet you and now I must leave."

She shook Tomas's hand and said something in German which made him blush. Beatrice escorted Eichhorn downstairs and saw her safely into a cab before hurrying back to the office to call London. She needed more time.

Outside the restaurant, Holger bid Adrian and Beatrice goodnight with kisses on both cheeks and a reminder of his address for tomorrow's lunch. They watched him cross the street and returned his wave before he descended into the U-Bahn. Adrian shoved his hands in his pockets and Beatrice linked her hand through his arm as they trudged back to the hotel. It was snowing again, this time tiny little balls that settled on his coat like polystyrene pellets.

"I have decided," Beatrice announced. "I like Hamburg. I'm quite partial to ports in general, but this city has something rather special about it. More waterworks than Venice, apparently."

Adrian corrected her with a wry smile. "Waterways."

"That's what I meant."

She'd been in an excellent mood all evening, discussing German artists with Holger, praising the rich food, teasing Adrian about his squeamishness regarding sausages and exulting in the fact she had permission to stay another week.

"Me too. I've had such a lovely day. Art, cakes and the market Holger showed me were so magical it was practically a Christmas fairytale. We must have a look at that tomorrow morning."

"After your description, I wouldn't miss it for all the Wursts in Hamburg."

Adrian laughed at her high spirits. "Is that really the plural of *Wurst*?"

"No idea. But I will always remember how to say *Blut-und-Leberwurst*, just in case I ever get the opportunity to eat it again."

"Oh stop. The name was enough to put me off. Isn't that typically German? Call it what it is in graphic terms, no matter how hideous it sounds. Blood and liver sausage. I don't know how you and Holger could face it."

"One could equally well say how typically British that we use a euphemism like black pudding instead."

"I wouldn't eat black pudding either. The pork chops were delicious and they looked far nicer than that monstrosity you ate. Funnily enough, I was just about ready for some meat. I'm glad Holger persuaded us. He is the perfect host."

"Lovely man. I have to say, I think he's definitely my favourite of your exes. Certainly one of the best looking. Those eyes!"

"True." He hadn't missed all those admiring glances from both genders in their direction in the markets, on the street, at the restaurant. "I do wonder occasionally if perhaps we gave up on the relationship too easily. Mind out, it's icy just here."

They picked their way over a patch of frozen overflow on the pavement and turned into Kirchenallee.

Beatrice looked up at him. "Not tempted to try again? He told me while you were in the loo that he's still single. I wasn't prying; it just came up in conversation."

Adrian gave her an arch look. "The day Beatrice Stubbs isn't prying will be the day hell freezes over. No, I think Holger and I make better friends than we do lovers. And anyway, he wants to be a father."

They walked in silence till they saw the lights of the hotel. Adrian was relieved. It had been a fabulous day, but after all those hours walking, shopping and standing around in galleries his feet were killing him, his face was smarting from the cold and that heavy meal of meat and potato made him yearn for his bed.

At the entrance, Beatrice stamped her feet to dislodge the snow. "If it's all right with you, I'll skip the nightcap and try to catch Matthew before he turns in. I feel I ought to explain personally why I need to stay a few more days."

"You read my mind. I'm going to turn in too. Being a tourist is exhausting."

Choral renditions of German carols were playing in the lobby as they entered. Beatrice said her goodnight with a light buss of his cheeks and trotted off down the corridor. Adrian took the lazy option of the lift. His bed had been made up, fresh fruit delivered and the mini-bar replenished. Best of all, it was warm. He hung up his damp coat and took off his boots. He was just undressing to get under a hot shower when he spotted a white envelope inscribed with his name lying on a silver tray. He slipped his finger under the flap and withdrew the typewritten message.

Go home.
You are not welcome here.
Go home.
Repent and ask forgiveness.
Go home.

All feelings of safety and comfort evaporated as the cold reclaimed him from the inside. He dialled Beatrice's room, but she was engaged. He threw the card on the table and called reception. After an interminable wait while they located the clerk on duty, he learned that the envelope had been delivered by bicycle courier.

Enough. This was tangible evidence. Someone was trying to frighten him and mess up his life. He replaced the card in the envelope and sat on the bed, staring at the silver salver.

He called Beatrice again. This time she answered.

"Yes?" Her voice was sharp.

"It's me, sorry. Were you asleep?"

"No, just about to call Matthew. I've not had chance yet. My bloody boss was on the phone and is insisting on coming here in person to ensure I'm not having a jolly at the Met's expense. The man is quite unbelievable."

"Oh no. When's he coming?"

"Wednesday or Thursday. I have to get this case either resolved or handed back before then. I will not have him breathing down my bloody neck. Anyway, I need to talk to Matthew now. What was it you wanted?"

Adrian hesitated. "Oh, nothing. I just realised I forgot to thank you for dinner."

"Don't mention it. See you at breakfast. Sleep tight."

The line went dead. Adrian replaced the handset, checked the door was locked, windows were secure and the wardrobe contained nothing more than his clothes. He took a scalding shower and wrapped himself in a bathrobe, then poured himself a gin and tonic while flicking through the channels to find some music, colour and comfort.

He got under the duvet with an extra blanket over his legs. The gin spread flames across his thorax and he clutched the glass in both hands. He didn't scare easily, but whoever sent that note had followed him from London. And that thought chilled him to the core.

Chapter 10

For a six-year-old, Asta had strong views on domestic creatures. She approved of the fact Beatrice owned no pets because she worked long hours and lived in a flat. It wouldn't be fair to the animal. A hamster might work, she suggested. Beatrice promised to take the matter under consideration.

Asta chewed on some coleslaw and regarded Adrian. He smiled with some awkwardness and shook his head.

"No pets either. I live in the flat under Beatrice's. But I have always wanted a Schnauzer. Maybe one day, if I move to Wales."

Holger addressed his goddaughter in English. "Bread, Asta?"

She shook her head without taking her gaze off Adrian, her Jean Harlow hair catching the light. "Thank you, no. Why do you want a Schnauzer?"

"I don't know. They have a lot of character. If I was a dog, I'd be a Schnauzer."

She placed her fork on the table, her left hand on her hip and her right under her chin as she studied Adrian. "No, you're not a Schnauzer. You're a Weimaraner. And Holger is a Labrador. He hates it when I say that, but it is true. Beautiful dogs, both of them, but a Labrador is more useful."

Beatrice and Holger burst into laughter, Adrian's eyes widened and Asta resumed her lunch.

"What kind of dog would you be, Asta?" asked Beatrice, helping herself to another slice of ham.

"I don't think I can answer that question. I can't see me from the outside. Even if I could, I'm only seven years old next birthday and not any kind of dog at all yet. In dog terms, I'm still a puppy."

Beatrice nodded, trying to maintain a serious expression. "Yes, you are very similar to a puppy. Bright, cute and with surprisingly sharp teeth. Ham?"

Asta turned to Holger. "*Was heisst* 'cute' *auf Deutsch*?"

"*Herzig.*"

She looked back at Beatrice and gave her a gracious nod. "Thank you. Yes please. One piece is enough. I always eat too much when I'm with Holger. He makes very good food and never tries to give me 'children's meals'. He knows I hate fries."

She grinned at her godfather with endearing warmth. He smiled back and Beatrice could almost see a cord sidewinding across the table, joining the two with a tangible commitment. Adrian shoved back his chair.

"Sorry, can I use your toilet?"

"Of course. First door on the left."

Adrian left the table and Beatrice turned to Asta.

"Holger tells me you speak Danish as well as English and German."

"Yes. My father is Danish and my mother is German. We spend our holidays in Denmark, so I can practise. When I am adult, I will live there all the time and have a farm with horses."

"And dogs?"

"Yes. Many dogs."

Holger stood up to clear the table. "Who would like some *Rote Grütze* for dessert? Beatrice, it's a kind of red fruit salad, served with cream. Quite light and sweet."

"Yes please."

"Asta?"

"Yes please. It's my favourite!"

"I know." He looked up as Adrian came back. "Adrian, dessert?"

"No thanks. But I wouldn't mind a coffee."

Beatrice studied her neighbour across the table. His eyes seemed bloodshot and his skin was the colour of dirty snow.

"Are you feeling OK?" she asked. "You look a bit peaky."

Adrian attempted a smile. "Tired, that's all. Couldn't get to sleep for ages and when I did, I had a succession of nightmares."

"You should have said. We could have skipped the market this morning and had a lie-in."

"We could, but I'm glad we didn't. I'm completely sorted for Christmas now."

Asta was listening and when Holger placed a bowl of berries in front of her, she tilted her face up to him.

"*Was heisst* 'nightmare'?"

"*Ein Albtraum.*"

Asta giggled, showing tiny white teeth. "Nightmare. *Ein lustiges Wort.*"

Holger raised his eyebrows. "Yes, I suppose it is a funny word. I never thought about it. Cream or vanilla sauce?"

"Vanilla sauce, please. When I have my farm, I will have a black horse and I will call him Nightmare." She giggled again and all three of them joined in. Beatrice gazed at her. She was the dearest little thing, a heart-shaped face framed by a dead-straight, silky platinum bob. Her eyebrows, mere hints of golden hair, danced above her crystal blue eyes as she looked from one to the other.

Holger offered Beatrice a jug of custard and spoke to Asta. "But what if he understands English? He might behave like a nightmare. You might be better to buy a white horse and call her Daydream."

Asta burst into peals of laughter and showed berry-stained teeth. "Horses can't speak English! I think I will have both. Nightmare and Daydream!"

"Your parents will think I've given you ideas. Come on now, eat your dessert. I'll make the coffee then we're off to Hagenbeck!"

Asta took a big spoonful of fruit and custard, her cheek apples shining as she gave Holger the thumbs-up. Beatrice turned to share a smile with Adrian, but he was checking his phone.

The Tiergarten Hagenbeck had an unusual system. The animals were separated from visitors and each other not by cages, but by wide moats, so one could see creatures moving in layers, part of a three-dimensional landscape. Asta, a regular visitor, knew exactly how to show guests the full experience. She took hold of Beatrice's hand, talking non-stop.

"Today is cold, so maybe we will not see everything. The animals sometimes stay at home. We start with the elephants. Then we go to the Africa panorama through the old door. Zebra, lions, monkeys, I like Africa. After that is the Ice Sea, with animals from Antarctica. Do you like penguins?"

"Very much."

"Me too. And then we go to my favourite place, the children's zoo. You can feed the animals and touch them and ride the ponies. But maybe not today. The snow, you know..."

"Probably a good thing. It's a long time since I went pony-riding."

Asta laughed, a clear bright sound like winter birdsong. "Me, not you! You're not a children. I must practise for my farm. Holger!" She looked back towards the entrance, where Adrian and Holger were strolling slowly behind, and indicated her intended route. Holger raised a hand in acknowledgement and inclined his head back to Adrian.

Beatrice watched them, deep in conversation, the Weimaraner and the Labrador, before Asta dragged her onwards. Adrian was not on his best form. Perhaps he really was lovesick. Since Holger, there had been very few boyfriends and none had lasted more than a month. A light inside him seemed to have dimmed and his innate joy in every pleasure life offered was lacking. She made up her mind to draw him out over dinner tonight. A small voice broke her concentration.

"Look, Beatrice! The elephants!"

Beatrice looked, astounded to see so many vast pachyderms within touching distance. Grey, leathery skin, long eyelashes, prehensile trunks and such expressive faces, the herd shoved and rubbed against each other, scooping up hay and tucking it into their mouths. A simply jaw-dropping sight in the middle of a North German city in the middle of winter. She widened her eyes, looked down at Asta and neither of them could stop laughing.

The zoo was larger than she expected and the wintry chill was so piercing that Beatrice wasn't surprised when after an hour Adrian suggested a break for coffee. Several refreshments areas were closed, due to the season. So they made their way back to the main restaurant at the entrance via the Himalayas and Australia, where Beatrice stopped to take a photograph of a kangaroo. She'd never seen a real one before. Holger engaged Asta in conversation while Adrian and Beatrice went to the counter to get drinks. The heat of the café warmed her cheeks and she decided on the ideal beverage to complete her restoration.

"Hot chocolate with cream. And you?"

"Triple espresso and a hot water bottle for my bum. I've never been so cold in my life."

"I'll get some cakes for us all too. If you're in Germany at Christmas, it would be a sin not to have *Stollen*, don't you think?"

"What?"

"*Stollen*. German Christmas cake. Adrian, what on earth is wrong? You look like death warmed up."

"Nothing. Sorry, just really tired and cold and in need of a sugar rush. Yes, let's get cake. Then can we go back to the hotel? I'll be useless company this evening if I don't have a nap."

"Of course we can. Holger needs to get Asta back to her folks by five, anyway. She's an adorable child, isn't she?"

"Yes, very sweet, if a bit precocious. I can see why Holger got broody."

Beatrice gave their order in halting German, but the cashier appeared to understand and rang it into the till.

Adrian nudged Beatrice out of the way. "My turn. And I'm taking you out to dinner tonight. Seeing as I can't cook for you on Monday."

"You'll be far too busy to cook, checking up on Catinca, the shop, the stock and comments on the website. Anyway, I'll be back Thursday or Friday. If you miss me that much, I wouldn't say no to a hot dinner when I get in."

He didn't respond. Beatrice looked up to see him staring at the doorway, a twenty-Euro note in his hand. She followed his sightline. Just a bunch of people coming in from the cold. A Sunday family, two nuns and one of the animal park staff wearing a fluorescent tabard.

"Adrian?"

"Yes? Oh, sorry, here." He thrust the note at her and Beatrice paid. She handed him the change, picked up the tray of drinks and jerked her head at the second tray with plates and cake.

"Are you sure you're all right?"

Adrian shook his head, his jaw tight. "Not here. Let's talk about this over dinner. I'm beginning to think I'm going a bit mad."

He led the way back to their table, past a young woman who was eating a doughnut with one hand and rocking a pushchair with the other. The rocking was doing nothing to soothe the infant. His face was screwed up and his lips were almost violet as he screamed with a shrill fury. Beatrice gave the woman a sympathetic smile. The gesture seemed to wake her from her glazed and vacant state. She looked down at the child, tore off a piece of doughnut and popped it into his mouth. The screaming stopped instantly.

"Asta has done a drawing for you, Beatrice." Holger held out a paper napkin on which was drawn a strange hunched animal with large ears, some sort of dorsal fin and foreshortened front legs.

"How lovely! Is it a platypus?"

Asta's laughter gurgled as she shook her head. "It's a kangaroo! There's its pouch and that's its tail."

"Of course. It's lovely. Look, Adrian."

His attention was distracted, so Beatrice touched his arm. He looked at the picture and smiled at Asta. "A kangaroo. You're very good at drawing animals."

"I'll do one for you too. How about a penguin?"

Adrian opened his mouth to reply but the screeching infant on the next table started up again. The bench began to vibrate, caused by Adrian's leg bouncing under the table.

"No, not a penguin. How about a tiger?" He raised his voice and his smile was forced. Beatrice caught Holger's eye and exchanged a look of concern.

"Coffee and cake, that's what we need," she said, distributing the drinks. She bit into her slice of *Stollen* and watched Asta concentrate on colouring in stripes on a big cat. Adrian wasn't eating, but had twisted around to look behind him. Beatrice assumed he was frowning at the heedless mother until he leapt up and jolted the table. Hot drinks spilt everywhere, scalding Beatrice's hand and soaking Asta's napkin. Holger's glass of green tea smashed to the floor.

Adrian whirled around to face two approaching nuns carrying trays.

"Leave me alone! Just leave me alone! What is your problem? Stop stalking me! This is harassment and I've had enough. I swear on everything I call holy – and I'll tell you now, it isn't the Bible – if I ever see you again, I'll report you to the police! Now FUCK OFF!"

Everyone else in the café fell completely silent, even the screaming child. Then Asta began to cry. The nuns' shocked faces showed a mixture of incomprehension and fear. Beatrice, clutching her throbbing hand, elbowed herself to a standing position.

"Adrian..."

His head snapped towards her, his eyes both haunted and

enraged. He looked at Asta, cringing beside Holger, as if seeing her for the first time. Then he picked up his jacket and stalked to the exit, ignoring the stares.

Chapter 11

The cafeteria staff applied a cooling spray and cling film to Beatrice's hand and covered it with a light bandage. The procedure absorbed so much of Asta's attention that her tears dried up. Holger apologised to the nuns, although Beatrice couldn't imagine what he could say to excuse such behaviour. People threw them curious looks as they left, but Asta recovered her chirpy humour and took Beatrice's undamaged hand to lead her out into the sunshine. There was no sign of Adrian.

"Does it hurt very badly, Beatrice?" Asta asked again.

"Not since they put the spray on. It feels sort of numb."

"Do you want to see the rest of the Tierpark?"

"I do, but not today. I should get back to the hotel."

Holger zipped up his coat. "Yes, good idea. And I'll take my favourite god-daughter back to her parents."

"I'm your *only* god-daughter!" Asta laughed.

"And my favourite," he teased. "Beatrice, I'll meet you at the hotel later. Can you find your way?"

"Oh yes, easily." She held out her bandaged hand to Asta. "It was lovely to meet you and thank you for showing me the park. I won't shake your hand but perhaps you could shake my finger as a substitute."

Asta grinned and with great care, moved Beatrice's index finger up and down. "Lovely to meet you too, Beatrice. Have a good time!"

No one mentioned Adrian.

By the time Beatrice exited the U-Bahn, the sun had sunk, leaving the streets colder and greyer. It matched her mood. The welcoming lights of the hotel offered a sense of relief and trepidation, but mostly warmth. She made straight for her own room, kicked off her shoes and dialled Adrian. After six purrs, he answered, his voice sleepy.

"Hello?"

Beatrice closed her eyes and exhaled. "You're there. Thank heavens for that. How are you feeling?"

He took a long time to answer.

"Not great. I took a zed."

"A what?"

"Sleeping tablet. I need to get some rest."

"OK, you do that. Just so long as I know you're here and you're safe. It's ten past four now, so shall I come round at seven?"

"Yeah, seven is good. Bye." The phone went dead.

Beatrice replaced the receiver and stared out of the window, replaying the afternoon's events until her stomach reminded her of the missed hot chocolate and *Stollen*. She picked up the phone and called Room Service.

At ten to seven, someone knocked at her door. She switched off the TV and hurried to unlock it, expecting Holger. It was Adrian, freshly shaved and dressed in a white shirt with an aubergine jumper. He held out a small box, marked with the hotel livery.

"Chocolates. As an apology for making you miss your cake."

Beatrice searched his face. Not the nervous wreck he'd been earlier, but his brightness rang hollow. "Thank you. I ended up having some back here, actually, but chocolate never goes to waste." She reached out for the box.

He saw the bandage. "What have you done to your hand?"

"You spilt coffee on it. A minor scald, that's all. Come in, we need to have a chat."

His brittle demeanour cracked. "Oh shit, I am so sorry. I hurt you, made Asta cry, pissed Holger off and terrified two people who couldn't even understand what I was saying. I feel so stupid and ashamed of myself."

On impulse, Beatrice stepped forward and pulled him into a hug. He clutched her to him, like a child with a teddy bear. They stood for several seconds, drawing comfort from the contact. He wore a spicy scent, like freshly plucked rosemary. She released him and looked into his face.

"Thank you for the apology. But I'd prefer an explanation."

He rubbed a hand over his face and sat on the sofa. "I owe you that. Can we have a glass of wine?"

She grabbed two little bottles from the mini-bar, poured them into glasses and handed one to her guest.

"Cheers." They raised their glasses and took a sip. For the first time in Beatrice's memory, Adrian did not comment on the wine. Instead, he released a huge sigh and began to talk.

Beatrice concentrated on his voice, reminding herself this was her friend, not a witness, not a complainant or a victim. But her police training could not be silenced for long.

"What did you do with the note?" she interrupted.

"Which one?"

"I meant the one delivered here, but both."

"Binned. I didn't occur to me to keep them."

"Can you remember if they were in the same kind of font, similar paper, anything to indicate they came from the same source?"

He shook his head. "They were typed, that's all I can say for sure."

"And when you were taken in for questioning about those accusations, you didn't tell the police about the Bible verse or the nuns?"

He rotated the stem of his wine glass. "No. I thought it would sound like paranoia, plus I wasn't even sure there was a connection. I just wanted to get out of there as soon as I could. I've got the sergeant's card though." He pulled his wallet out of his back pocket and flicked through the cards. "Do you think I should call him and report all this?"

Beatrice hesitated, weighing up the situation through the eyes of a detective inspector. It didn't look good. If a man made a complaint about being stalked by a nun with almost no evidence, Beatrice would have asked a lot of questions to ascertain his plausibility. Catinca could confirm the graffiti but no one else had seen the notes and as for the nun sightings, it could be coincidence. Before she could formulate a reply, there was a knock at the door. Adrian's demeanour changed from nervous to downright fearful.

Beatrice opened the door. "Hello Holger."

"Hi Beatrice. I just came from Adrian's room. There was no reply."

"He's here. Come on in."

Beatrice only half listened to Adrian's apology and summary of the situation for Holger while she looked up Detective Sergeant Quinn on the police database.

She tuned back in to the conversation and the contrition in Adrian's voice. "So when I saw two of them today, I lost it. I'm really sorry for making such a scene, especially in front of Asta."

Holger shook his head. "Asta's fine. It's you I'm worried about. This doesn't make any sense. You think a nun put graffiti on your shop?"

"I know. It sounds insane. But I promise I'm telling the truth. Someone is trying to scare me and has travelled from London to follow me here. Don't you find that weird?"

"The nuns at the zoo. Did you recognise either of them?"

"I've never got a good look at the one who's been following me, so I couldn't be sure. Although they did seem a bit older."

Holger shook his head, frowning. "It just sounds so..."

"Unbelievable? This is exactly why I didn't say anything to the police. I'm having trouble believing it myself. It's a horrible feeling when you don't trust your own mind. And now the two people I thought I could trust suspect me of delusions."

Holger, sitting on the bed, looked across at Beatrice. "I don't suspect you of anything. Beatrice?"

Beatrice closed the laptop and came to sit on the arm of Adrian's chair. She'd have been more comfortable next to Holger, but with what she had to say, it might look like they were ganging up.

"I think we should look at this in two ways. Firstly, we take the idea of a stalker seriously and keep any evidence that someone is following Adrian. If we're going to report this, we'll need something more concrete than what we've got. Secondly, when is the last time you had a holiday? You've spent so long building up the shop and working late and worrying, I wouldn't be surprised if you were feeling a bit burnt out. Why don't you go somewhere lovely, get some sunshine and take a week off? Now you've promoted Catinca to assistant manager, there's nothing stopping you."

Adrian stopped fiddling with his glass. "So you think I'm imagining things and it's nothing a week in Tunisia won't cure."

"No. I believe you're unsettled by what's happened and could do with a break. Not least because if someone is behind this, they're unlikely to follow you to a holiday destination. Anyway, some distance from your routine might add some perspective."

He didn't reply, still staring into his wine. Holger caught Beatrice's eye while they waited for a response.

Adrian finally answered. "I can't take a holiday now. Christmas is around the corner, Catinca's only just started in the assistant role and I'll never be able to book anything at this short notice."

Beatrice hid her satisfaction. If his objections were only practical, the thought had already taken root. Holger clicked his fingers and pointed at Adrian.

"I have an idea. It's not Tunisia and the weather is even worse than here, but my grandparents have a holiday house on the island of Sylt. They usually spend the summer there. It's right on the beach and a beautiful, wild, peaceful place. Anyone in my family can use it whenever they want, but my brother and I are the only ones who do. I can call my grandmother now to see if it's free. Trains go every hour so I could take you there tomorrow. No traffic, no Christmas songs, just waves and seagulls. The perfect escape."

The faint sound of the train station tannoy and occasional honk of a horn could be heard outside the silence of the room. While they waited for Adrian to respond, Beatrice's stomach growled. She shot a glance at the chocolates. Now was not the time.

A smile crept across Adrian's face and he looked up at Beatrice. "Funnily enough, I just bought some hiking boots yesterday. Looks like it was meant to be."

"Fantastic! Holger, call your relations. Adrian, get onto Catinca. Let's get this organised and then can we go out to eat? I'm absolutely starving."

Chapter 12

Tomas Schäffer had clearly worked all over the weekend. His results were broken down across several spreadsheets and in two languages. It took over an hour to explain his analyses. As he could not stop talking, Beatrice finally asked for some time to let the information sink in, ideally with the aid of some coffee. He conceded and left for the canteen.

The amount of data was intimidating. She started with the smallest set, planning to work her way up to the rest. *Neue Sachlichkeit*. New Objectivity. Five artists, the locations of most of their works, insurance cover, security measures and likelihood of theft. She focused on individual collections first, since they weren't sure if the museum robbery had skewed the inquiry.

The names Frau Eichhorn had suggested featured prominently. Schad and Grosz, alongside Dix, Schlichter and Beckmann, were available to view at various galleries around Northern Europe. Only two known examples of Grosz were in private collections, one in Bremen, another in Geneva. Several homes boasted a Schad, at least two in Berlin, one in Munich and another in Salzburg.

She called Ranga's mobile, specifically to avoid Hamilton, and got permission to approach Interpol. Then she spent twenty minutes talking to Herr Meyer. He said surveillance at six properties was impossible but if intelligence provided sufficient reason, he would fund one. Finally, she sent a message summoning Schäffer back. She wanted him in the room before calling Frau Eichhorn.

He arrived so quickly she suspected he'd been hovering outside the door. She called the ex-professor, whose voice rang out from the speakerphone.

"*Detective Inspector Stubbs. I was expecting your call. Herr Schäffer's material is very interesting.*"

Beatrice shot a look at Tomas and muted the microphone. "You already shared this with her?"

His expression was defensive. "It's mine. I didn't include any police information, only the art-related elements. Sharing my own research is legitimate."

Eichhorn continued, oblivious. "*All these works are potential targets so I suggest adding extra security to each home. If it was up to me, I'd ask each owner to put a fake in its place, but I understand time and effort may not allow for that.*"

"Which ones do you think might be the most likely targets? I doubt I'll get funding to supervise all these places, so if I have to choose, I'd like to make an informed decision."

Tomas's eyes flickered over hers as they waited.

"*Schad. If they go for a Grosz, others might make the connection to the verists and increase security levels. In my opinion, the thieves will take a Schad next and wait for calm. That could take years. Then they'll steal a Grosz and the set will be complete.*"

"Thank you, Frau Eichhorn. I appreciate your help and I'll be in touch."

Beatrice hung up and turned to Tomas whose fingers were already flying across his keyboard.

"What are you doing?"

"Searching for images of the Schad paintings."

"Good idea. Pay special attention to those with eyes. I'm going to find Detective Stein and ask if I can officially borrow you for the week. If that's OK with you?"

His focus didn't shift from the screen. "Of course it's OK with me. What do you mean about those with eyes?"

"Check out the other thefts. I have a feeling there's something to do with gaze, eye contact, windows to the soul and all that."

"You have a hunch?" he asked, his lips twitching.

"I don't believe in hunches. What I have is an instinctive feeling with no supporting data."

His eyes met hers for a full two seconds before he returned to his computer with a poorly-concealed smile.

Stein's agreement was easily obtained and Beatrice sensed an enthusiasm in his voice. Whilst grateful for his acquiescence, she declined his invitation to lunch and waited till Tomas left for the canteen before settling down to read Frau Eichhorn's book in peace. She needed time to immerse herself in this world, to let her subconscious loose.

Each page drew her in. Unable to read the German commentary, Beatrice absorbed the artworks for what they were. In the quiet of her glass-walled room, the pictures became both familiar and more strange. Many of these pieces she'd seen before, in galleries and as reproductions, yet now she looked at them through a different filter. The sensation reminded her of an occurrence on her daily commute. A young man who had shared the same route for years suddenly broke their unspoken etiquette – a brief nod of acknowledgement and return to their respective newspapers – and struck up a conversation. She recalled the feeling of breaking glass, a simultaneous sense of possibility and dismay for something that could never be the same again.

Tomas returned and stood in the doorway, his expression unusually bright. For the first time, he made direct eye contact and did not look away.

"Good news."

Beatrice put down her book. "Just what I need. Come in and tell me."

"BKA intel just in. WBC with two owners of Schads at fifteen hundred. Can you be there?"

"I think I'm suffering from some kind of sugar withdrawal. My brain processed almost nothing in that sentence. Something is happening at three o'clock? In which case, I will rush out for a sandwich and come back so you can explain slowly in small words."

"I brought you a brown bag lunch package from the canteen. Sandwich, fruit, dessert and juice. I know you have had no time to eat. And I can bring an espresso from the machine when you finish."

Beatrice held out her hand for the bag. "That is most considerate and welcome. Now start at the beginning. We have some new intelligence?"

The six-person web conference ended at twenty minutes to four. Tomas and Beatrice were joined by Stein in person, Meyer from Wiesbaden and the two art collectors on video link. The threat to their artworks was made clear by Meyer, the danger to their loved ones clearer still by Stein. Both German speakers, the two collectors had myriad questions, which Stein and Meyer handled, while Tomas muttered translations for Beatrice's benefit.

The team identified Frau Kruger as the most vulnerable. Her property had easy access from a prestigious Berlin street and her painting, *Die Wolken*, had recently featured in a high-profile Schad retrospective. She eventually agreed to an extra security patrol and the installation of an alarm system.

Regardless of the practical considerations, however, Beatrice knew that Frau Kruger's painting was not the target. The minute Tomas indicated the next picture – *Nina in Camera* – a jolt of recognition shot through her. The eyes. Huge, liquid, limpid and exaggerated, the girl's gaze induced a feeling of vertigo. They were eyes you could fall into. Viewing the painting under glass, you would see the reflection of yourself in the velvet depths of her irises. A powerful conviction took hold that this painting was linked to the others by more than just the art movement.

So she paid particular attention to Tomas's translation when the painting's owner was speaking. Herr Walter would put his own security team on high alert, since he was currently skiing in Davos. Beatrice twitched and whispered a question to Tomas.

"When did he leave Munich?"

"*Entschuldigung, Herr Walter, wann sind Sie nach Davos gefahren*?"

"*Freitag abend. In privatjet. Wir kommen am Mittwoch morgen züruck*."

Tomas whispered to Beatrice. "They flew Friday evening and will come back on Wednesday morning."

Stein met Beatrice's eyes with a certain curiosity. He waited till Meyer thanked the participants for their time and the guests had disconnected before speaking.

"According to Herr Meyer, we can afford to carry out surveillance on only one of these paintings. Which would be your choice, DI Stubbs?"

She didn't hesitate. "Munich. The owner is absent, it's a Schad and it's got the eyes connection. I am quite convinced this is the next target. If he's away for a couple of days, now is the perfect opportunity for the thieves to act. On top of all of that, it's just two days of watching the property."

Meyer, on screen, nodded. "That's all in order. I will talk to the Munich force and ensure they are fully briefed. I will also follow up with the other potential burglaries. Congratulations everyone, this is good work. Have a nice afternoon."

The screen went dark, Tomas's attention reverted to his computer but Stein was still watching Beatrice.

"Coffee, DI Stubbs?"

"What an excellent idea."

She reached both arms behind her head to massage her neck. It was like kneading stale bread.

Stein asked Tomas a question in German, picked up the phone and as far as Beatrice could understand, ordered coffee. Then he stood behind her.

"That won't work. If you have tension, you need another pair of hands."

He brushed her hands away and applied his own to the solid knotted mass of muscle between her shoulders. Soothing palms, hard thumbs, pressure and warmth unlocked all kinds of physical reactions. Thankfully, he continued talking, so that Beatrice's little moans could be disguised as grunts of agreement.

"Herr Meyer will organise extra patrols in the area of the Munich house. We can implement a similar intelligence search for all the other pieces by Schad and Grosz, adding addresses, owners and other terms in our database. Isn't that right, Herr Schäffer?"

"Exactly what I'm working on right now," Tomas replied, hunched over his screen.

"So what we need to do is mine the data. Find the cross references... oh sorry, did I hurt you?"

"No, just found a hot spot. Carry on."

His hands spread across her back again, manipulating the musculature. Heat moved across her skin. He continued talking but her concentration was divided between her neck, where his thumbs applied pressure to either side of her atlas vertebra and his voice, saying something important about mapping.

Her phone rang, seconds before she dissolved entirely, so she was actually grateful to see Hamilton on caller display.

"Thank you, Herr Stein. You're rather good at that. I must take this call. It's Detective Superintendent Hamilton. Excuse me."

She took the phone outside, hoping the wintry air might cool her cheeks.

"Good afternoon, sir. How are you?"

"Stubbs. Any progress?"

"Some. Just finished a phone conference with the Cultural Crimes unit and two potential targets. We'll be collaborating with forces in Berlin and Munich to add extra levels of protection. Everything is under control and even if I've made no progress by Friday, I'll hand over to Herr Schäffer to pursue the investigation. Whatever happens, I'll fly back to London on

Friday evening and be back at work on Monday."

"That would be appreciated. Going to need all hands on deck next week. But I will be in Hamburg on Thursday and thought you and I could have dinner."

"Dinner, sir?"

"Yes, Stubbs. A meal one traditionally has in the evening. See if you can't find a decent restaurant and book a table for two. There's something I need to discuss with you."

Beatrice's heart sank. Not only an evening spent making small talk with Mr Irascible, but he'd probably insist on talking shop, putting out feelers on the whole replacement Superintendent issue. A horrible thought struck her. Would he expect to accompany her back to London?

"Certainly, sir. Have you already booked your return flight?"

"Onward flight, in point of fact. Flying out again on Friday morning."

"Oh, I see. Is that for business or pleasure?"

He took a moment to respond. "This is not work-related."

In other words, mind your own business. Beatrice changed the subject. "Are you feeling any better now, sir?"

"A little. Thank you for your concern. Now when you book a restaurant, make sure it serves something other than fish. Steak, ideally. See you Thursday, Stubbs."

"I'll look forward to it," she lied.

Chapter 13

Tell the truth and shame the devil, his granddad used to say. Get the weight off your conscience and rest easy. So after sharing all his fears with Beatrice and Holger, arranging business as usual at Harvey's Wine Emporium and anticipating an impromptu holiday while escaping the excesses of Christmas preparations, Adrian thought a good night's sleep should be his by default.

It didn't work like that.

Once under the duvet, he turned out the light with a sigh, only to switch it back on within seconds. He made a note on the hotel notepad: *security system – remind Catinca to change password.* He spent the next ninety minutes envisaging every possible disaster which could befall his business and finally, at ten past two, decided to cancel his trip. He would call Holger at seven and say he'd changed his mind. Go to the airport, get a flight to London City and be back behind the counter of Harvey's Wine Emporium by lunchtime. Decision made, he set the alarm, switched off the light and willed the onset of sleep.

Two hours later, sweaty, clammy and with a sore throat, he woke from a nightmare. The dream had taken place in his hotel room, with shadowy figures around his bed, pressing down on his limbs. He'd tried to scream, but it felt as if his mouth had been glued shut. He put the light back on, checked the door was locked and searched the room thoroughly. Prickles and itches all over his skin made him scratch, so he took a shower and decided he may as well pack.

By the time he'd shaved and was completely ready for his return home, it was four-thirty in the morning. He turned off his alarm as he had no hope of sleeping anyway. Finally, fully clothed on top of the duvet, he drank a camomile tea and watched music videos with the sound down.

Traffic. Car horns. A siren. The dawn chorus. Adrian opened his eyes and realised the hotel room phone was ringing. His watch said twenty to nine.

"Hello?"

"Adrian, it's Holger. I'm downstairs in the lobby. Sorry I got here a little late. I stopped off at the main station to get our tickets. I thought we could have breakfast on the train. Are you ready?"

Adrian blinked at his suitcase and dismissed his night frights in an instant.

"I'll be down in two minutes."

The journey lasted almost four hours and Adrian loved every second of it. The crisp blue light of winter, the landscape growing wilder by the mile, the rail causeway to the island, sweet houses that reminded him of Amsterdam and ever-changing but always thrilling views of the sea.

They arrived at the island's main town, Westerland, and switched to a bus to take them north along a coast road. Adrian was in awe. He'd never seen a winter beach before. The composition of dune grass against blue ocean trimmed with pristine white snow seemed like a fairytale setting. He could imagine a unicorn galloping through the surf or out towards the horizon, a dolphin leaping out of the water in a slow-motion arc.

He constantly exhorted Holger to look, which he duly did. Holger seemed to enjoy Adrian's excitement and offered insider tips on the *Strandkörbe* or beach basket-seats, the expensive celebrity holiday homes in Kampen and the marine life so treasured by the islanders.

Just after one o'clock, the local bus service deposited them at the end of a sandy track. Adrian felt as if he'd arrived at the end of the world. Once the bus had gone, he stopped to breathe the clear cold air and to listen. Other than seagulls, the wind through the dune grass and the distant sound of the rolling sea, the peace was complete.

Holger inhaled and stretched. "I miss this place. This is my first time back since the summer. Come on. Let's get to the house and light a fire. The wind is sharp."

They set off in the direction of the sea.

"Just remember, this is a holiday house. Don't expect too much. There are all the basic conveniences and unbeatable views, but it is pretty simple. List, that town we just went through, has shops and restaurants and everything you need, only a twenty-minute bike ride away. You know, I never spent time here in winter. It feels very different. I hope you will be OK. This is not London."

Adrian took a huge breath of sea air. "Thank God for that. Stop worrying. All I want is nature and solitude and this looks like the place to find plenty of both. Oh! Is that it? No way!"

The house at the end of the lane had a peaked roof, descending from a top point to flick out over the eaves like a schoolgirl's hair. The red brick seemed warm and inviting against the backdrop of windswept dunes and the bleached horizon. Shuttered windows gave it a sleepy look, as if it was dozing until their return.

"Yes, that's it. When we were kids, we lived every summer at this house. This place is my childhood."

Gulls screeched as the wind buffeted them towards the building, encouraging them onward. Beyond the rectangle of garden lay the empty beach and constant tumbling waves, rushing up the sand and receding in a soothing rhythm.

Adrian inhaled and closed his eyes. "I'm going to like it here. I already know."

"I hope so. Strangers sometimes suffer from *Inselkoller* – island rage. Just remember you can leave at any time. Buses to Westerland are regular and then you can catch a train back to

Hamburg. Don't stay if you feel uncomfortable."

"You should have been a travel agent. 'How to Sell a Place', by Holger Waldmann. Let's get inside, my face is freezing. I need some tea."

Holger unlocked the door, switched on the lights and deactivated the alarm. Adrian heaved his case over the threshold. It was almost as cold inside as it was out until the door slammed, shutting out the wind. A vague aroma of vanilla drifted through the air.

White walls, a driftwood sculpture, an open-plan living-room with a corner sofa, a beech wood kitchen with an island hob, parquet flooring with pastel rugs and sunken spotlights illuminating the cleanest, most Adrian-friendly environment he'd ever encountered outside his own flat.

"I don't believe it. This is the original IKEA house!"

Holger looked around as if seeing it from Adrian's perspective. "It is pretty Scandi, I guess. My grandparents bought this place way back in the 60s. They lived in it for twenty-seven years. If they sold it now, it would be worth millions. The decor is their taste. Light, clean and functional, but my grandmother has a homely eye. Come upstairs. I will switch on the heating and show you the bedrooms."

Patchwork quilts on ironwork beds and a pine grandfather clock. The final detail to convince Adrian he should live here and never move for the rest of his life. Holger went around the building, opening all the shutters, and lit a fire. Adrian hummed Doris Day's *Just Blew In From the Windy City* as he unpacked the food and assembled a picnic lunch on the dining-table. The sun shone directly into the living room, turning the wooden floor the colour of honey.

As they ate the cold meats and cheeses with a white loaf and gherkins, Adrian encouraged Holger to reminisce about his childhood summers on the island.

"What did you do here as a kid? I want to hear stories. Tell me!"

Holger gave a dismissive laugh. "Nothing to tell. Same as every kid, I was an explorer. My brother and I were mad about making things. When we were very small, it was a den or a wigwam or a tree house, where we'd occasionally be allowed to sleep. Whenever we did, my sister wanted to come with us but she never lasted the night. She always got scared and had to be taken back to the house. Then we discovered the sea. Growing up in Bavaria, we had forests and castles and mountains, but the sea was something almost foreign. We built kayaks and learned how to sail. One year my grandfather bought an old wooden sailboat which we fixed up. I got so sunburnt while we painted it I had to stay indoors for two days. At that age, it felt like forever."

"Are you the oldest?"

"No, I'm the one in the middle. My sister's the oldest by five years. Joachim and I were born within a year of each other and we're extremely similar in looks and temperament. People often thought we were twins. He's the one member of my family who still treats me exactly the same way since I came out. It honestly doesn't matter to him."

"What about the rest of your family?" Adrian asked.

"My grandparents, the ones who own this place, are cool with it but sort of too much, if you know what I mean. Always asking if I've met a nice man. Very interested in you and excited that I'm bringing you here. They just want me to be happy. My sister, Patricia..."

Adrian cut another slice of bread and when Holger didn't continue, offered a prompt. "Your sister doesn't want you to be happy?"

"She is a person of extremes. She made a lot of effort to make me change my mind. I refused and now she will not speak to me. My parents are accepting but worried."

"Why are they worried?"

"They fear I'll be beaten up, they think it's a phase, They wonder what they did wrong, and they believe I'll suffer from prejudice or AIDS. The usual."

Adrian shook his head in exasperation and poured more tea. "They expect the worst. You have a duty to show them the best. Make them happy for you."

Holger tore a chunk from Adrian's bread and bit into it. "I want to make me happy first. The family comes later. Finished? Are you ready to look around?"

"Have we got time for a walk on the beach?"

With a glance at his watch, Holger stood up. "Maybe later. Now I want to show you how everything works. We can walk back to the bus stop in an hour. Come. You're going to love the sauna."

They strolled up the lane as the sun sank into the sea, the sky all the shades of a volcanic eruption. Adrian was speechless. Almost.

"It beggars belief. I've never seen such an outrageous sunset in my life and I've been to Bali twice. I really can't thank you enough for introducing me to this place, loaning me the house and not giving up on me. You're so patient. I know I've not been the best company these past few days. When you talk to your grandparents, please tell..."

A car horn beeped as they reached the main road. A Jeep pulled to a halt and the window rolled down to reveal a bearded face with a big smile.

"Daan!" Holger dropped his rucksack, the driver jumped out and the two men embraced. Despite not understanding a word either said, Adrian deduced from the smiles and easy affection that this was a long acquaintance. The big hairy man looked at him with curiosity. He had deep-set green eyes and a monobrow.

"Daan, this is Adrian, a friend of mine from London. Adrian, meet Daniel Knutsen. We met when we were eight years old. Daan lives on the west coast and repairs boats for a living."

Adrian took Daan's outstretched hand and returned the strong shake.

"Pleased to meet you."

"Hello Adrian, you too." He had a wide, generous smile with teeth like tombstones. He reminded Adrian of Captain Haddock crossed with Bluto.

Daan pointed an accusing finger at Holger and spoke in English. "Why didn't you let me know you were coming?"

"Because we only decided last night. I'm not staying, I have to work. But Adrian will be here for the week to get away from it all. Maybe you could come over once or twice? Just to make sure he is OK?"

"Sure. I'd be happy to do that. If you feel like some sightseeing, Adrian, I can give you the guided tour."

"Thank you. I definitely feel like some sightseeing." Adrian hoped it wasn't just a friendly platitude.

"Holger, when are you leaving?"

"As soon as the bus gets here."

"Get in the truck. I'll take you to Westerland and we can have at least half an hour to talk. It's been too long."

Before Holger could reply, the bus came down the road. Daan rushed back to his Jeep, which was blocking the way. Holger hugged Adrian, picked up his bag and jumped into the passenger seat. Within twenty seconds, the two men drove off, waving and miming phone calls. Adrian watched the truck turn the corner, followed by the bus, and he was left alone.

He gazed behind him at the sunset for a moment and strolled back along the track to his holiday home. The sun had dropped below the horizon and the sharp twilight air brushed his neck. He was glad they'd left the lights on. The glow reassured him, as did the motion sensor triggering the outside floodlight. *I feel safe and comfortable. I will not get spooked by any strange noises. I have an alarm and a security system. I am perfectly safe.* He closed the door, checked all the windows and doors, put on the Scissor Sisters to drown out the sounds of the North Sea wind and started unpacking his case. He was going to be absolutely fine.

Beatrice left the office early, in a hurry to get back to the hotel in time for her scheduled telephone chat. This was one conversation she wanted to have in private.

"Hello James."

"*Beatrice, good to hear from you. I was surprised to receive a phone call request so soon after our last session. How are you?*"

"Fine, completely fine. Mindful, self-aware and taking the tablets. Thanks for making the time for me. The thing is, I need some advice, in a sort of 'off the record' kind of way. This isn't about me, you see. But don't worry, I'll pay for this as if it were an official session."

"*I see. Before we go any further, I can't offer any professional insight on a police investigation. It would...*"

She interrupted, well prepared for his objections. "... be completely unfair to even ask. This isn't about my investigation, I assure you. But a friend of mine is displaying peculiar behaviour and I wondered if you could offer some guidance as to where I could seek help."

There was a pause. "*What precisely does 'peculiar behaviour' mean?*"

Beatrice smiled. She'd expected more resistance. Her counsellor was punctilious in his professionalism so she'd thought long and creatively about the exact phrasing to excite his curiosity. Her deviousness had paid off.

She outlined the episode at the zoo and tried to deliver Adrian's later explanation without leaving out any crucial details. James, as always, began with questions.

"*Has your friend had any previous experiences like this?*"

"Not that I know of."

"*As he's joined you and his ex-boyfriend for the weekend, I assume he's not displaying antisocial tendencies.*"

"No. Quite the opposite. He was outgoing and lively until Sunday."

"*I don't suppose you know if he's having trouble sleeping?*"

"He did mention he'd had a bad night, yes. He was very tired and irritable and sort of disengaged. And I found out yesterday he's taking sleeping tablets."

"*Any other recent behavioural changes?*"

A familiar instinct to hide, dissemble and protect surfaced. Beatrice fought it, knowing that without honesty there could be no help. That applied to Adrian just as much as it did to her.

"He's been jumpy. He thinks his post went missing, he worries about who's coming into the building, he seems much more nervous than usual and contacts me on a daily basis. Just cheerful little check-ins, but that's not normal."

"*Hmm.*" Rustling scratchy noises indicated James was writing. Beatrice visualised the white-blond head bent over his paperwork in his light, white room and longed for her next appointment. Once a month seemed far too infrequent.

"*I'm going to send you a list of people he could see when he gets back to London. Many are experts in the field of paranoia but some simply use CBT to realign thinking patterns. I suggest you present the idea to him as physiotherapy for the mind. Interesting as this case is, I can't take him on, as there's an obvious conflict of interest. I hope he finds the right person, but if not, come back to me.*"

"Thank you, James. He won't be back for another week, as he's spending some time in his ex-boyfriend's holiday home. I wish I could go too. A remote island in the North Sea where people speak Danish and wear patterned jumpers."

"*He'll be with his ex-boyfriend?*"

"No, Holger has to work. And Adrian could do with a bit of time out. He hates the whole Christmas excess, crowds, pressure, food, so a week alone on an island is just what the doctor ordered."

"*As I said, I can offer no diagnosis on your friend. But with my background and understanding of mental health I feel that if someone is suffering a depressive episode and potentially experiencing anomalous incidents, the last thing he needs is a week alone on a remote island where he can't even speak the language.*

My advice would be to get him back to London and into a specialist's surgery. I'll send an email with contact details immediately. I'll leave it up to you how to deal with that."

Abashed, Beatrice said nothing.

James picked up on her silence. "*I don't mean to be alarmist. However, the fact you had enough concern to call me indicates this man is important to you.*"

"He is," she agreed, only then realising how true that was.

"*Beatrice?*" His voice changed register, a more urgent tone than his usual practised distance.

"What?"

"*Remember how important your friends have been during your low points. At the time you found them bullying and controlling, but now you appreciate their loyalty. They stuck around. They held on no matter how much easier it might have been to let go. If this person is important and he needs your help, be a bully if you have to, but don't let go.*"

His words hit home. "I won't. Thank you, James."

After fifteen minutes repeatedly trying Adrian's mobile and receiving the unobtainable message, she tried Holger. The only number she had was for his work, a studio in a shared building. A brusque, male voice answered and she left a semi-comprehensible message in jumbled German. She faced facts. She'd left it too late. Adrian had already gone.

Chapter 14

On Tuesday morning, Beatrice awoke in a terrible mood. A wretched night of fidgeting till four in the morning led her to oversleep and miss breakfast. She was worried about Adrian, regardless of his cheerful assurances. The investigation was too big, too complex and as concrete as a spider's web. It was all bloody pointless. She considered handing over everything to Tomas and just going home. Better her tail between her legs than her head against a brick wall.

She'd no sooner opened her office door than Stein followed her in, carrying two cups of coffee.

"Good morning, DI Stubbs. It seems you were right."

Beatrice unbuttoned her coat. "Good morning, Herr Stein. Is one of those for me?"

"Yes." He helped her out of her coat and hung it on the chrome stand. "Latte macchiato. I know you can't think before your first coffee."

"You have no idea how grateful I am." She took the cup and inhaled. "Right about what?"

"The painting in Munich. The owner left a message for me this morning. He instructed his security team to be extra vigilant and in response they mentioned some unusual activity. The normal routine is that one officer patrols the grounds, while the other sits in the security lodge, watching the camera footage. One of these cameras is trained on the road outside the house.

It seems a black van with Dutch plates parked outside on three consecutive nights around four in the morning. No one got in or out, and the van drove away just before six."

Beatrice wiped some foam from her lip. "That's very interesting. I wonder..."

"You wonder what?"

"We now have extra reason to believe this piece is an imminent target. Therefore it might be worth investing in more than surveillance. The thieves are looking for the easiest time to pull a heist. That's likely to be overnight. Basic security cover, fewer potential witnesses, cover of darkness for vehicles. We even have a probable timescale. Could we stage an operation with a secondary undercover cordon to ensure we trap this gang in the act?"

He sat down and rotated his coffee cup, thinking for a moment or two.

"We can present Meyer with a suggested plan and then approach the Munich force. We'll need BKA support or they'll never agree."

There was a knock on the glass and Tomas entered with his laptop bag slung across his shoulder and two cups of coffee in his hands. He glanced at Stein and nodded to Beatrice.

"Morning, Tomas. What's the news?"

He held out a cup. "I got you a coffee. Herr Stein told you there's an update on security of the Munich painting?"

"Thank you." She took the cup and placed it placed it next to the one Stein had given her. She smiled inwardly at the courtesy of her foreign counterparts, remembering the kettles and the jars of pound-shop instant in her own office, the open milk cartons she'd have to sniff before risking. "Yes. We were just discussing if it is feasible to set a trap."

Tomas set up his computer while talking. "All the signs point to this theft happening over the next two days. Setting up a trap is a lot of expense and effort but on this occasion, it might be worth it."

Beatrice picked up her first coffee and drank from it. "Herr Stein, what do you think? Increased surveillance and a team on standby?"

"That sounds practical but expensive. Let's work out what to say to Meyer and if he agrees, I'll need to talk to Munich as soon as possible. This means a lot of work for them. If we go ahead, I'd like to be there in person. I want to be present when we catch this group. Would you like to come with me?"

"Yes, please. Catching these violent thugs in the act would make me very happy. Not to mention convincing Scotland Yard I'm not a timewaster." Beatrice sampled the other coffee, in the interests of fairness. "Tomas, anything else we need to know?"

"The Swiss and Austrian police have warned the owners their paintings are at risk. They gave no more detail apart from telling them to take 'extra precautions'. Frau Doktor Eichhorn sent me a message last night with factors regarding composition. She confirms your feeling, DI Stubbs. Of the six items we have identified as being on a possible hit list, only two Schads and one Grosz have subjects looking directly at the observer. One of those is *Nina in Camera*."

"The one in Munich. What about the other two?" asked Stein.

Tomas typed some commands on his keyboard. "There's a Grosz we already know about in Bremen. It's called *Äusserer Schweinehund*. But one other Schad we hadn't considered. This one is in Lübeck. Not in a private home but in a small gallery shared by a group of collectors. Less expensive than the others, although it's insured for a million Euros. It's called *Jäger,* which means hunter. You can see it here."

Beatrice and Stein moved closer to look at the screen. Once more, eyes dominated the picture even though this was a full-length portrait. Hard and somehow malign of feature, the man wore a felt coat and a green hat, peaked at the front and uptilted at the back. His britches were tied at his knee and the nuanced nature of the paint gave a vivid reality to both colour and texture. His right foot rested on a dead boar, gutted and muddy. His grey eyes challenged the viewer to congratulate him as he cradled his shotgun over his knee. The sensory power was such that Beatrice could not only feel the fabric of his coat, but smell the ripe gamey odour of the wild pig. She hated it.

"Not what I'd want in my living room, but each to his own." She took the other coffee once again and swigged. "Do you have an image of the Grosz?"

Tomas reached for the mouse and stopped.

"What is it?"

He spoke without turning from the screen. "This is not nice. Sometimes, you wish you hadn't seen something. Are you sure you want me to show you?"

Beatrice swallowed more coffee, managing nerves, curiosity, irritation and a refusal to be patronised. "Thanks for your concern, Tomas. A detective's job is to turn stones. We may not like what we find underneath them but it's our duty to look."

Tomas gave a sharp nod. He clicked a few times and a garish image filled the screen. A caricature of a fat man, dressed in a three-piece suit, with porcine eyes and florid cheeks, a cigar protruding from lips pulled back in a grin, showing his stained teeth to the viewer. His right fist held a rope, the end of which was tied around a woman's neck. She was on her knees, her arms hanging limply by her sides. She wore a gauzy top, torn so her left nipple was visible, and no underwear apart from stockings, revealing a dark triangle of pubic hair. Her face was covered by a white bag. The fat man's left thumb jerked behind him, at two figures in uniform bending over a bloodied body on the ground. One muscled arm was bringing down a club, the other's foot was drawn back for a kick.

Beatrice found it repulsive, but she refused to react. She focused on the fat man's eyes. Once again, they had a message for the viewer. *Look at this. Feel shock. Feel injustice. And there's nothing you can do*. It was a direct challenge.

Stein took a deep breath. "As a social commentator, Grosz didn't hold back. DI Stubbs, does this fit the pattern you and Frau Eichhorn identified?"

"I think it does. I'd like to discuss it with her again because I see a transactional factor in these works. A gauntlet laid down by artist to viewer, communicated by the eyes. Thanks, Tomas, I've seen enough. You're right, though. Some things you wish you could unsee. What does the name *Äusserer Schweinehund* mean?"

Stein frowned. "It's hard to translate. *Innerer Schweinehund* is a common expression, meaning 'inner pigdog'. The lazy demon inside you that makes you stay in bed rather than go jogging, who offers excuses rather than encouragement. It tells us not to try anything because we will fail. We all have to overcome our pigdog if we want to achieve anything. Naturally it's 'inner' because it's a part of us we keep hidden. *Äusserer Schweinehund* is a twist on that expression which would mean 'outer pigdog'. My interpretation is Grosz is making a statement – here is the worst part of humanity openly exposed."

"Sounds like a rational analysis to me. Right, gentlemen, let's get to work. I need to call Berlin."

After calling Frau Eichhorn, Beatrice made some notes for Tomas, who was still on the phone to Herr Meyer. She signalled ten minutes and made a little walking gesture with her fingers. Tomas nodded and she went out into the street. She didn't go far as the cold made being outside more of a struggle than a pleasure, but she needed time to think. The concepts she'd discussed with the art professor batted around her mind and her solar plexus glowed with the conviction she was right. With Eichhorn's help, the police were now able to think like the art aficionado who employed such vicious means to assemble his collection. And therefore stay one step ahead. They were going to catch this gang and find where the trail led.

Yet not all the optimism and excitement she experienced was related to the case. She had just discovered a powerful weapon to wield in her own fight and wanted a few moments to process the idea. Stein's description of the *Innere Schweinehund* – the personal demon – thrilled her to the centre of her being.

Beatrice had always prided herself on clear-eyed self-assessment – she knew she was nothing special. Hard work and application had enabled her to rise through the ranks of the Met, because her intelligence was no more than the upper end of average. Talent, kindness and wit, albeit mediocre, were in evidence, as were selfishness and greed. Her looks would never turn heads, apart from her hair, and that caused more alarm than admiration. She lacked vanity despite possessing a sizeable ego, but on the whole she'd always quite liked herself.

Since her diagnosis with bipolar disorder, that had changed. In the same way she might regard an old friend in a new light after a betrayal, she realised she could no longer trust herself. She had become her own enemy; one who would never give up trying to destroy her. One who had almost succeeded by convincing her the only thing to live for was endless misery and offering an escape route via a bottle of pills. Those black dogs who padded around the peripheries of her subconscious, waiting for their moment to attack her soft, white underbelly were her own monstrous creations. She had long since lost her grip on the leash.

Now this exhausting battle had taken on a new dimension. The unpredictable mood swings, the energy-sapping inertia, the conviction of life's futility against an incessant tide of cruelty and injustice, the hyper-cycling euphoria which would drop her at any second into a void of numbness, the smothering duvet of absence – none of these was Beatrice Stubbs. Her enemy now had a name and an otherness. An *Innere Schweinehund* she could visualise, personalise, separate and therefore defeat.

She had a Pigdog.

Chapter 15

In the upmarket area of Gruenwald in Munich, the streetlights remained on all night. Not that it was necessary. High walls and electric fences bristled with security cameras and movement-triggered floodlights. These luxurious villas and their occupants and contents could not have been better protected. Especially this evening, as a dozen plain-clothes police officers were stationed around the vast corner property on Waldstrasse. Most officers carried the badge of the Munich City Police, apart from two, who were sitting in the back of a surveillance van, drinking coffee. The time was 04.41.

Stein checked in with all units, and although Beatrice didn't understand the German, she picked up the bored intonation over the airwaves. Nothing happening. The operation was due to run till eight am but everyone knew the optimum hours would be between four and six. Tension built and the clock seemed to slow. *Do it. Do it now!* Beatrice closed her eyes and willed their targets to act.

"DI Stubbs, if you need a rest, you could lie down on the bench for half an hour. I'll wake you if anything happens."

Her eyes flew open to see Stein's brown eyes and shadowed jawline angled towards her with a kind expression of concern.

"Thank you. I'm fine. How about yourself? More coffee?"

"No more coffee. I need to freshen my mouth. Perhaps there's water or juice in that fridge behind you. Only another three hours to go. We will survive."

Beatrice gave a tired laugh and opened the mini-fridge to find cold water, all kinds of energy drinks, a variety of juices and assorted chocolate. She selected two bottles of juice and a bar of Lindt to share between them. They sat side by side, watching the screens, listening for input and snacking on their impromptu picnic. Waiting, watching.

Stein spoke, his focus on the monochrome images of gates, doors, gardens and streets on screens.

"It's like looking at an empty stage. This is the place where anything could happen."

Beatrice swallowed some chocolate. "I know what you mean. The stage is set and we're all in anticipation. But when nothing happens for hours on end, it's no more exciting than watching pants dry."

Headlights swept across the screen and they both sat up, stowing their drinks. The car drew closer and Beatrice spotted the unlit taxi sign on the roof. She got a clear view of the driver and passengers while remaining invisible, thanks to the police vehicle's tinted windows. A couple kissing in the back seat, an uninterested driver and nothing to draw their attention. Nevertheless, Beatrice followed its trajectory. At the junction, the cab turned right, not left and removed itself from suspicion. The clock read 04.53.

"Coming home at this time of night? Munich is obviously a party city." Beatrice rustled open the rest of the chocolate.

"Less so than Berlin or Hamburg, unless it's Oktoberfest. Isn't London even more of a twenty-four hour party zone?"

"Probably. I wouldn't know. My clubbing days never really began. Even in my twenties, I was usually in bed by eleven."

Stein raised his eyebrows with a smile.

"To clarify, in bed with a good book. Are you a party animal, Herr Stein?"

"Sometimes. I play guitar in a band at weekends, so late nights and socialising are part of the package."

"Really? What kind of music do you play?"

"Jazz, funk, some of our songs are more pop, but it's all easy listening. The important thing is that when I'm playing, I'm completely absorbed, concentrating on what I'm doing at that moment. I can forget whatever happened during the day and focus on the music. It always makes me feel better. In a job like ours, I find that's vital."

"I agree. One can get very weary when dealing with the less attractive side of human nature on a daily basis."

"And you? What do you do to relax after..."

The floodlights around the house burst into life, throwing a harsh brightness across the grounds. Stein picked up the radio and checked in with each patrol. After a few moments, a security guard exited the gatehouse and made a circuit of the garden, checking the gates, shining a torch into corners and generally putting on a display of 'doing my job'.

A realisation dawned, draining all the tension from Beatrice and leaving in its stead a sense of being played for a fool. "We're onto a loser here. The security team know we're watching and this is all part of the show. Nothing's going to happen."

"But it was the security team who alerted us," said Stein. "That doesn't make any sense."

Beatrice sighed with frustration and tiredness. "No, it was *one* of the security guards who reported the activity. Probably a senior member of the team. Then we told the owner we'd be here tonight, watching. Despite our warning him not to do so, he's obviously told the security firm. Look at that bloke. He's acting the part! If the thieves have one of the guards on their payroll, which is highly likely, they know they're under surveillance and they're miles away, laughing at us or stealing someone else's painting."

Stein watched the poor performance and nodded slowly. "I think you might be right. *Scheisse*!"

Five hours sleep and one flight later, Beatrice was fractious and upset. During the telephone conference, Herr Meyer did not mince his words and called the Munich operation 'poorly planned' and 'rushed without sufficient thought'. He asked for a full report and analysis before committing to further surveillance. It was a rap across the knuckles and Beatrice could only hope Hamilton would not get to hear of it before he arrived on Thursday. Fat chance.

She spent the rest of the afternoon incorporating Eichhorn's expert opinion, Tomas's data analyses and her own unsubstantiated views into a report and delivered it to Stein. His face seemed shadowed and fatigued, but the warmth in his eyes was genuine as he thanked her.

She left the office at five and walked to the hotel, wishing Adrian was still in residence. She needed to offload. On a whim, she took a detour and jumped on a U-Bahn to Holger's studio. It would have been polite to call first, but he had no mobile. If he wasn't there, she'd go to his flat. Further than that, she hadn't planned.

The studio complex, *Made im Speck*, was an old brick building which showed signs of a previous life as an industrial plant. She looked for a bell or door knocker, then pushed open the door and called a hello. No reply. The place seemed empty, although all the lights were on. It didn't surprise her. These collective art/work spaces seemed to operate on a very relaxed system of trust. Beatrice wandered from studio to workshop, encountering all kinds of eye-popping creations, but not a single artist. No caretakers, no security guards, no Holger.

Finally a bearded male in overalls emerged from a doorway, smelling so strongly of dope that she reeled.

"*Guten Abend. Ich bin...* um... *Holger Waldmann*?"

He spoke in English with a Mancunian accent. "Holger? I don't think he's here today. You can check his studio. Up the stairs, second door on the left."

"Thanks."

She found Holger's workspace more by luck than the hipster's directions. The second door on the left was a photographer's studio, containing some rather disturbing nude close-ups. She closed the door in a hurry and checked the other side of the corridor. The second door on the right opened into a viaduct arch with a carpet of wood shavings and sawdust. This was the right place. The body of a violin lay on the workbench, oddly vulnerable without its neck. Unvarnished, limbless, bare of strings: an instrument embryo.

Beatrice stroked its curves with one tentative finger, before drawing back out of respect. The room gave little away. Tools hung from the walls in neat racks and a wooden chest of drawers, each compartment neatly labelled, reminded her of a spice cabinet. She smiled. A scent of pine, nutmeg and tar ebbed and flowed as she wandered the room, a fine dust disturbed by her footsteps. A workshop, a place to use one's hands, with few indications as to the craftsman himself.

On a small table in the corner, there were books and papers and several box files in no discernible order, and a selection of photographs pinned above the desk. Photographs of guitars, violins, a double bass. A smiling Holger with two men in overalls holding a certificate of some kind. Another one showed Adrian and Holger on a London bridge. She pulled out the pin and picked it up, looking past their beaming faces to ascertain which bridge, but the background was out of focus and indistinct. As she went to stick it back in place, she spotted a postcard which had been obscured by the one in her hand.

The image looked like a monastery, austere and withdrawn from the world. Old-fashioned script under the picture read *Kloster St Ursula, Rosenheim, Mai 2009.*

On the back were hand-written words.

Open your heart and return to the path of righteousness. Forgiveness is yours for the asking.

Voices could be heard echoing in the yard below, so she reached for her phone, took a photograph of the back and the front of the postcard, then replaced both images as she had found them. Time to go. Her urge to seek a friendly face had melted away in this peculiar building. Now she had an insistent need for some uninterrupted thinking space. In any case, Matthew would be home from university in an hour and she could bend his ear instead.

Outside in the frosty air, she hailed a taxi and gave the driver the address of the hotel. First priority, order room service. Then Matthew. After that, a little bit of research on Kloster St Ursula in Rosenheim.

Chapter 16

In forty-eight hours, Adrian had not spoken to a single person – apart from the checkout staff at the supermarket in List, a couple of texts exchanged with Catinca, a call to Holger, two to Beatrice and a bit of banter with friends from the Gay Men's Choir on Twitter. He was practically a hermit.

Being alone was such a grounding experience. He walked on the beach, paying attention to detail by collecting beautiful shells and jewel-like pebbles. He paid homage to the immense and ever-changing canvas of sky with photographs which caught a mere sliver of the colours and expanse. He cooked meals for one with local ingredients, some more successful than others. Herrings, he decided, would never be a cupboard staple. He read his book, cycled along the coast road and adjusted to enjoying experiences for their own sake, rather than capturing them to post on Facebook. He had changed gear, put himself in a different kind of Cruise Mode.

In the evenings he lit a fire, poured a glass of red wine and caught up with some European films on his must-get-round-to-watching list. He slept deeply and could remember none of his dreams. His island escape was working wonders and he made up his mind to escape the commercial horrors of Christmas every year.

A storm hit the coast on Wednesday, which put paid to any cycling as the rain lashed the house and a gale shook the building with the force of a meteorological tantrum. When a Jeep bounced down the track late Wednesday afternoon, he was surprisingly relieved to see another human being. He opened the door to greet his visitor and recoiled at the strength of the wind.

"Hello Adrian!" Daan yelled as he slammed the driver's door shut. His shaggy hair whipped across his face, obscuring his smile. He swept it away in practised gesture of exasperation and crammed on a trapper hat, then advanced with his hand outstretched.

"Remember me? Holger's friend? I'm on my way home after buying some food. So I thought I'd ask if you want to join me. Let's go indoors. Shouting over this wind is a waste of time. What kind of crazy person comes to Sylt in December? Have you got any beer?" He grabbed Adrian's hand and shook it with an alarmingly powerful grip.

"Hello! Nice to see you again. Come in, come in, you're getting soaked!" He closed out the screeching gusts and punishing rain. "My God, Sylt really knows how to put on a show."

Inside the house, Daan seemed even larger. His black beard, waterproof jacket and ear-flap hat seemed to fill the small hallway, carrying a smell of the sea. Although he had brought the outdoors in, his smile radiated good humour and warmth.

"It's going to be like this for a couple of days. That's why I stocked up at the supermarket today. If I have to stay indoors, I want to enjoy myself. Good food, plenty of drink and entertainment. So, where's that beer?"

"Oh, yes, sorry. I don't think I have any beer, but I have got a smooth red wine which is very warming. Shall I get you a glass?"

Daan narrowed his eyes. "No beer? OK, good job I went shopping first. You don't mind dogs?" He didn't wait for an answer, but opened the door and battled his way back to the truck, using his shoulders against the wind like an American footballer. Adrian watched from the threshold as he hefted a case of cans in a fireman's lift and threw some items into a carrier bag. He jerked his head and a husky leapt from the back seat, ran straight past Adrian's legs and shook itself in the hall.

The door banged wide open and Daan blocked out the light. He held out the case of beers with another huge grin. "If I'm cooking for us both, here is as good as anywhere." Adrian lugged the cans into the kitchen while Daan took off his outdoor gear.

"The dog is called Mink, but just ignore her. Don't try to make friends. She doesn't have a lot of time for humans. If she likes you, it's her decision. Just put down a bowl of water where she can see it and let her make up her mind. Are you Jewish?"

Adrian filled a ceramic bowl with water and solemnly placed it in the hallway, observed by a pair of ice-blue eyes. He considered the relevance of the question and tried to answer honestly.

"Um, no, not committed to any religion to be honest, but..."

Daan, now in thick socks and a fisherman's sweater, gave him a powerful pat on the back. "Nothing to do with religion. But on the menu tonight is my speciality. Pork, parsley and potatoes. How does that sound?"

"Lovely! I eat everything. It's very kind of you..."

"I like to cook for people. And I should have called you before. Holger said you were alone. How about we have dinner this evening and if the storm is over, I'll take you on a tour of the island on Friday? Mink and I will sleep in the spare room tonight if that's OK. I never drive drunk but never eat pork without beer and akvavit. Shit! The pork! We need to switch on the gas. The meat takes at least two hours and it's getting dark already."

He barrelled into the kitchen, leaving Adrian and the dog in the hallway, both avoiding eye contact.

Daan moved around the kitchen with an easy familiarity, talking and drinking beer as he prepared the joint of meat. Mink watched from the doorway, her glacial gaze fixed on Daan's hands as he massaged spices into the scored pigskin. In an attempt to be useful, Adrian sat at the table, peeled the potatoes and listened.

"Yes, I've known Holger for years. We met when I was around

eight years old. His family and mine spent summers here, which I hated at first because I had to leave my friends at home. In fact, it was because I wanted to play with him and his brother that I learned German."

"How come you didn't speak German?"

"I'm Danish. Daan the Dane from Odense. Do you know Odense? It's a port. I grew up with boats and the sea and never wanted to do anything else. I did my apprenticeship in maritime technology in Britain, you know. A boatyard in Plymouth."

"Plymouth? How funny. I thought you had a touch of a West Country accent."

"I loved Devon! And Cornwall. Cornish pasties are the best invention in the world. But I always planned to live on Sylt. As soon as I got my diploma, I moved here to start my own business. The island changed a lot, but no matter how many rich idiots in SUVs swarm here in summer, it's still wild and natural."

As if to prove the point, a machine-gun volley of raindrops hit the window with impressive force. Had Adrian been alone, the ferocious weather would have unsettled him. Daan's company was most welcome.

"Holger mentioned you repair boats. So your work is also your passion. Same with me. I sell wine. It's never going to make me rich, but I love what I do."

"Exactly!" Daan heaved the meat into the oven and clanged the door shut. He set the timer, stamped on his empty beer can and flung it into the recycling bin before opening another. "Beer for you or are you staying with the wine?"

"I'm fine with this, thanks. How many more potatoes do you need?"

"Do the whole bag. Even if we don't eat them tonight, they are delicious cold. Yes, I love what I do and I'm good at it. On Sylt, I can make good money. All these wealthy fools who think this is their playground are very careless with their toys. In the summer months, I often have too much work, fixing their stupid mistakes. So I earn as much as I can in the summer which takes me through the winter, when there's not much demand. Why did you choose wine?"

He sat at the table and picked up a paring knife to help Adrian.

"To show off, at first. But then I found myself reading more and more on the subject and accidentally became the go-to guy for wine recommendations. I got a job in an upmarket hotel and learned from a master sommelier."

"Sommelier? What's that? A wine waiter?"

"Well, a bit more than that, but yes, an expert on wines. Then I became a buyer for a chain of off-licences and the manager of one of their stores. Eventually, I took the risk of starting my own business and this is the first real holiday I've had since then."

"Why did you and Holger split up? You two seemed perfect for each other."

Adrian stopped, surprised at the sudden lurch towards the personal. Daan continued peeling, an open expression of enquiry on his face.

"We have... differing hopes for the future. Basically, he wants kids. I don't."

"Shame. You make a lovely couple and I know he was mad about you. But I'm with you on the kids thing. Didn't even want a dog, but she was abandoned by some selfish moron and left to starve. Typical of these people. They dabble. Buy a boat and all the gear, sail a couple of times, damage it through incompetence and move on. Get a dog, expensive pedigree, don't train it or give it enough exercise, so it gets bored and starts causing damage. Then they chuck it out. Bastards."

They both turned to look at the wolf-like shape in the doorway. Since the meat had disappeared, Mink lay with her nose on her paws, watching the two men.

"She is a beautiful animal. I've always wanted a dog, but living in London..."

Mink got up, stretched her front paws out with her bottom in the air and walked over to Adrian. She sniffed at his foot and up his calf, rested her chin on his knee and looked up into his eyes.

Daan grinned. "That means you're allowed to touch. Offer her the back of your hand and give her a stroke. Under, not over. Don't go for the top of her head. It still scares her."

Adrian nervously obeyed the instructions and caressed the soft fur under her jaw. He did feel a bit stupid speaking to her in English, but hoped she understood the tone.

"You're a gorgeous girl, aren't you? Look at those ears. What a fabulous coat. Like a Siberian landscape in the shape of a canine. Oh my God, her tail is wagging."

"And if you give her a piece of your pork crackling later, she'll love you forever. Right, that's the potatoes done, now we can have a break before I start the sauce. Why don't you prepare a fire and I'll make up my bed in the guest room. I know where everything is, don't worry. And I might just break with tradition tonight, seeing as I'm dining with an expert and drink wine with the pork. Choose something for us. Mink! *Fuss!* Come on, we need to sort out our bed."

The dog loped after him, wolf following bear, and Adrian found himself smiling.

The meal was an unqualified success. Moist, succulent pork, perfect roast potatoes and a piquant parsley sauce accompanied by a chilled dry Riesling all worked in harmony to deliver comfort, taste and balance. Mink lay in front of the fire, sated by her plate of leftovers and crackling. Adrian's usual urge to clear the table and tidy up immediately had deserted him, and the two men sat amongst the remains of the roast, savouring the satisfaction of a great meal and pleasant company.

The weather continued to batter the house, but inside the atmosphere glowed. Daan had a disarming technique of engaging in small talk one moment and segueing into politics or personal details the next.

"What did you see of Sylt so far?"

"Why do the British always put fruit with meat? It's weird."

"When did you realise you were gay?"

"What was your impression of Hamburg? Full of dickheads?"

"Why are the British so hung up about class?"

"Have you ever been sailing?"

Adrian thought about that one. "I've been on a boat but I wouldn't call it sailing. To be honest, it wasn't an experience I'd want to repeat."

"Let's see how the weather behaves. I'd like to show you a different side to the island, if it calms down. Mink won't even get on the boat when the sea is choppy. That dog has good sense. We can tour the whole of Sylt in the Jeep whether this storm continues or not, but the boat is best. I want to show you my place. It's nothing sophisticated, apart from being the most beautiful location in the whole Northern hemisphere, I guarantee."

"And you live alone? Apart from Mink?"

"Yes. I have relationships now and then, but my last girlfriend told me there is no room in my life for a partner. I can't argue with her. Company is great, but on my terms. I need time alone to feel rooted. Not many people understand that and end up getting frustrated or angry with me. Best to keep it casual. With plenty of variety." He laughed loudly and clapped his hands together, waking the dog. "Now! Time for the akvavit!"

Adrian stacked the plates and took them into the kitchen, while Daan uncorked the hooch. When he came back, his guest was standing at the fire, peering at pictures on the mantelpiece. He thrust a glass at Adrian.

"Here! Cheers! I hope Sylt brings you everything you want."

Adrian threw back the firewater and coughed.

"Sip it. There's a taste as well as an explosion. Here, look at this. Do you recognise me?"

The mantel was covered with framed photographs of children, dogs, boats, happy family units and picnics. Adrian scanned the various assemblies and spotted a dark-haired child on top of an upturned canoe. Every other head was blond.

He pointed. "You're not the average Dane."

"Marauding Celts along the coast. Powerful genes. How many generations does it take to fade black hair and green eyes? Not to mention charm. You ready for another?"

"Go on then. Is that Holger?" He indicated a white-blond kid holding a paddle.

"No, that's Joachim, his brother. That one's Holger." Another white blond, cross-legged in the sand, squinted at the camera. "We spent that whole summer on the beach, rebuilding a boat."

Other pictures showed freshly-caught fish, seventies fashions and family meals. There was another blond, a girl with plaits who stared out of the pictures with a resentful glare.

"Is this Holger's sister?"

Daan's smile shrank to nothing. "Yeah. Patricia. Horrible sow."

His terminology made Adrian laugh, attracting Mink's attention as she raised her head from her fireside spot. Daan poured two more glasses of akvavit.

"She was! She ruined everything. Always hiding and listening to us so she could run to Mummy and tell tales. Whenever we had an adventure planned, she'd want to be part of it, but as the dictator, not part of the team. She spoiled everything. Bossy, sneaky, poisonous. We used to lay Patti-traps, early warning signs that she was near. That was my first close-up experience with women. It's a surprise I didn't turn gay."

Adrian laughed harder. He suspected he might be borderline drunk.

"What?" Daan demanded.

Adrian attempted to focus his thoughts. "I don't think it's a negative experience with a particular gender that flips a switch. I see it as more of a positive thing, like good taste. I know the kind of wines I prefer which suit a particular dish. I know the kind of people I prefer who suit a particular experience."

"Good point. Cheers!" They toasted again. This time Adrian repressed his cough because Daan had already launched into a story about the time the three boys tried making their own alcohol.

"So sick, all of us. My stomach wasn't just upset, it was outraged!" He thumped his thigh and laughed, a huge infectious booming sound which made even Mink's tail thump.

The evening passed so pleasantly in terms of conversation, food and ambience, Adrian was amazed to see it was after one in the morning. He was warm, happy, expansive and pissed.

"Daan, I need to go to bed. I'm drunk as a skunk. God knows what's in that akvavit but I'm not surprised it gets you through a Scandi winter. Are you and Mink OK to put yourselves to bed? I need to douse the fire, locks the checks and make sure we're safe."

Daan bellowed with laughter and clapped his hands. "How about I lock the checks? Yes, you're obviously new to akvavit. Go to bed, we'll make sure the house is safe. See you in the morning for the full Danish. I hope you have some decent coffee. Sleep well, Mink and I will be fine. Drink some water before you go to bed or your head will hurt tomorrow."

Adrian did as he was told, dimly conscious of Daan chuckling and talking to the dog as he secured the doors. He filled a beer mug with water and ricocheted up the stairs to his room. After taking off his clothes, he did a lazy mouthwash, drank some more water and hit the pillow like a manatee.

Adrian opened his eyes and ran an inventory. Head throbbing, stomach queasy, mouth dry and a pressing need to urinate. He sat up and drank several gulps of water, registering the LED digits. Just before six in the morning. The storm had either taken a break or blown itself out.

He got up and fumbled his way to the toilet in darkness. He emptied his bladder and washed his hands with his eyes barely open. On the way back to his bedroom, he stopped, listening to an unfamiliar sound. Snoring. He walked on the balls of his feet to the door of the guest room, which was wide open. Inside, lit by strips of moonlight lay the wolf and the bear, back to back, one on top of the duvet, one underneath, both snoring. He tiptoed away to his own room and as he turned the door handle, he heard a more familiar sound. The creak of the front door.

The sound took a second to register, by which time his eyes were wide open. He stood still and listened in the gaps between snores, feeling the cold wood of the landing beneath his bare feet. He switched on the hall light and padded down to the living room. Nothing. In the fireplace was a mound of ash, the front door was locked and empty glasses littered the table. Down here it was warmer and Adrian's heart rate returned to normal. He checked the kitchen, just to be sure, and stood in the hallway wondering what else could have made the sound he'd mistaken for the door.

That was when he saw the mantelpiece. All the photographs he'd looked at a few hours earlier had gone. Instead, right in the middle, was a large wooden crucifix.

Chapter 17

"It was an inside job."

Judging by the number of empty cups, Tomas had been in the office for some time. Cables snaked across the desk to two laptops and a third device which looked like something from a Bond movie. He didn't even look up when she entered the room but delivered his evaluation directly at his screen.

A thought crossed Beatrice's mind. If she had set Tomas onto the connections between Holger Waldmann and a nunnery in Rosenheim, she need not have wasted last night chasing one dead-end after another in front of her screen. But she shook off her personal preoccupations and focused on work.

"Good morning to you too. There was no 'job', inside or out. What do you mean?"

"The security guards tipped off the thieves minutes after the conversation with Herr Walter. Look at the timeline. Incoming call from the boss advising extra security at sixteen ten. Outgoing call from same mobile at sixteen twenty three. The number dialled is located in The Hague. Three more text messages from that number that afternoon and evening. The metadata shows us this Dutch number is the kingpin."

"*Was soll denn das werden? Was fällt dir ein?*"

Beatrice and Tomas both jumped as Stein's voice whipcracked around the room.

A rapid-fire exchange in German ensued with Stein repeatedly indicating the Bond box. Tomas's body language gave the impression of defensiveness but without apology. Stein repeated the word 'knee' three times with all the conviction of the final word. She watched the exchange like a tennis match, mildly entertained and admiring the sparks off Stein.

Tomas jerked his head towards Beatrice. "*Was meint die Chefin?*"

Stein's expression turned volcanic. "DI Stubbs, I'm sorry about this. I needed to say something to Tomas regarding his unauthorised use of police equipment."

Tomas protested. "It is authorised. The Munich force has clearance to use the FlyTrap for specific purposes. And I am permitted to use the data. This meets all the official..."

"*Halt die Klappe!* This surveillance equipment is still restricted under European law. Our policy is to use this only in cases of terrorist activity, human trafficking and drug smuggling. Art theft does not qualify."

"That's not for you to say! DI Stubbs is in charge of this investigation."

Beatrice held up her hands in surrender. "I have no jurisdiction here and in any case, I feel under-informed. Can one of you tell me what the problem is? Tomas, explain this box of tricks."

"The FlyTrap. You don't know it? This is an IMSI device which captures data from mobile phones. It intercepts mobile traffic by imitating a base station. You can listen in to conversations and read all SMS data, in fact anything going out of or coming into a mobile. This technology is controversial, especially since Snowden, because you don't need a warrant. This is why Herr Stein is uncomfortable."

Beatrice exhaled, relieved she was not as far out of the techno-loop as she imagined. "Yes, I'm familiar with the technology. We just call it by a different name."

"So you know that it is legal and one of the best techniques we have to track the electronic communications of organised gangs."

"Which is exactly what we're dealing with. So your issue is

the legality of data-gathering, Herr Stein?"

"No. I know it's legal. I'm far more concerned about civil liberties and privacy issues. Just because we believe a painting to be under threat, the police have no right to listen into conversations coming from that house."

Tomas shook his head. "Herr Meyer disagrees."

Stein's head snapped round with a furious glare and Tomas looked away.

Beatrice cleared her throat. "I'm confused. If this imitates a mobile phone base station, how can it possibly work from here?"

Tomas was eager to explain. "The data didn't come from this machine. I asked Herr Meyer if we could use this technology as a back-up to the physical surveillance. He gave the instruction to the Munich team, not me. All I have is the data they gathered. It takes a long time to find the relevant information and I had to ask a communications analyst, but I found it and we are in a far better position than before. The only problem is here in Hamburg. We have the technology." He indicated the box. "But Herr Stein refuses to let me use it."

"If Meyer and the BKA approved its usage, I don't see the problem. Herr Stein?"

"Munich can make decisions regarding data-gathering according to their own policy. Ours is only to use communications interception in clearly defined circumstances. This is not one of them."

Beatrice sat down, partly to defuse the tension but mostly because she had not yet recovered from a night drinking coffee and watching an empty house. She yawned.

"If I understand you correctly, this FlyTrap shows a certain amount of telephone activity from a mobile phone belonging to one of the security officers at the Munich house. We assume it was a warning to potential thieves not to attempt the heist that night. If that's the case, and as yet we have no other evidence, surely we'd want to use this machine to eavesdrop on the Netherlands operation. So I don't see why you need it here in Hamburg."

Tomas, eyes glittering, tapped a couple of commands into his screen. "Listen to this. It's in German, but I will translate."

A voice recording came from the computer's speakers. Beatrice made out a few words but kept her attention on Stein's face. His frown eased as he listened and as the speakers ended their conversation, he nodded.

"That's clear. The caller doesn't identify himself but says their 'appointment' for the evening must be postponed because his boss asked him to do overtime. The person at the other end, who speaks German with a strong Dutch accent, asks if the caller is being watched. The caller says that eyes are everywhere. He then suggests an opportunity over Christmas, when the place is empty. The Dutchman says he'll talk to his people but confirms our suspicions by saying 'Tonight, Nina stays home'. Tomas, you said there was an SMS?"

Tomas tapped at the keyboard, his complexion pink with excitement. This man evidently loved his job. "The first one is from the same mobile and more or less the same location, on the outskirts of The Hague. It says 'Due to increased levels of interest, his client prefers to withdraw his offer. Thanks for your help and I will be in touch." The security guy replies 'A temporary withdrawal, I hope? As mentioned, access over the Christmas holiday will be no problem.' There's a two-hour gap in communications before the Dutchman sends a final text. 'Other options I need to investigate. Thanks for the information and I will contact you if we decide to proceed'. So, they're looking at other paintings. This means we have to get as close as we can to the other pictures on the list."

Stein sat opposite Beatrice, his expression thoughtful. "DI Stubbs, how do you see it?"

"I assume we know who owns the Munich mobile, Tomas?"

"Yes. The other calls and texts show it is the younger security guard, Udo Katzmann."

"So in theory, we could bring him in and lean on him a little. He's obviously an amateur or he'd have used a separate mobile for communication with this gang."

Stein shook his head. "That risks alerting the nucleus we're onto them. Tomas has a point about using the FlyTrap, but I cannot authorise this. Nor can you, DI Stubbs. I will ask Herr Meyer for his decision and we can proceed in conjunction with the Netherlands police."

"That's fine with me. On the same issue, Tomas, employing a secondary tactic was an interesting idea. However, it is totally unacceptable to do so without asking permission from Herr Stein or myself. Going over our heads to Meyer was a poor decision and I'm surprised Meyer allowed it. It will not happen again. This unit functions as a team, and as such it offers its members the courtesy of full disclosure."

She resisted the urge to ask for agreement and opened her laptop. She could feel Stein's eyes on her, but kept hers down.

The morning passed quietly with the three officers absorbed in their own tasks. Apart from the occasional request for confirmation, they worked in silence. Stein's phone rang just before eleven. He picked it up, glanced at the display and left the room. Beatrice decided it was coffee time.

"Tomas, I'm going to the canteen for my caffeine fix. Can I bring you anything?"

He looked up. "Thank you. I'd like an espresso. And..." He hesitated.

"Yes? I'm having a pastry so I'm happy to get one for you too."

"No, not a pastry. I want to apologise. Meyer told me to inform you and Herr Stein about using the FlyTrap. It was my choice not to do that because I know how much Stein hates the idea of covert interception. He would have stopped it and we'd have zero results after last night."

"That doesn't sound much like an apology. More of an excuse."

"It's both. I am sorry I didn't inform you." His eyes met hers, slid away and looked back from under his brow.

"Accepted. I hope you'll do the same to Herr Stein. It might be a good opportunity to talk about your different approaches to the FlyTrap. As I understand it, he's only following the official policy for the region."

Tomas waved his head from side to side, in an 'I'm not so sure' gesture.

"Well, I'll leave it up to you. But we're working as a team, so no secrets. Now do you want a pastry or not?"

Tomas caved in and requested a Berliner.

On the way to the canteen, Beatrice stopped at Margrit's desk. The girl looked up from her screen with a bright smile.

"Hello DI Stubbs. How's it going?"

"Very well, thank you. I wondered if I could ask you a favour."

"Of course. I'm on Herr Stein's team so it's not a favour, it's my job."

"It's not actually work-related. You see, I've been looking into retreats for my holiday next year. I want somewhere peaceful, where I can meditate and contemplate but nothing overly religious. Someone recommended this one in Rosenheim, but the website's all in German. Would you mind having a look and tell me what you think?"

Margrit took the piece of paper with the URL written on it.

"Sure. Do you want me to do it now?"

"No, there's no hurry. Just when you have a spare five minutes. Thanks Margrit, I appreciate it."

By the time Beatrice got back with the cakes and coffee, Stein had returned. She approached the room with caution, trying to read the body language between the two men. Tomas's humble posture and Stein's relaxed attentiveness suggested an apology was in progress, so she went back to the canteen and added a latte and a croissant for Stein. On her return, both men were working on their computers so she decided it was safe enough to enter.

"Elevenses time!"

Stein smiled, his face unlined and open. "A good time for a break and a discussion of procedure. Thank you, DI Stubbs. That was Herr Meyer on the phone. He's spoken to detectives in The Hague and the decision has been taken at the European level to commit to telecom interception in three locations: the house in Bremen which houses the Grosz, the gallery in Lübeck with that Schad painting of a hunter, and at the location in The Hague. It's been identified as a light industrial unit which imports and exports fruit. We're responsible for Lübeck and Bremen. As Tomas knows the FlyTrap pretty well, I suggest he oversees both operations, keeping us informed at all times, naturally."

A look passed between the two men.

"Good. Glad to see you two have buried the ratchet. I agree, I think Tomas deserves a role of responsibility after all the effort he's put in."

A look of confusion passed across Stein's face but cleared as Beatrice passed him his coffee. Tomas bit into his doughnut, careful not to sprinkle sugar on his keyboard.

"I have one area of concern," said Stein. "Do we warn the owners of the house and the gallery? They are potential victims, not suspected criminals, so perhaps they should be aware that every personal call or SMS might be scrutinised."

Beatrice thought about it as she tucked into her apple strudel. "Did Herr Meyer have an opinion?"

"He said that after the Munich non-event, he would advise not informing them. We might be sabotaging our own operation by doing so."

Tomas nodded vigorously. "Exactly. We don't know if the security teams and owners are involved in some way. This is our chance to find out. I say no. We listen, assess any relevant data and pinpoint the next target. From there, we can use traditional methods of surveillance."

"I tend to agree," said Beatrice. "We delete any information which is not pertinent to this case, but we listen to all of it." She rammed home her point. "We are very close to identifying a gang who don't simply steal works of art but use violent means to do so, ruining lives in some cases. As far as I'm concerned, we put every possible means we have into catching these people so we can find who pulls the strings. I believe we owe that to the victims."

She was pushing Stein's buttons, she knew. Evidently, so did he.

"Thank you, DI Stubbs. I had not forgotten the victims. It seems I'm in the minority, so I'll accept that. For this operation, we do not warn innocent people their personal conversations are being monitored. Tomas, can I leave you to arrange the two local units and report back to DI Stubbs and myself on how you plan to analyse the volume of data?"

Shoving the rest of the Berliner in his mouth, Tomas nodded, still chewing, and started work immediately.

Stein's gaze rested on Beatrice's face. "I'd like to discuss a few points with you in more detail. Do you have plans for this evening? I think it might be a good idea to get out of the office and share our thoughts on the management angle of our collaboration."

Beatrice flushed. There was something extremely intimate about the way he used the word 'you' instead of her name. This was practically asking her on a date. Then she remembered her commitment and grimaced.

"Oh hell. I'd really love to, but my boss is arriving tonight. He wants to have dinner and I'm not in a position to refuse. Could we do lunch instead?"

"Your boss is coming from London? Must be important. Of course we can have lunch instead. But we get out of the building, OK? I know a nice place a short walk away. Can we say twelve-thirty?"

"Yes, I'll look forward to it. I had planned to speak to Frau Eichhorn about the paintings in question, but under the circumstances, perhaps I shouldn't mention them. What do you think?"

Stein gazed at her until she began to feel awkward. "Shuffle the cards. Ask her about a lot of paintings and slip those into the middle somewhere so as not to attract attention. Oh." He leaned forward and picked a piece of apple strudel off her jacket.

"I was saving that for later," she said.

"Too late!" he replied and slipped it into his mouth. "See you at lunch."

She watched him walk away with a heartfelt sigh, the scent of his aftershave lingering in her nostrils. It was probably for the best they couldn't have dinner together. Her imagination was likely to run away with her. Instead, she had to spend several hours with Hamilton. Her smile faded.

Chapter 18

Daan wrapped his hands around the coffee mug, took a sip and swallowed, his gaze resting on the mantelpiece. He shook his head again. A scratch at the door indicated Mink was ready to come in. Adrian opened the door and she bounded back across the threshold, leaving wet pawprints in her wake. Outside the light was weak and yellowy, but the storm had gone, at least temporarily, leaving a trail of broken branches and drifts of tobacco-coloured leaves in its wake.

Back inside, Daan was still shaking his head. "This makes no sense. We both stood here last night, looking at those photographs. We identified me and Holger. I even remember noticing the dust when I picked one up. Last night, those pictures hadn't been touched for months and there was no crucifix anywhere in this room. This morning, the pictures are gone, the surface has been cleaned and there's a huge cross in the middle."

"And the door was locked. When I thought I heard it close, I came down and checked. It was locked. I'm one hundred percent certain."

"Two people in this house with the door locked. So it must have been you or me. I don't think I've ever sleepwalked. Even if I did, I wouldn't know where to find a cross in this house. Holger's grandparents don't have such a thing, as far as I know. They're Calvinists and reject all kinds of iconography."

Adrian rubbed his face. "It wasn't you and it wasn't me and it certainly wasn't Mink. I wonder why she didn't bark?" The dog's tail whisked back and forth across the floor as she faced the two men.

"Because she sleeps like the dead. Useless guard dog."

"That's true. When I heard the door close, it was impossible to hear much at all over you two snoring. You were both out cold, like I'd been. Where did the pictures go? Where did that cross come from? Who the hell has access to this house and why would they come in during a massive storm to replace family photos with a crucifix? And what's up with Mink?"

The husky's eyes were fixed on Daan and her tongue lolled as her tail made rhythmic sweeps of the rug. Daan broke his focus on the cross and shifted his attention to the dog.

"She's hungry. Me too. We should have some breakfast and then I need to... shit, look at the time! I've got to go! No time for the full Danish. I'll shower, you fry an egg and put it in a pork sandwich to take with me. Give Mink some leftovers. No bones! I don't want her farting in the Jeep all day. We have a long drive."

He thundered up the stairs, cursing the time. Mink followed Adrian into the kitchen and watched as he prepared her breakfast.

"Here you are, girl. Eat up. I'll wrap some bones for later. Now, he wants a fried egg and what?"

The mechanics of making the sandwich only occupied half of Adrian's attention. His gaze was drawn to the window and the patterns in the swirling leaves conjured by the wind. Someone was trying to scare him and doing a pretty good job of it. Staying on a stormy island in winter was perhaps not the smartest move. He should be at home, with friends, with crowds, London Transport, Catinca, the shop. He shouldn't be alone.

Daan barged into the kitchen, poured himself another half cup of coffee and drank it in one. "Sandwich ready? You fed the dog? OK, listen. I don't know how that happened." He jerked his head in the direction of the living-room. "But it is a bit freaky. At this time of year, Sylt can be a bleak place. I have a job today, otherwise I'd stay. Still, there are two things we can do. One, I've just set the CCTV cameras to record. They don't usually run during the winter, but this counts as special circumstances. If anyone is creeping about the place, we can see them. Two, how about I leave Mink with you? At least you'll have some company."

Mink's head angled at the mention of her name. Daan dropped to his haunches and spoke soft words, unintelligible to Adrian, as he scratched her neck. Her tail drooped and her ears folded back. She didn't want to stay.

"Are you sure? She doesn't look happy."

"She'll sulk for half an hour. Then take her for a walk on the beach. Give her a bone when she gets back if you can cope with the farts. Take her out again this afternoon and feed her when you eat. She'll be fine. Make sure she has water and I'll come by on Friday morning to pick you up for the tour. OK? I have to go. Thanks for dinner!"

He grabbed his bags, scratched Mink's chin, hugged Adrian and ran out the door. They watched as he executed a three-point turn and drove off with a toot. Adrian looked down at Mink.

"Do you want to go for a walk? Walkies?"

Her head dropped, she turned tail and curled up in the corner of the hall, refusing to look at him. Adrian locked the front door and before he could dither, removed the cross from the mantel and put it in the cleaning cupboard. His stomach rumbled and he decided Daan's breakfast recipe sounded intriguing. He set some butter to melt in the pan and started shredding some pork. He'd got halfway through a rendition of *To Know Him Is To Love Him* when he sensed a presence at his side. A pair of serious blue eyes studied him as Mink's nostrils flared in the direction of the counter. Adrian unwrapped a bone and placed it in her gentle jaws. She took it into the hallway and started gnawing.

"Eat that now and then we can both fart outside."

The wind was still powerful as Adrian and Mink crested the dunes and he had to lean into it to make any headway. Mink ran ahead, chasing sea birds with a gleeful bark. The cold air blew away the last traces of his hangover and he ran down the other side of the dune to join the dog. The vast arc of beach stretched away towards the distant town of List to his right, with a spit of sand curving out into the sea. The voices of two horse riders reached him, as they conducted a shouted conversation as their mounts kicked through the surf. Further along, a man threw sticks for a small scruffy terrier. To his left rose a headland topped with dune grass, deserted but for gulls.

He whistled to Mink but his breath was whipped away. He trusted her to follow and picked his way across the beach, his boots sinking into the soft white sand, to the edge of the sea where the footing was firmer. Clouds tumbled across the sky set to fast-forward, creating constant patterns of light and shadow on the ground below. Adrian shielded his eyes from the sun and gazed out at the waves.

The colours of the sea changed constantly, from a brushed steel grey to the dark blue of a naval uniform, only to break into bubbles of white as the water crashed on top of itself and rolled up the sand. He took a step to avoid getting his feet wet and Mink charged past him, straight into the water. She pranced, bouncing off her front paws, and landing with a splash, again and again. Adrian laughed aloud at her playfulness. After a few minutes she trotted out of the water and shook herself so hard her face seemed to rearrange itself. Then she pushed her shoulder to the ground and fell into a roll, wriggling and kicking her legs in the air.

"You're going to get filthy!" Adrian yelled against the wind, but she was on her feet and rushing into the sea once more. They proceeded along the beach like this until she found a piece of wood in the shallows. She picked it up, threw it with a sideways jerk of her head, grabbed it and shook it before bringing it to Adrian and dropping it at his feet. She didn't look at him but stared intently at the wood, nosing it towards him. He picked it up and flung it along the sand, watching her rush after it. When she was almost upon it her forepaws lifted and she leapt into the air to dive on it in an almost catlike pounce.

Adrian wiped away tears of laughter. For such a serious animal, she certainly knew how to have fun. Man and dog kept each other mutually entertained all the way to the set of rotting posts stretching into the sea, presumably the skeleton of a long-destroyed pier. Even in their ruin there was something beautiful about them, like standing stones.

The cold air, so bracing and clean at first, now began to infiltrate his jeans, so he turned back to the house, wondering if there was an old towel he could use to dry a large, wet, sandy dog. He planned to make a hot chocolate, read his book and maybe have a nap on the sofa. Being awake since six after a drunken sleep was not sufficient rest. But his fear and paranoia in the small hours was under control. Tonight, he would have the dog and security cameras, and Daan would be back in the morning. He might even take a sleeping tablet to catch up on his rest.

A bit of digging about in the laundry cupboard unearthed an old blanket and a towelling sheet with holes in it. Adrian used the latter to dry Mink, amazed at how much water a dog's fur could hold, and made a blanket bed for her in the middle of the rug. She circled it several times, dug it into an acceptable shape and curled into a ball, her nose on her tail. Adrian's mobile beeped. A text from Beatrice, asking him how his holiday was so far. He sent a rapid reply.

Weather dramatic, scenery divine, food and company excellent. Ax PS: I want a husky!

He checked the doors were locked and made a hot chocolate, then settled down on the sofa under a fleecy blanket to read. Within five minutes, his eyelids started to droop.

When he awoke he was sweating and couldn't move, and a damp and putrid stench filled his nostrils. He turned his head to see a mound of grey fur, each hair tipped with black, beside his head.

"Mink!"

A furry tail bounced off the cushions, followed by more of the revolting smell. Adrian struggled upright and shoved her onto the floor.

"Oh my God, Daan was right about the farts. Why did you have to point the business end in my direction?"

She scratched behind one ear then shook herself again, the cloud of fine hairs she released visible in a shaft of sunlight.

"Right. Time for lunch, another walk and then I'd better clean up after you. I had no idea you'd be such a full-time job. Come on."

Omelette for him, a tin of meatballs for her and *OK Go* playing on his iPad, with sunshine streaming onto the pale wood of the kitchen. All these elements combined to put Adrian in the best mood he'd enjoyed for weeks. Then he bundled himself up in his warm jacket and took Mink out to explore the other end of the beach. They walked over the headland and looked out at the tip of the island with its lighthouse. Adrian threw sticks, watched a distant ferry heading for Denmark and gawped at what he first assumed was someone swimming in the bay, until he realised it was a seal. He'd never seen one in the wild before. The seal was joined by several more and they bobbed and dived in the waves before heaving themselves onto the sandbank to enjoy some rays of afternoon sun. He wished he had binoculars.

A cloudbank swelled from the east and the sky on the horizon seemed to join the sea in a wall of smoky grey. Mink was digging in the dunes but lifted her sandy snout out when Adrian clapped his hands. She dashed to join him as the first fat raindrops pockmarked the beach and they broke into a run through the dune grass and back to the house. They weren't fast enough. All his efforts at keeping her out of the sea were wasted. She was now as rain-soaked as he was. Puffing and dripping, he dried them both in the hallway and went upstairs to change his clothes. From his bedroom window, he saw the cloudbank chase the last tiny sliver of sunshine until it was swallowed by the sea. Raindrops pelted the roof above him and he hoped there were enough logs downstairs that he wouldn't have to go back out to the wood stack.

Once he was dry, he checked all the windows and made Daan's bed. It occurred to him he had no idea where the Dane was or how to make contact. He'd just have to wait till he reappeared tomorrow.

It was already darkening when he got downstairs so he switched on the lights and dragged the vacuum from the cleaning cupboard. Mink disapproved of the sound, slinking out of the room with her ears flat. The wooden floors were easy to clean and the whole floor took only twenty minutes to restore to photo-shoot charm, with a quick spray of Febreze to counter the whiff of wet dog. He put the vacuum back and froze. That morning, he'd taken the wooden crucifix from the mantelpiece and put it in that very cupboard. Now it had gone. He rushed back to the living-room. The mantel remained empty.

He searched every room in the house, in wardrobes, under beds, behind doors, but found no trace of the cross. Mink found the whole exercise a game, trotting after him, nosing under beds and snuffling behind furniture, occasionally glancing at him as if to say, 'What are we looking for?' A vein in his neck pulsed and his breathing became laboured.

He returned to the lounge and lit a fire, less than reassured by the pile of logs that remained. He'd have to go outside again later. Mink curled up on her blanket and Adrian took a moment to breathe deeply and think. This tornado of thoughts was blinding any attempt at logic. He imagined explaining the situation to Beatrice, which calmed him. He sat at the table and wrote down the facts.

Pictures removed, crucifix substituted. Daan could bear witness to that. Crucifix relegated to cleaning cupboard, now disappeared completely. No witnesses, apart from a very clear memory of shoving the vacuum to one side so he could fit it in.

That's how he'd known where to find the cleaning materials this afternoon. Doors locked on both occasions. It was pointless to wonder why, he just had to focus on how.

Perhaps someone had been hiding in the house last night? But how did they lock the door after leaving? There was no one here now; Adrian had just spent the last half hour searching the entire building. The only occupants were himself and a large snoring husky.

So whoever it was had a key. He checked the doors again and noticed the front door had a chain. So even if someone did have access, he could stop them getting in. The back door didn't, but it was opened by an old fashioned key, so all Adrian had to do was leave his key in, tilted so it couldn't be pushed out, and no one could insert one from the other side. No one was in the house. No one could get into the house. Bingo.

Now the question remained, who had a key to the property? Holger said his grandparents lived here in the summer and loaned it as a holiday home the rest of the year. The logical thing would be to leave a key with a local. Adrian checked the time and called Holger at home. No reply. He left a message on his answerphone.

Hi Holger, just checking in from Sylt. Everything's lovely and the place is a delight. Daan and his dog came round for dinner and we're off on an island tour tomorrow. One odd thing, a crucifix appeared on the mantelpiece overnight. Bit weird but generally I'm fine and feel safe. Can you give me a call when you get this? Bye bye.

How can anyone on the planet survive without a mobile? No wonder they were incompatible, the man was a troglodyte. He pondered calling Holger's studio, but you never knew who would answer the phone. Instead, he uncorked one of his favourites, a Châteauneuf-du-Pape, and took some photos of the label, the ruby glass aglow with firelight and the sleeping dog in the background in a set of still life images guaranteed to inspire envy. At least he could make his life *look* perfect.

Chapter 19

From the sublime to the ridiculous. Lunch with Herr Stein had been everything she needed. Their surroundings were not exactly five star – an upstairs room in an Imbiss – but the fact they were alone, dropping bits of kebab and lettuce on the paper plates and eating with their fingers seemed to fit the occasion. Gloves off.

Stein appeared relaxed and willing to share his thoughts, with the proviso that she did the same. Their conversation was a delicate two-step, each exchange a quid pro quo. He acknowledged her detective work and hoped she understood his adherence to policy. She complimented him on his ethical standpoint and emphasised the importance of compromise and mutual respect in multi-national collaborations. He praised her instincts regarding his team and suggested unified thinking on their plan. Then she got a chilli caught in her throat. He leapt to his feet and patted her back till she stopped coughing, then poured her a glass of water.

"Thank you. You obviously have healing hands. Sorry, I was attempting to agree with you. We have no choice but to join up our thinking. We need the Dutch police, the BKA, two teams on the ground here in Germany, ourselves and Tomas overseeing the data. Do we..."

"Trust him?"

Beatrice shrugged in apology.

Stein shrugged back. "In the interests of mutual respect, I don't honestly know. Tomas is untried in the field. My hope is he will rise to the challenge, but I've never seen him under pressure, making decisions with human beings rather than data. Having said that, I noticed he brought you coffee and a lunch bag this week, and volunteered an apology. Not a big deal for most officers, but in Tomas it shows an unusual sensitivity and awareness of other people's feelings."

Beatrice chewed the last of her kebab and ruminated. "If you want my nine eggs, everyone needs the chance to prove themselves. Tomas's data is the cornerstone of this investigation, so he should be central to the investigative team. He'd benefit from guidance when it comes to fieldwork, but you can watch over him."

Stein opened his book and made a note. "I'll make arrangements. Would you like anything else?"

"No thanks. Apart from that awkward chilli, I enjoyed that. How was yours?"

"Dirty but satisfying. I'd planned to take you to a sophisticated Asian restaurant tonight. Instead, we're in an Imbiss, eating a kebab which nearly killed you."

Beatrice sighed. "I have nothing against dirty and satisfying. Nor sophisticated Asian either. If I had a choice, I'd much rather have dinner with you than get the third degree from my boss. But when it comes to Hamilton, no is not an option."

"Why is he coming here?" Stein asked, gnawing on a toothpick.

"To check up on me. He thinks I keep taking foreign assignments to run away."

"Run away from what?"

"Reality, I suppose." Beatrice rubbed her eye and immediately wished she hadn't. The remnants of chilli irritated her cornea and made her eyes water. "Sorry, I need to wash my face."

"Let me see."

Stein in close proximity to her garlic breath was a horrifying thought. "No, no, all I need is a rinse. Shall we get the bill?"

"You're invited. I'll pay while you use the bathroom. That chilli's determined to get you one way or another."

Beatrice thought back over their conversation as she stared at her reflection in the mirror over her hotel room desk. Tomas did have many of the identifying features of a geeky misfit with antisocial tendencies. But as Stein said, he was also showing behaviour which counteracted that. Apologising. Engaging. Bringing her coffee. She agreed with herself. He was certainly worth trying out on an operation. Apart from anything else, it would broaden his horizon from theory on a screen to action in the field.

Her hair was disobedient and the dour black dress made her look like a Portuguese fishwife. Good job she'd be sitting opposite her own crotchety boss, rather than Germany's equivalent to George Clooney. Hamilton would only take exception if her outfit contained any colour.

She applied lip salve but not gloss, put in her black pearl earrings and gave herself a final check in the floor-length mirror by the bathroom. Sober, boring, steady and anything but a loose cannon. She would do. In her handbag, she slipped an executive summary of the case to save her a lengthy explanation and give her a few minutes off the hook. With a deep sigh, she left her room and went to find a taxi.

When she arrived at Estancia, Hamilton was already sitting at the bar. She was five minutes early and only a third remained of his water, so he'd been waiting a while. His expression was neutral as he watched her approach. His greeting took the form of an inclination of the head.

"Stubbs." He pulled out a bar stool.

"Good evening, sir. Sorry I'm late."

"Five minutes early, for a change. Drink? G&T if memory serves?"

Hamilton proposing alcohol? She kept her eyebrows under control and gave a gracious nod. "Thank you, sir, that would be just the thing. Are you joining me or sticking with water?"

"Don't mind a drink when not on duty. This is my second." He drained his glass and a whole new level of concern opened up. She'd never seen Hamilton drink and had no idea what might happen if he did. These uptight sorts were often the worst when they let their hair down. He gave some kind of hand signal to the barman as if he were at home in his club, while Beatrice hauled herself onto a bar stool.

"Did you have a good flight, sir?"

Hamilton ignored her in favour of watching the ceremony of drink preparation.

The barman presented two tall glasses: ice and lemon and an innocent looking fizz. "Two gin tonic, sir. On the tab?"

"Yes, thank you. Here you are, Stubbs. Cheers!"

"Cheers to you too." She took a small sip and studied Hamilton's posture, colour and general demeanour. "You look better, sir. How are you feeling?"

A silence ensued and Beatrice's stomach sank in dread. A whole evening of these social power games. Her trying to make small talk, him refusing to engage. To think she could be chatting to Herr Stein over spicy noodles.

"How am I feeling? Surprisingly good. Yourself?" He didn't look at her, but studied the array of optics behind the bar.

"Optimistic. I believe this case could be solved within days. We have a great deal more information and a cross-border collaboration agreed. I wrote a summary for you, if you'd like to read it?"

"Not now, Stubbs. In fact, hang onto that and give it to Jalan. I'm taking some time off."

Irritated, she shoved the folder back into her bag. "So I understand. Is this a holiday, sir? I imagine you could do with one."

"Not exactly. Planning to catch up with some old friends."

He beckoned the maître d' to enquire about their reservation, forestalling any further questions. Beatrice bit her lip, sipped her drink and watched the beautiful people enjoying themselves.

A waiter escorted them to their table, insisting on carrying their drinks, and parked them in an alcove, next to an impressive pillar. Hamilton sat with his back against the wall, forcing Beatrice to sit opposite, with little to absorb her gaze other than her boss and some decorative cow horns attached to the wall. She snapped open the menu and looked for the most expensive dish.

"Stubbs, I've already decided on the food. We'll have the best quality steak and chips. Medium rare for me. You tell the chappie how you'd like yours. Might want to decide on an appropriate wine while you're at it. That's one area where your expertise outstrips mine."

Her molars pressed together, tensing her jaw, as she scanned the wine list. In point of fact, she did want steak and chips, but loathed it when others decided for her. She took her revenge via the wine.

When the waiter arrived, he gave their order. She added a Malbec with a hefty price tag and instructed the chef to cook hers medium to well done with a pepper sauce. In the last year, she had gone off bloodied meat. The napkins, the tasting of the wine, the addition of cutlery and the enormous effort it took to find a suitable subject for small talk wearied her and she decided she'd had quite enough of eating in restaurants for a while. Tomorrow, she would go to a supermarket and picnic in her room.

"Did you get the chance to have a look around Hamburg, sir?"

Hamilton tasted his wine. "That's jolly pleasant. Good choice. No, all I've seen is the interior of a taxi and my hotel room. Too damned cold to go exploring."

"It's certainly chilly. Perhaps you'll have a bit of time tomorrow. There are some lovely spots along the..."

"Doubt it. Flight at midday. I'm not here as a tourist, you know."

Not as a tourist, not as her boss, so the question was unavoidable. Why was the crabby old bastard here?

He narrowed his eyes. "Something wrong?"

"Not at all, sir. Trying to store the name of this wine, that's all. It's very good."

"So it should be, for the amount it costs."

She did not retort, but sat back and surveyed their surroundings. Let him come up with some chit-chat if he could be bothered.

"If you could choose anyone across the team, including yourself, who do you feel would make the best Superintendent?" he asked, his focus on his glass.

Hardly chit-chat, but better than sitting there in silence. She'd been expecting this and needed to tread a careful course between pretending she had no idea what he was talking about and pushing the idea of Rangarajan Jalan as the ideal.

"I thought you were planning a break, sir, not leaving us altogether."

"Playing for time, Stubbs? Answer the question."

"Not playing for time, sir. I've no reason to do so. Personally, I believe Rangarajan Jalan has all the management experience, diplomacy, decisiveness and interpersonal skills to be an outstanding Superintendent. If all you wanted was my opinion on a successor, sir, you could have asked me over the phone and saved yourself a trip."

Hamilton smiled, with all the warmth of a shark. "How odd. When I asked Jalan, he recommended you. Some sort of pact, I ask myself?"

Beatrice's temper changed colour. Up till now, she'd been in zone amber with the occasional flare of red. Now she shifted into magnesium white-hot. This arrogant, upper-class arse chose to make assumptions and patronise her as if she were a sixth-former. He'd already spoilt her evening and would continue to do so unless she showed her teeth.

"Sir, can I just say something?"

"No. Just for once, Stubbs, shut up and listen. I asked you to take over Operation Horseshoe for more than one reason. One, I thought you were perfect for the position and could learn a great deal about diplomacy from DCI Jalan. Two, I hoped the engagement would reignite your enthusiasm for policing in London and quash your desire to leave the force. Three, the role would be closely observed by the Chief Super and the board with a view to a promotion. Can you not see that I was trying to do you a favour by manoeuvring you into the job? But with your usual short-sighted urge for immediate gratification, you wriggled out of it to come here. I care very much about who will take over as Superintendent and the only possible candidates thus far are both determined to retire. Frankly, I find it very disappointing when an officer hasn't got the mettle to finish the job."

The man had offended Beatrice on every possible level and she considered simply getting up and walking out. Perhaps throwing her wine in his face to boot.

"Ah ha! Finally, the food. Move your elbows, Stubbs. Medium to rare? That's for me. The overcooked one with sauce is for her. Can you wait while I try this? Then I can send it back if not to my taste."

He sliced into the middle of his steak, parted the meat to check the colour and cut off a small section and chewed it with care. He looked up at the waiter.

"Cooked to perfection. The chef should be commended. Top up, Stubbs?"

Beatrice said nothing but watched as the waiter poured.

"Thank you." She spoke only to the waiter.

Hamilton lifted his glass. "Bon appétit. Cheers!"

She reciprocated, unsmiling, took a sip and returned her attention to the food. The sauce came in a mini jug beside a huge lump of meat and the chips looked crisp and chunky. At least she could enjoy the food, if not the company. She attacked her plate with vigour. He nodded his approval, apparently at ease, and they ate in silence. The sound of conversations, laughter, crockery and high heels on tiles eddied around them, filling the gaps.

After a while, Beatrice noticed how little Hamilton had eaten. She was a good two-thirds through this beautiful piece of meat, but he'd barely had more than a few mouthfuls.

She looked into his face. "Not to your taste, sir?"

"The food is delicious. As is yours, evidently." Hamilton leaned back, rotated the stem of his wine glass and fixed his stare on hers. "You want to know why I'm here."

"I did wonder. It seems a long way to come for a chat about human resources." She carried on with her chips.

"What did you expect?"

In her head she said *power games and politics.* Aloud she said, "I expected you to grill me and demand proof I'm not wasting police time."

"Are you wasting police time?"

"No, sir."

"Good. Consider yourself grilled."

He picked up a fat chip, reached over and dipped it in her sauce. He bit it in half, chewed and swallowed. Beatrice began to wonder if he was drunk.

"Not bad, if a little heavy on the cream. Fact is, Stubbs, I'm sorting out my affairs."

Beatrice refused to react. Hamilton always had loved his melodramatic language and half-statements, with the express intention of eliciting a question.

"Really? I found it rather well balanced with the Marsala to add that touch of punch and sweetness."

He topped up her glass, without asking her. "Not to my taste. As I say, I'm ticking boxes and dealing with unfinished business."

She put down her knife and fork and stared him in the eye.

"Sir, if you have something to say, please say it. All this 'sorting out affairs', 'unfinished business' sounds very dramatic."

Hamilton looked directly at her, all geniality gone. "It does rather, doesn't it? Truth of the matter is, I'm dying."

Chapter 20

It was always bittersweet to reach the end. Adrian closed his book and lay back on the sofa to consider the sense of loss. Reading is a strange experience, he thought. You dive into the world of another, adjust to their terms, begin to feel at home and then it's over. You're alone with a bundle of emotions and no means of return. Rather like a failed relationship. Or being kidnapped by aliens.

The fire's earlier blaze had dwindled to a glow, so he got up and checked the weather. Darkness limited his view but it didn't seem to be raining. He seized the moment to go wood-gathering. He borrowed a waxed jacket and an Aussie-style hat then grabbed the hatchet from the tool cupboard. Cold wind hit his face as he opened the back door and he was glad of the porch, keeping the rain off and providing enough illumination for him to work. He loaded the log basket then set about chopping some kindling on a wooden block. The effort warmed him and he found himself relishing the swing of the blade and the split of the wood as he indulged his inner lumberjack. After one last look at the starless sky, he lugged the loaded baskets back inside, locked the door and attached the chain. Mink was sitting in the hall, her tail thumping as she awaited his return.

He looked at the clock. Five past seven. "I've been out for less than fifteen minutes, you soppy creature!"

She ran to him and bunted her head against his legs.

"Yeah, OK, I missed you too. Come on, let's build the fire. Then I need a shower before we think about dinner."

He knelt by the fireplace and built a tepee of kindling around some scrunched-up copies of the *Sylter Rundschau.* While he selected some dry logs, an odd sensation crept up the nape of his neck. He was being watched. He snapped around to the window facing the sea. Nothing but navy darkness. He looked behind him into Mink's blue eyes and caught the smallest movement at the kitchen window. Without switching on the light, he walked silently across the hallway and up to the glass. Balletic grasses swayed in the wind and trees waved their branches as if in some sort of interpretive dance. The floodlights hadn't been activated so it was probably something light blowing past, like a plastic bag.

He returned to his task and finished his preparations. Then he ran up the stairs, peeled off his layers and jumped into the shower. He rejected the creeping fear of a stalker, determined to conquer his own paranoia. Focus was essential. He mentally began preparing two quite different meals for himself and his guest.

Daan worked late to get the job done. It hadn't been a good day. The first attempt at repairing the damaged section of the gunwale had resulted in bloodied knuckles and a good deal of swearing. All because the imbecile had given him the wrong dimensions. He drove to a nearby metalwork shop to get a replacement panel cut to fit, then started again. Finally, he tightened the last of the screws and looked at it from all angles. A professional job. He was hungry as hell and just as soon as he'd done clearing up, he was heading for his favourite restaurant in Rømø. Tonight, he planned to enjoy live music and a large burger. He'd missed the last ferry, so he'd have to sleep in the Jeep and get the first one in the morning. Without Mink, it was going to be a cold night.

He was sweeping up the last pieces of detritus when his mobile rang.

"Daan Knutsen."

"Daan, it's Holger."

"Hey! How are you?"

"Good, thanks. Just calling to ask if you've seen Adrian at all."

"Yeah, we had dinner last night. Nice guy, although for a wine merchant, he can't really hold his liquor."

"How did he seem to you?"

"Nice, like I said. We had a fun evening. I can see why you liked him. If I was gay, he'd be just the sort I'd go for."

Holger paused. "I can't imagine you as gay. No, what I meant was his behaviour. When he was in Hamburg, he seemed a bit paranoid and nervous. He sometimes imagines things. Today he left a message and said something which worried me. I hoped the rest would do him good, but I think he's still having these delusions."

"I didn't notice anything strange, but I've nothing to compare it to. He was good company. I cooked my pork speciality, we got drunk and I stayed over. He was a bit freaked this morning but he wasn't the only one. All the pictures on the mantelpiece had been moved and there was a wooden cross there instead. Weird."

"You saw that?"

"Yeah. He must have done it himself, sleep-walking or something, The brain can do some weird shit."

"Daan, will you keep an eye on him for me? I'm really concerned he's having some sort of breakdown and all this... stuff… is a cry for help."

"Of course. I'm taking him on a tour of the island tomorrow, in fact. And I left Mink with him."

"What do you mean?"

"He's got the dog. She's not a Rottweiler or Doberman, but she'll help him feel more secure tonight."

"Why, where are you?"

"Rømø. Doing a shitty job in some crappy village but at least there's a good restaurant. I wanted to get back this evening, but the last ferry's already gone."

"…"

"Holger? You still there?"

"Yes, just thinking. I called Adrian a few minutes ago, but there's no answer. That's not normal. He's always got his mobile nearby. I'm wondering if I should get up there."

Daan looked at his watch. "I don't think you'd make it. What time is the last train? Anyway, Mink is there to keep him company. If he is ill, being responsible for an animal is a good thing. It switches his focus away from himself."

"Maybe. Listen, I'm going to call him again. If there's still no answer, I'll check the trains and see if there's any way of getting there tonight. I can't help feeling I've made a mistake. I thought calm and isolation would be the best for him. Now I'm not sure he should be alone."

"I'll be there first thing tomorrow, so don't worry too much. Let me know if I can do anything."

"If neither of us can get to Sylt tonight, we'll just have to put our trust in Mink."

Two days' growth had given him more than stubble. Adrian spent ten minutes checking the advance of grey, trimming the edges of his not-quite beard and cleaning his fingernails. In the last two days, his attention to personal grooming had seriously slipped. Fortunately, like a well-kept lawn, the damage was easy to repair. He hummed along to the sound of Lady Gaga coming from the living room as he clipped his toenails. Mink barked. And again.

At first his body tensed before he understood this was a request for attention, not a warning.

"Demanding dog," he muttered. He wrapped a towel around his waist and came out onto the landing. "What?"

There was no reply. He pattered halfway down the stairs to see her sitting at the bottom, her tail wagging.

"Nearly done. Then we'll have dinner."

Toilette complete, he dressed in jeans and a long-sleeved

T-shirt, and descended the stairs with enthusiasm. Mink was waiting, tail sweeping the parquet floor like a windscreen wiper.

"I know, I'm hungry too. Where are you going?"

The husky trotted into the living room and sat in front of the unlit fire, an expectant look on her face.

"Yes, yes, when we've eaten. Come on, it's dinner time!"

She bounded ahead of him into the kitchen, her collar tinkling. He put enough rice on for both of them and prepared a chicken piri-piri à la whatever was in the cupboard for his dinner. She would have chicken scraps and rice with a handful of peas. He was opening a bottle of Chilean Sauvignon Gris when he happened to look into the reflective surface of the oven and saw a white face at the window. He whirled round, pinching his skin in the corkscrew. The window was completely dark; there was nothing more than raindrops on the other side.

Pain drew his attention. His right index finger was already sprouting a blood blister and he realised he was clutching the bottle so tightly his nails had imprinted livid grooves in his thumb. The house was silent, apart from rice bubbling in the pan.

This had to stop. He turned the gas down and walked all around the house closing the blinds. He lit the fire and switched on some random news channel, just to feel a connection to the rest of the world. Then he unplugged his phone from the charger. The screen blinked on and announced two missed calls from Holger in the last half hour. He hit redial as he went back to the kitchen and ignited the heat under his chicken. The phone rang for a full minute. Holger was not at home.

The DVD selection was surprisingly eclectic. Presumably each family member had contributed some of their favourites. Adrian discarded anything at all scary, opting for the familiar and well loved. He was debating over *The Grand Budapest Hotel* versus *Brokeback Mountain* when Mink started growling. Her hackles stood up in a ridge along her back and her attention was fixed on the front door. Adrian's hairs rose too.

"What is it, girl? Did you hear something? The wind, I expect. It's still pretty lively out there. Nothing to worry about." He was reassuring himself, he knew, but the dog's ears twitched towards him and she laid her muzzle back on her front paws, still watching the door. He set up the film and picked up another log to throw on the fire. That was when the doorbell rang. Mink burst into an alarming volley of barks and Adrian dropped the log on his foot.

"Ow! Shit! Mink, shush now. MINK! It's probably Daan. Sssh. Come here."

He caught hold of her collar with one hand and opened the door, chain on, with the other. The porch light was still on from his wood collecting foray but there was no one at the door. He craned his head to see alongside the house, but all was in darkness. Mink thrust her nose through the gap and sniffed.

"Hello? Hello?" he called, his voice sounding feeble against the wind.

He pulled the dog back, closed the door and switched off the porch light. She was still growling. He checked the back door. Locked, with his key inside. He tried Holger again. No reply. He went into the unlit kitchen and looked out at the blackness. It was a long way to come to play knock-down ginger.

The blackness. If someone had rung the doorbell, why hadn't the floodlights come on? Thinking about it, he realised they hadn't come on while he was chopping wood, either. At the time, he'd been absorbed in his task with the porch spilling enough light on the log pile. He had no idea where the electrics were or how to operate them. He picked up the phone to dial Beatrice and dropped it in fright when a hammering came at the side window. Mink went berserk, barking and scratching and digging at the front doormat.

Adrian chickened out of approaching the window. If someone was there, a face at the glass, his heart would probably give out. Instead he crept into the kitchen and looked out. Light from the living-room lamps glowed through the windows onto the wooden walkway. No one in either direction, as far as he could see. Mink's barks grew angrier. He snatched the hatchet from the tool cupboard once more.

"No, I'm not opening it. No. You can't go out there. Somebody is playing silly buggers and trying to scare us. No, no, come and sit down now. I need to find a number for Daan."

He sat on the sofa and tried to think above the thumps of his heartbeat and Mink's incessant growling. There must be a phone book. He dug through the magazine rack with shaking hands and found a local directory. But Daan the Dane was unlikely to be listed. Had he ever heard Daan's surname? He must have, when Holger introduced them. What the hell was it? Mink padded out into the hallway and gave the front door a thorough sniffing, then commenced another marathon growlfest.

Perhaps under boat repairs? What was the German for boat? Or repairs? The only person he knew on the island who had even entrusted him with his dog and he didn't even know the man's name or number.

But the dog did.

"Mink, come here. Come, there's a good girl. Now sit." He reached around her neck, trying not to tremble, feeling for the small silver disc he had seen on her collar. He found it and tilted her to the firelight to read. One side was engraved with a single word: MINK. On the other, another word and some digits. He couldn't read at this distance and Mink had begun to growl once again. He knew it was directed at the disturber of their peace but wasn't comfortable with his face so close to hers.

"Can I take this off? Good girl. I only want it for a minute. There's a good dog."

He unbuckled the leather and drew it slowly through her fur. She seemed unconcerned and returned to her lookout post while he read the disc. Knutsen! That was it. Adrian reached for his phone when Mink released a volley of enraged barks. A jolt of fear rushed through him as he heard the unmistakeable sound of running footsteps on the wooden porch, which sent Mink into a frenzy.

He pocketed his phone and stood behind the door, trying to listen over his ragged breathing and Mink's noisy outrage. With a double check the chain was still on, he opened the door and something thudded at his feet. The crucifix was back. It must have been propped against the door and now it slid sideways into the gap, preventing him from closing the door. He tried shoving it away with his foot, impeded by Mink shoulder-charging him out of the way.

He reached for her collar to hold her back, rolling his eyes at himself when he realised it wasn't there. Instead he pushed her backwards and told her to sit. He squeezed the door as near to closed as it would go and released the chain. Then he opened it enough for him to crouch down, pick up the crucifix and fling it off the porch. The next second a massive blow to the back of his knees shoved him onto all fours. Twenty-two kilos of furious Siberian Husky shot past him and away round the back of the house.

"Mink! MINK! MINK!!!"

He went back inside, pulled on his boots and a coat, checked the back door was locked, then picked up a torch and went out through the front in search of the dog.

He could hear no barking and she was nowhere near the house. He did three circuits, cupping his hands round his mouth to call her name. He struck out towards the beach, his increasingly desperate calls snatched away by the wind.

Chapter 21

Beatrice set down her knife and fork, searching for the right words.

"Sir, I'm so sorry. I don't know..."

"... what to say? Not many do. Generally speaking, 'That's a shame' is preferable to 'Thank God for that'. More wine?"

"I had no idea things were so serious. I mean, I know you've been ill, but none of us was sure what the problem was."

"Not really a topic for the water-cooler. Cancer of the prostate. Unpleasant but rarely a killer when diagnosed in the early stages. When it isn't, one is subject to many more complications, especially when it spreads. I'm part of the latter unhappy band of souls."

Beatrice took a sip from her freshened glass. She tasted nothing. Hamilton's restless eyes moved from her plate to the window, to his plate, to the bar but rarely made it to her face.

"Eat up, Stubbs. Just because I've put a dampener on the evening, no need to let good food go to waste. In fact, I'll give that sauce another go. May I?"

She nodded and instead of using one of his own untouched pile, he purloined one of her chips with an uncharacteristic smile.

"You could hardly say no. Denying a condemned man his last wish."

Beatrice faked a laugh. But the shock of Hamilton's news had not sufficiently sunk in for her to appreciate his gallows humour.

"What about treatment, sir? I understand the complications, but surely there are things they can do?"

"Hmm. Still say that's overly rich for such a beautiful piece of meat. Less is more, Stubbs. Unless it comes to the wine." He studied the label and emptied the bottle into their glasses. "Yes, there are things 'they' can do. Alleviate my symptoms, prolong my time, ease the pain, providing I'm happy to spend my remaining days in an oncology unit."

"You said 'remaining time', sir. Would it be incredibly crass of me to enquire as to what that means?"

Hamilton smiled for the second time in two minutes, a warmth suffusing his face as he looked at her, his eyes softened by the candlelight glinting off his red wine.

"Crass, no. Blunt, impetuous, direct and classically Stubbs, but not crass. That, never. As for how long this thing will take to kill me? The consultant says I should celebrate this Christmas to the hilt. That, combined with words such as 'palliative care', 'will and testament', and 'keep me comfortable', indicate this is likely to be a matter of months. Like that Pratchett fellow said about his own illness, it's an embuggerance."

Tears flooded Beatrice's eyes and she reached into her bag for a tissue. Her phone screen indicated a missed call but now was not the time to check. She dabbed her eyes as discreetly as she could while the waiter cleared their plates.

"Sir, I can't tell you how sorry I am. I just want you to know that if there's anything I can do to help, although I have no idea what that might be, I would be honoured to do so. You only have to ask. I'm sure the rest of your team would say the same."

Hamilton stared into his glass. "I should like a coffee and a dessert. But first I must find the bathroom. Order whatever you want and something with chocolate and cream for me. Obviously accompanied by an espresso and a quality port wine. Then we do have something to discuss."

He levered himself to his feet with an almost imperceptible wince and gave her a polite nod. Beatrice sat back, staring at the ceiling, her thoughts and emotions a mess. Twenty minutes ago, she'd have cheerfully killed him with her bare hands. Now his vulnerability and attempts to promote her after he'd gone brought a painful lump to her throat and she scrabbled for another tissue. The vibration and glow of her phone caught her attention. Adrian. She picked up the dessert menu and her handset at the same time.

"Adrian? Are you all right?"

For several seconds she could hear nothing but breathless sobs and incoherent babbling, occasionally punctuated by recognisable words.

She sat bolt upright. "Adrian! I can't understand what you're saying! Are you all right? Has something happened?"

He was silent for a second and Beatrice thought she'd lost him. Then he repeated his story, still panicky and breathless, but with more attempt at being understood.

"Slow down, I can only catch about half of this. What dog? When? Where are you now?"

The waiter approached the table and Beatrice held up a hand to indicate she needed more time.

"Adrian, listen. "Go back indoors immediately. I'll call Holger and I'll call the local police. Get in and stay there. Don't move till I call you. Adrian… Adrian!" but the line had gone dead.

Beatrice was still shouting into the phone when Hamilton came back. Other diners' heads began turning towards their table. She looked up at Hamilton, saw his eyebrows arch in an unspoken question as he registered the concern on her face. She slammed her mobile down onto the table with too much force, then picked it up again and called Holger's home number.

"Something the matter, Stubbs?" Hamilton asked.

"A friend's having a crisis. He came with me to Germany… oh, shit!" she said as Holger's answering machine cut in. "Sorry, sir. I was trying to get help from a mutual acquaintance but he's not home."

"By friend, you mean your partner, I assume?"

"What? No, not Matthew. This is my neighbour. I think he's having some kind of breakdown. He's on his own and he needs my help."

"Then you must go to him, DI Stubbs."

"But sir, your news..." Beatrice was torn, uncertain of how to react to such an unprecedented situation.

"Go," Hamilton ordered. "There's nothing I have to say that won't wait. Might just pop some thoughts on paper, in fact. Probably best, can't stand a fuss. Go to your friend, Stubbs, that's an order."

Beatrice made up her mind. She shouldered her handbag and picked up her phone. "I am so sorry."

She looked up at her boss and saw his face had lost all the warmth of earlier. She wondered if she'd imagined the light in his eyes.

"Sir, this is terrible timing and I wouldn't dash off if it weren't an emergency. I really am sorry. Thank you for such a lovely meal. I just want to say again I'm shocked and saddened by your news but you can count on my full support. Have a lovely break and I look forward to seeing you on Monday." She held out her hand.

Hamilton shook it and held on for a moment. "My flight leaves at lunchtime. Perhaps we might have breakfast, presuming all is well with your friend?"

"I don't think I'll make that, sir. I need to travel north tonight, towards the Danish border. See you bright and early Monday morning."

A waitress arrived with a large chocolate cake. Beatrice gave it a lustful once-over then allowed the waiter to help her into her coat.

"Thanks again for dinner. Your pudding looks delicious."

"Thank you for being with me. Goodbye, Stubbs."

"Goodbye, sir." She hurried to the door, pressing the waiter for advice on the nearest taxi rank while tapping her phone for directions as to the best way to get to the island of Sylt.

Stein entered the station bar, peeled off his thick navy coat, hat and gloves and strode towards Beatrice. She put down her phone and pulled out her earpiece, so relieved she could have hugged him.

"Thank you so much for coming! I'm sorry to disturb you so late, but this is uncharted territory for me."

"Any news since we spoke?" he asked.

"Yes, I managed to get hold of Adrian a few minutes ago. He's in a terrible state. He thinks someone got into the house while he was looking for the dog. I told him to get a taxi into the town but he won't leave while the dog is missing. And I can't see a way of getting there tonight. Is it possible the island is actually cut off overnight?"

"Train and ferry access stops overnight. But it's not exactly cut off."

"But if the causeway is railway only, it's not possible to drive onto the island. So I have no chance of getting there before morning? What about a helicopter?"

"DI Stubbs, would you authorise use of a Metropolitan Police helicopter for a nervous man and a runaway dog? Out of the question. We cannot get to List tonight. But he is not cut off. I called the Sylt police force and asked officers from Westerland to attend the scene. They will ensure he is safe and assist in looking for his dog. I suggest we have a coffee and wait for their report."

"How close can I get? To List, I mean. If I can get nearly there, I could get the first train in the morning. Herr Stein, this is important to me. I need to get moving. Is there a train that will take me most of the way?"

Stein rubbed his eyes. "I'll drive you. Come on, let's get a coffee to go."

"Are you sure? That's so kind of you. I'd feel much better with you beside me. Right, you order the coffees but I insist on paying. A small sort of thank you."

She picked up her phone to tell Adrian the good news.

Chapter 22

Daan wasn't answering. Twice his calls went to voicemail, but Adrian couldn't find the right words to leave a message. He paced from front door to back once again, peering into the darkness, willing a lupine shape to appear.

Since Mink had disappeared, the disturbances had stopped completely. He'd wandered up and down the beach, combed the length of the lane and called the dog non-stop. Without gloves, his hand soon became too cold to hold the torch, so he alternated. One in his pocket, one shining a light across the darkened dunes. He returned to the house every ten minutes to check if she was there, afraid she would miss him and run off again. The fourth time he came back, he saw a rectangle of light spilling over the wooden steps leading to the kitchen. The front door was wide open. As he approached, the floodlights came on. That was when he called Beatrice.

The relief of hearing her voice burst his bubble and his voice cracked as he tried to explain. Practical as ever, she told him to go indoors and call Holger. He did as he was told, reluctant to disconnect and lose the human connection, especially as he dreaded what might be inside. He locked the back door, went straight into the kitchen and grabbed a jointing knife, feeling foolish and prepared in equal measure. Apart from the open door, nothing seemed altered. No crucifixes, front door locked and embers glowing in the hearth. No Mink.

He phoned Holger, expecting the answer machine, which was exactly what he got. Then he searched the house, knife in hand, working himself into a state of terror every time he opened a wardrobe door. The house was empty. No one, nothing under the beds, behind the shower curtain, in the utility room or standing between the rack of winter coats. He steeled himself to open the back and front doors and found no huskies, religious icons or murderous psychopaths lying in wait. He stood on the front porch and stared out into the night.

Icy crystals hit his face as he watched snowflakes swirl in changing patterns at the whim of the wind. Where the hell was Mink? She'd freeze to death out there. Siberian Husky she may be, but this was a domesticated dog who loved the fireside. A bitter blast of Nordic wind made him recoil and he retreated inside. No Daan, no Holger, Beatrice hours away and that beautiful dog out there in the dark and cold at the mercy of whatever kind of freak was tormenting him. A bone-chilling shiver ran through his whole body and he wondered if he'd ever feel warm again. If he could transport himself to a Moroccan hammam... He stiffened as he recalled a snatch of conversation.

"You're going to love the sauna."

Adrian stopped his pacing between the two doors to the house. What sauna? By the time Holger had shown him the heating system, the bathrooms, the spare blankets, the oven and how to use the entertainment console, it had been time to catch the bus. He'd never seen a sauna in the house and had no idea where it was.

He took one more look outside and walked back along the hallway. There was no room unaccounted for, so unless the sauna was in some kind of outbuilding he'd yet to see, there was only one place it could be. Underground. He'd seen no unusual doors, no indication of a cellar or access to a basement. He stopped to think. If you have a sauna, you will get hot and sweaty and need a shower. He made for the downstairs bathroom.

Whiteness, pine furniture, stone tiles, a toilet, bidet, dual sinks and a shower big enough for two. It was large, as bathrooms go. But no evidence of another door. He ran his hands along the walls, a cursory examination, his ears attentive to any sounds anywhere in or outside the house. Two wall panels had a circular disk at handle height. Adrian bent to study them more closely. Silver recesses with a semi-circular pendant. He hooked his finger into the loop, pulled it out and twisted it. The door opened smoothly, revealing shelves of towels, toilet paper and disposable guest slippers. There was also a pine bucket with a wooden ladle. Exactly the sort you'd use to pour water on the coals of a sauna.

He tried the second door. A silent black space which made him clutch his knife tighter until he saw the rattan flooring and a dangling pull switch to his right. He pulled and saw a spiral staircase leading down to a bright, whitewashed room, two pine recliners and several artificial plants. The atmosphere was so wholesome and enticing he'd got halfway down before he realised he was enacting exactly the kind of horror movie cliché he despised. He scuttled back up the stairs, switched off the light and jumped as his phone rang. He closed the door and answered the call.

"Beatrice?"

"Yes. Just to let you know we're on our way. The local police should be paying you a visit shortly to check out the premises and help you find the dog. Are you all right?"

"Umm. Yes and no. I just discovered a sauna in the basement. A whole room I didn't know existed."

"Is there anything down there?"

"Not sure. I was just checking it out when you called."

"Don't! Can you secure the door or block it in some way till the police arrive? And did you get hold of Holger or the owner of that dog?"

"Holger and Daan aren't answering. The sauna room is inside a bathroom so I'll lock the door from the outside. How long will it take you to get here?"

There was no answer.

"Beatrice?"

"We're not going to get there till early tomorrow morning. I'm estimating six o'clock. But local police will be with you as soon as they can. Adrian, listen to me. Stay safe. Don't open the doors to anyone unless you see police ID. Not even the dog. It could be a trap. The dog will find a place to shelter and we'll find it tomorrow. Do not open the door unless it is to a police officer. Is that clear? Secure that basement now and I'm going to call you every half an hour to make sure you're fine. I'll be there in the morning, I promise."

Adrian looked at his watch. Eleven pm. Seven hours to go. He locked the bathroom door and went back to his vigil, peering out of the kitchen window, back to the living-room, checking his phone, waiting for something to happen. Every gust of wind rattling the door, each creak of the roof or pockets of wet wood popping in the fireplace set his nerves jangling. Pacing between one side of the house and the other, he had to pass the locked bathroom door, which wound him up to snapping point. He wanted to listen to music, drown out the silence and distract himself, but needed to be alert. He had to be ready. His promise to Beatrice was hollow. If Mink returned, he would let her in and deal with the consequences.

Twenty minutes later, he was straining to see out of the front window when a flash of headlights lit the dunes. A car bumped down the track, frequent red glows from the brake lights indicating the driver's caution. Adrian's tension became a trembling anticipation of relief. The police patrol car pulled up and two officers got out. The driver stayed in the car. Adrian watched from the window as they approached the house and he rushed to open the door, forgetting everything Beatrice had said.

Both officers were tall but there was no mistaking who was in charge.

"Mr Harvey? My name is Herr Rieder and this is my colleague, Frau Jenssen. We understand you had some problems this evening. Can we come in?"

Adrian opened the door wide, relief at human contact and the presence of authority rendering him unable to speak.

It took over an hour to give a full statement of recent events, during which time he and Herr Rieder drank two pots of mint tea and Beatrice called twice. The policewoman and driver went out looking for Mink while Adrian sat on the sofa and tried to be as chronologically clear as he could. That meant he'd already been talking for fifty minutes before mentioning the locked bathroom and sauna.

Herr Rieder's disbelief was evident. "If I understand you correctly, there is a locked room in this house which may contain the dog?"

"No, I told you. Mink went outside. She couldn't possibly have got back in the house on her own, let alone open the sauna door. I doubt there's anything at all down there now, but it is somewhere a person could have hidden. I didn't dare open it alone, I just locked it and waited for the professionals."

"Show me, please."

Adrian led the way to the bathroom, wishing he had some kind of excuse not to accompany the man. He unlocked the door and jolted as he saw Herr Rieder remove a gun from his holster. His nerves approached hysteria and he began to sweat. Rieder motioned him away, shoved open the door and switched on the light. The bathroom and its mirror reflected innocence and emptiness. The reflection of his washed-out self and an armed cop seemed ridiculous in the spa-like sanctity of the space.

Rieder found the door to the sauna without instruction. Perhaps most houses had a similar arrangement, Adrian thought. He watched the officer open the door, call an order in German and wait. No response from the darkness.

Rieder entered and switched on the light. The wooden staircase creaked with each step as he descended into bright cleanliness. Adrian followed on tiptoe. The room was empty, peaceful even, with the one area of uncertainty. The sauna itself. The small wooden block, like a sinister Wendy House, sat in the corner with its one window in darkness. Adrian's hair stood on end and every sense screamed at him to retreat. Rieder did a 360° check and moved towards the sauna. Adrian held his breath. The officer threw back the door with his left hand, keeping his gun cocked in his right.

Silence. The door swung back and forth from the momentum but afforded enough visibility to see the space was empty. The only thing apart from pine slats, a heating unit with artificial coals and a laminated instruction sheet was a pile of picture frames. Rieder took out gloves to examine them and the photographs they contained. He showed them to Adrian.

"Those were the ones on the mantelpiece. My guest will tell you. We stood there and talked about them."

"The guest who stayed the night?"

"Yes, I told you, the owner of the dog. Daan Knutsen."

"Who gave you so much strong alcohol you had to go to bed, leaving him downstairs. A man very familiar with this house, who would know about the sauna."

"Daan didn't do this. He was as freaked as I was. And he left me his dog!" Desperation roughened his voice and he bit his lip, determined not to cry.

A loud knock sounded from upstairs, making them both start. Rieder indicated Adrian should take second place as he climbed up the staircase.

"My colleagues. I hope they have your dog."

The door opened to three people. Two cold, tired, snow-dusted police officers and in the middle, Holger. An optimistic shot of adrenalin pumped though him at the sight of his friend but he could not help but scan the background for Mink.

Frau Jenssen shook her head to dash any hopes. "We looked everywhere, including the owner's house in case he made his way home, and sent out an appeal to officers nearby. Don't worry, he'll be fine. In this weather, he will find somewhere to hide."

"It's a *she*," said Adrian and fell into Holger's arms.

The officers sat by the fire and took a statement from Holger while Adrian made more tea. Beatrice called again to announce her arrival in Knee-Boo or something, which was where the car shuttle would begin at five am. She and her colleague had checked into a motel to catch a few hours' sleep. The news of Holger's arrival seemed to ease her mind and she advised him to get some rest.

When he got back to the living room, the police had gone and Holger was poking at the embers in the grate.

Holger looked up, his face full of concern. "Are you OK?"

"I feel a whole lot better since you arrived. Where'd the police go?"

"They answered another call. We can go into the station tomorrow to add to our statements. Anytime, doesn't have to be early."

"I have to be up before first light. Beatrice will be here at six." Adrian placed the tray on the table and sagged onto the sofa.

"Beatrice? I didn't know she was coming to Sylt."

"I called her when I couldn't get hold of you." Adrian had barely enough energy to lift the teapot.

"I couldn't get hold of *you*! After I got your message, I phoned you twice. When I got no answer, I decided to come here. You always answer your phone. When you didn't, I assumed there was a problem. Then I phoned Daan but he's on a job in Denmark. So I ran for the train. And if you use this as another opportunity to persuade me to get a mobile..."

"You spoke to Daan?" Adrian rubbed his itchy eyes. "Did he tell you about the crucifix?"

"Yes, he mentioned it."

"See, it's not just me! Daan saw it this morning and didn't understand it either. He thought it was creepy. That's why he put on the CCTV cameras and left me Mink. And what did I do? I went and lost her."

Holger stared at him. "Daan activated the cameras? And you didn't tell the police?"

A huge sense of embarrassment followed by relief washed over Adrian. How could he have forgotten the CCTV? Finally proof that he was not imagining things.

"I forgot. I was worried about Mink."

"Stay here and listen for the dog. I'll check last night's recording and find out what the hell is going on." Holger stomped up the stairs.

Adrian poured more tea but didn't drink it. Instead, he checked the thermometer on the kitchen window. Minus 7°. He paced round all the windows, imagining Mink outside, shivering in the snow and freezing rain, the light in her blue eyes growing duller.

A warm hand on his shoulder woke him.

"Adrian?" Holger crouched by the sofa. "Do you want to get ready for Beatrice? It's nearly seven in the morning."

He blinked several times and took in his surroundings. He was lying on the sofa, covered by a fleecy throw. The fire had gone out. His brain circuits crackled into life. "Mink?"

Holger stood up and shook his head. "She's still not back. No point in going out yet, it's still as dark as the inside of a cow's arse."

"What did you see from the cameras?" Holger shrugged and looked away.

Adrian sat up. "What? What is it?"

"The camera footage shows nothing. No one going in or out of the house. No one outside the building. No dog. Nothing registered between 18.00 and 21.00. The first images show up at 21.39 when you arrive at the kitchen door."

Adrian rubbed his eyes with his palms. "Wait, what? No footage at all? None on me collecting and chopping the logs? None of the crucifix? You're not telling me it didn't pick up Mink knocking me flat. I ran round the house three times, it can't have missed that!"

Holger knelt beside him. "We'll work this out later. I'm as

confused as you are. Something's wrong, I just don't know what."

A light flashed outside the window and by the time Adrian had risen to his feet, he could hear the sound of an approaching engine.

"That must be Beatrice. Listen, Holger. I agree that something's wrong. But it isn't me. This is not my imagination."

Chapter 23

On the journey across the sea and up the island, Beatrice bounced between various emotions. Concern for Adrian, for his well-being and mental health. Residual guilt at abandoning Hamilton after he'd taken the time to deliver his news in person. Professional embarrassment at dashing off across the country with a senior detective just as her case was coming to a head. Irritation at how Stein appeared lean, rested and fresh while she had all the appearance of an uncooked doughball. And an undertow of worry about her medication, left behind in her Hamburg hotel bathroom. A day or two will make no difference, she told herself, trying to block out an image of James shaking his head.

Stein spoke little, which suited her. For all she could see in the inky pre-dawn, Germany's picturesque playground for the rich and famous could have been a back road in Norfolk. Blackness, a bit of sea, a glimpse of village and more blackness. A flash of irrational anger blazed at Holger for suggesting somewhere so remote and impractical for Adrian's rest cure. Occasional sleet showers spattered the windscreen as she checked her phone again. Nothing new from Adrian. She gnawed at her thumbnail and leant over to see the SatNav.

Stein spoke. "Three kilometres, DI Stubbs. We're there, almost. Are you OK?"

"Yes, thank you… No, not really. Four hours sleep and no

idea of what's really going on is making me extremely nervous. You shouldn't be here, for a start. I've already broken an entire file of protocols by asking my colleague to drive through the night to help a possibly delusional friend of mine. In the cold light of, well, not-yet-day, I think my judgement was off. I should not have..."

"You asked me for advice and I gave it, as your colleague. I offered to drive you here as your friend. I'm very happy you accepted. Attention! Here's the turning. Look out for the dog."

The car bumped down the track to the isolated house at the end. Silver streaks of dawn were just beginning to pierce the night sky as they parked. The door burst open and Adrian rushed out to meet them. He hugged Beatrice.

"I am so glad you're here."

"Are you all right?" she asked.

"Yes, since Holger turned up I feel much safer. Still no sign of Mink though. The police searched but found no trace of her."

"We'll look again when it's light. This is Herr Stein of the Hamburg police. He very kindly drove me all the way here. Herr Stein, Adrian Harvey."

The two men shook hands. "Pleased to meet you, Mr Harvey. Let's go inside, you must be cold."

Holger, standing in the doorway, raised a hand in greeting. Beatrice made the introductions and Holger closed the door, shutting out the wind.

Stein glanced around the interior and said something in German. Beatrice couldn't pick up any of the words but recognised the appreciative tone. Holger nodded and replied, then said a word Beatrice certainly did know.

"*Kaffee*?"

"Ooh yes please," she said.

"I'll make coffee for us all and let Adrian tell you... his story."

Adrian shot him a look Beatrice couldn't read.

Ever the professional, Stein took notes while Beatrice pressed

Adrian for precision. "How long did it take you to get dressed to go after the dog?"

"Only a couple of minutes. I put on my boots, grabbed a coat and found a torch, locked the door and left."

"Was the crucifix still there?"

"I don't know. I didn't see it, but it must have been. I only just chucked it off the porch. But it was dark and..."

"No outside lights?" asked Stein.

"They weren't working. The first time they came on was when I got back and I found the kitchen door open."

Stein made a note. "And that was at what time?"

"I can check," said Beatrice, scrolling through her phone. "Here it is. 21.41."

Holger entered with a tray. "Yes, that matches what's on the CCTV footage. I can clearly see him pacing and talking on his phone at that time."

Stein looked up. "There's CCTV?"

"Yes. But the problem is that it shows nothing. I checked everything it recorded from six o'clock last night. The first activity it picked up was Adrian leaving by the back door." He looked at Adrian. "I'm sorry."

Beatrice frowned. "How is that possible? Are some of the cameras faulty?"

Holger shrugged and shook his head. "They recorded the police arriving, me turning up and everything. Just no dog, no activity outside apart from Adrian."

The room fell silent and Beatrice sensed Stein's surreptitious assessment of Adrian. She tried not to do the same, despite her urge to study his face and gestures for clues. To give herself time to think, she poured coffee for everyone. Sunlight crept across the room and the only sounds were the stirring of spoons and ticking of the clock for several minutes. Then a creaking, bouncing and honking of a horn announced the arrival of a vehicle.

"It's Daan," said Holger. He stood up. "I'll go and tell him what's happened."

"No. I'll do it. I lost his dog, so I should be the one to tell him." Adrian pushed himself to his feet and went to open the door. He looked utterly wretched.

The big Dane took the news in his stride. He greeted everyone with a general wave and listened to Adrian's explanation with every appearance of calm.

"Probably chased off after something and got lost. Maybe she tried to make her way to my place. I'll go home and check. It's a shame she's not wearing her collar, but many people would recognise her anyway. You go out, look around and call me if you find her. If she's not at home, I'll be back to help in around forty minutes."

He jumped straight back into his Jeep and rattled off up the lane. Then his brake lights came on and he began reversing. He rolled down the window.

"Take her collar with you!" he bellowed.

Holger gave him the thumbs up and he rumbled away.

Adrian, Holger and Beatrice prepared to search, while Stein left to talk to the local police. Since the sun had come up, Beatrice could appreciate the beauty of the place. Last night, it had seemed bleak, miserable and almost deliberately inaccessible. This morning, the expanse of golden pink sunrise reflected on a snowy beach would have taken her breath away if the cold hadn't got there first.

She took the stretch of beach to the left, reaching towards the headland, leaving Adrian to cover the middle and Holger to take the right. As she crested the dunes, she could see the rough outline of a coast in the distance and she wondered whether it was still part of Germany or if she was actually looking at Scandinavia. Birds screeched and swirled, and the early sun highlighted the drifts of snow on the leeward side of the dunes. The wind whipped her hair across her face, but her eyes scanned the landscape and she let out her infamous whistle. Two fingers in her mouth, a lungful of air and she could make an impressive noise.

But no dog or anything else came running. She'd covered the headland and was making her way back towards the house when she saw the Danish man's Jeep pull up outside. She squinted and watched him jump from the cab with some kind of box in his hand. He strode off down the beach. So the dog hadn't made it home yet. Chilled by the wind and pained by her impractical footwear for beachcombing, Beatrice decided to explore further inland. She kept up her whistling while turning over the nagging worry that Adrian's story was only partially true. There had been a dog; the collar was evidence. But if it hadn't gone missing when he said it had, what had really happened? Why would he go to such lengths as to bring Holger all the way here from Hamburg, to worry Beatrice herself enough so that she would travel half the night?

Half an hour later, her eyebrows frosted and thighs like slabs of ice, she returned to the house. As she opened the front door, she heard Holger's voice, speaking German. His head whipped round when he heard Beatrice come in, so she shook her head regretfully, so as not to raise his hopes. She removed her outerwear while he finished the call. He lifted the coffee pot in enquiry.

Beatrice was just about to answer with enthusiasm and politely suggest some toast when her phone rang.

"Adrian?"

"*We found her! She was shut in a shed. She's OK but she seems a bit woozy. Daan's carrying her back. Where are you?*"

"Oh that's wonderful news!" She took the handset from her mouth. "They've got the dog!" Holger closed his eyes and sagged with relief.

"I just got back to the house. Holger's here too."

"*Good. Can you find some blankets and stuff so we can keep her warm? What? Oh, Daan says to heat some milk too. We're about ten minutes away.*"

"I'll do it now. See you in a bit."

By the time the odd procession reached the porch, Beatrice had assembled a bundle of blankets, put some milk in a pan over a low flame, instructed Holger to light a fire and was waiting at the door to welcome them.

The dog, a great furry thing like the ones that pull sleds, bobbed along in its owner's arms, wrapped in his puffa jacket. Adrian's lips were blue with cold, but his recent worried frown was only a trace of itself and in his hand was a box of dog biscuits.

Daan laid the dog on the blankets and removed the coat. Beatrice fetched the milk and gave it to Adrian, who crouched beside the two big hairy heads.

"Mink? Here you go, girl. I expect you're thirsty. Nice warm milk for you."

The dog's sleepy blue eyes watched him set the bowl down and she got unsteadily to her feet. Her back legs remained in a crouch but she sniffed the milk and began lapping. Four humans watched, each wearing an indulgent smile.

Holger spoke first. "Where did you find her?"

Adrian looked up from his kneeling position. "In one of the outbuildings on the next farm. Daan was calling and whistling and we heard her bark. Just once. So we searched all the barns and found her in what looked like an old chicken coop."

Daan nodded. "You know it, Holger. That shed on the Lemper farm. We all used to play in there as kids. Though I can't remember the Lempers ever having chickens."

"How did she get in there?" asked Beatrice.

Daan's voice deepened, although his focus remained on the dog. "She didn't. The door was bolted from the outside. Someone shut Mink in there deliberately. My guess is she went after some meat. She'll do anything for food."

Beatrice was beginning to feel the same way.

"It looks like she was drugged or sedated somehow," added Adrian. "See, it's just like she's come round after an anaesthetic."

The dog had finished her milk and seemed to have dozed off, still standing up.

"Perhaps she should have a check-up," said Beatrice, partly out of concern and also to disguise her rumbling stomach.

Daan guided the dog back down onto the blankets, mumbling gentle words in a foreign language. Then he got to his feet and smiled.

"Let's see if food, time and a warm fire make her feel better. If there's no change in two hours, I'll take her to the vet. First, I need coffee and breakfast. Dog-carrying on an empty stomach is never a good idea. I'm hungry and I don't think I'm the only one." He grinned at Beatrice. "Adrian, will you stay with Mink? Beatrice and I have work to do in the kitchen."

He rubbed his hands and led the way. Beatrice followed without hesitation. She had already decided she was going to like Daan.

After a substantial plate of smoked salmon and scrambled eggs with toast and a large milky coffee, Beatrice felt fully restored. So, apparently, did Mink. She appeared in the kitchen doorway, nose twitching, followed by Adrian with an empty plate.

"She's already had half of mine but I think she fancies seconds."

Daan studied the dog with a smile. He opened the fridge and tore off a few strips of chicken, under a pair of blue watchful eyes. Her tail wagged and she sat obediently as he fed her one slice after another.

"Let's see if she keeps that down. I have a feeling she will be fine." He looked at Adrian. "Can we postpone our island tour till tomorrow? I should stay home and watch her for the next twelve hours or so."

"Of course. She needs to be supervised after such a horrible night. I'm happy to wait till tomorrow."

Beatrice stared at him. "Adrian, you can't possibly be thinking of staying."

"Why not? If you and Holger are here..."

Holger shook his head. "I have to get back to Hamburg today.

I have a meeting this afternoon and a lot of work to catch up with. You should come back with me. You can always visit Sylt again in the summer."

"He's right," Beatrice agreed. "I can't stay either, because I'm in the middle of a major investigation. I could get myself and Herr Stein in trouble for being here now. Why don't we all go back to Hamburg together?"

Adrian's face fell and Holger reached over the table to put a hand on his arm and give it a squeeze. "It wasn't my best idea, leaving you up here alone. Especially when you're unsettled. Better to come back to the city."

"What do you mean by 'unsettled'? There's nothing wrong with me."

Beatrice could sense trouble brewing. "Adrian…". Her appeal to common sense was curtailed before it could begin, interrupted by the ring of her mobile. "It's Herr Stein. Excuse me."

She stepped over the supine dog and went into the living-room to take the call. "Hello, Herr Stein?"

"DI Stubbs, we need to get back to Hamburg. Our sources indicate that this evening will be of vital importance. I'm coming to pick you up now. Can you be ready?"

From the kitchen she heard voices rising and tried to eavesdrop and converse with her colleague simultaneously.

"Yes, of course. How long have I got?"

"Thirty minutes. Maybe a little more, I need to stop for fuel. Is your friend fine? Did he find his dog?"

She dropped her voice. "The dog's here, but I'm not sure whether he's fine or not. If I can persuade him to come, do you think we can take him and Holger back to Hamburg with us?"

"That's probably the best thing for him. Sylt is not an easy place in the winter. See you in half an hour."

"See you then."

She rang off just in time to hear the words 'pig-headed and stupid!' and the front door slammed. As she hurried to the kitchen, Adrian stormed past her and took the pine stairs two at a time.

In the kitchen, only one man and his dog remained. Beatrice boggled her eyes at Daan. He rolled his head in a loose, evasive gesture.

"They had an argument. Adrian wants to stay, Holger wants him to go. Adrian asked if he was throwing him out and then I messed up."

"What did you do?"

"I said he could stay at my place."

"But Holger wants Adrian to go for his own good."

Daan slumped against the sink. "I'm better with dogs than people." He looked down at Mink, who thumped her tail once. "Shitty shit, this is the Friday from hell. I'll find Holger, you talk to Adrian. If you think it's best for him to go, I will support you. I trust what you decide. You remind me of my mother."

With that non-sequitur, he went into the hall to don his outdoor things.

"Mink! *Fuss!*" he commanded. The dog padded to his side.

Beatrice checked her watch and trudged up the stairs. She stood in the doorway of a bedroom, watching Adrian pack in an obvious rage. He must have been furious or he'd never have treated cashmere that roughly. She waited a few seconds to allow him to ignore her or shout, but he whirled around and glared.

"You've come to tell me I'm not right in the head as well?"

"You think I'd ever say something like that? To anyone?"

He faltered for a second. "I had a row with Holger. He's playing the 'I know best' role, which I hate."

"Yes, well, that's between the two of you. On a practical note, there's space in the car if you want to join us on the journey back to Hamburg. I won't push you, but I will say this. I'm short-tempered and fractious because I had very little sleep last night. Didn't we all, you might say. Yes, but I left my boss in the middle of dinner, possibly exposed a colleague to criticism, drove through the night and spent several freezing hours wandering a North Sea island looking for a dog. Why? Because I was worried about you. Tonight, I may well be involved in a complex operation which I will be unable to leave at the drop of a cat. So I'd feel vastly more relaxed if I knew you were safely across the city in a cosy hotel room, rather than on an inaccessible island five hours away, in an empty house which scared you half to death last night."

Adrian had the good grace to look ashamed. He continued packing and spoke through a clenched jaw. "You're right. I am scared of being alone. But I won't be chased away."

"Well, what are you going to do?" she asked.

"Daan says I can stay with him."

"Why is it so important to..."

"Because I will not be fucking bullied! And..."

"And what?"

"And... no more running and hiding. I've reached the end of the line. I'm going to stay and face this. It's not just the fact that someone's stalking me, I need to get my own head together. This is the right place, I can feel it."

They stared at each other for a second until the sound of Daan's mighty lungs reached up to the first floor.

"Beatrice!"

She gave Adrian a reproachful look and trotted down the stairs.

Daan stood in the hall with Holger's bag. "I'm taking him to the train station. He wants to get back. What's Adrian going to do?"

A voice came from above her. "Adrian is going to stay, if you don't mind."

Daan looked up the stairs at Adrian, back at Beatrice and shrugged his enormous shoulders. "Right, fine. I'll be back in an hour or so. Beatrice, do you need a lift?"

"My colleague is due in about twenty minutes, so I'll travel with him. Nice to meet you and Mink. Look after him." She jerked her head up the stairs.

Daan embraced her in a smothering hug. "Short but sweet. *Tschüss!*"

As he yanked the door closed, Beatrice wondered exactly what his words were referring to.

"Beatrice!" Adrian hissed.

"What? I feel like I'm in some horrible nightmare where voices keep calling my name and I have no idea what they want."

"You understand security. Come up here, quick!"

She ascended the stairs again. "Stein will be here soon."

Adrian's voice came from a different room. "I know. Get a shift on!"

The room was an office and Adrian sat in front of a computer with various icons on the left hand side. "CCTV. How do I check the footage from last night?"

"Holger already did."

"So he says. I want to be sure."

Beatrice didn't like the tone of paranoia in his voice. "All these systems are different, I'm not sure I can..."

"Just try." He vacated the seat and batted a hand at her.

It took her a good five minutes to familiarise herself with the recording system, and only then because she recalled a case in Finsbury Park where cameras had proved crucial. Last night's footage was broken into three-hour chunks. She started at 18.00 and watched a minute in real time before fast-forwarding. The system had 'markers', indicating when some kind of motion had occurred. The two cameras were fixed, showing one view of the front and one of the back porch. The light changed as the night grew darker and once an owl or piece of paper flapped past the front camera. Other than that, nothing.

She sped the tapes back and forth, finding no activity on either. She opened the next batch – 21.00 till midnight. The first thirty minutes showed nothing until Adrian arrived at the back door at 21.39. They watched him, a strange sensation. She on the other end of that line, trying to calm him. He, obviously frantic, desperate for help. Where had he been? The tape sped on to the police arrival and Beatrice hit pause.

"He's right. There's nothing on here."

"That's just not possible." Adrian rotated the chair so that Beatrice was facing him. "I know you think I'm unreliable or attention-seeking or having a breakdown. All those things might be true. But you must believe me about last night. I chopped logs, someone banged on the windows and rang the doorbell, someone left a crucifix on the porch, Mink ran off barking and I stood there calling her. All that really happened, I swear. I don't know why the camera didn't film it and I almost feel like I can't trust myself." He paused for a moment. "I wish Mink could talk. She'd vouch for me."

"What time did you chop the logs?"

He thought about it. "Before my shower. Around seven, I think."

Beatrice located 18.50 on the timeline and let the footage run. Nothing. She fast-forwarded, stopping occasionally to watch the rain spatter the empty porch. She peered hard at the ghostly monochrome image, trying to search every detail. She looked at the time counter and noticed the date. 11.12.15. The eleventh of December. She rewound to where the section began, at 18.00. The date was the same. She skipped to the next section, in which Adrian appeared on the porch. This time the date read 12.11.15. Twelfth of November? Unless...

She minimised the open windows and searched for the security system's user manual. The company's address was in Palm Beach Florida. She brought up the footage from between six and nine last night. 11.12.15, according to American date stamping was the twelfth of November. Everything else the cameras recorded was from yesterday evening, except one chunk, which was recorded one month ago. Beatrice scratched her forehead, thinking.

"What? Adrian demanded.

"Ssh," she replied. She found the files from November the twelfth and compared the six till nine recording with yesterday's in a split screen. Frame for frame it was exactly the same. It even had the movement marker in the same place when a piece of white flashed over the porch roof. The Recycling Bin showed no sign of the missing footage and recent activity had been erased. An expert would be able to find it, no doubt, but...

"Am I right in thinking the only person who accessed this computer since yesterday was Holger?"

"Yes. He went through it last night while I was downstairs waiting for Mink. Why?"

"One section of footage has been removed and replaced with film of the same three hours in November. Same sort of weather, dark, no change to the layout and the dates are so similar, most people wouldn't notice. Whatever the cameras recorded last night has gone missing."

Adrian stared at the computer. "I don't understand."

"Nor do I. But I think it might be best if you stay with Daan for the next few days."

The sound of a doorbell made them both tense.

"That'll be Stein. Go and let him in while I clear my traces. I need some time to figure this out. Adrian! Say nothing about this to Daan or Holger or anyone."

His face grew paler. "I won't."

"Go and answer the door. Tell Stein I'll be a few more minutes. Say I'm attending to my natural needs. That always shuts men up."

Chapter 24

The journey down the island, across to the mainland and back to the city of Hamburg should have provided Beatrice with plenty of time to think, but Herr Stein had other ideas. As soon as they'd established that Adrian and dog were well, he guided her attention towards their case.

The surveillance operation had borne fruit. Coded conversations and increased activity between the Hague and Bremen aroused enough suspicion to refer the transcripts to a specialist intelligence officer in Wiesbaden. She described the code the thieves had used as 'laughably simple' and analysed the messages in under an hour. She was able to give them specifics as to the planned theft. *Äusserer Schweinehund*, a George Grosz in a private home was the target for Saturday night. The family had gone to London for Christmas shopping and one of the security guards was in communication with the Dutch theft ring. He would disable the alarm, ensure the gang could access the property and allow them to leave with the painting before the police were alerted.

"And we will let that happen," said Stein.

"We will?" Beatrice asked.

"Yes. We don't just want the thieves, we want the whole organisation. The intelligence service in the Netherlands is working with us and Wiesbaden. We're planning a double attack. How do you say...?" He took one hand off the wheel and mimed plucking something with finger and thumb.

"The pincer effect. How will that work?"

"The gang intend to take the painting to Osnabrück. There they will hand it over to a middle man, who will travel back to the Hague and place it in storage until it's safe to transport it to the collector. The thieves themselves will return to their hole until their services are next required. Except they won't get that far."

Beatrice folded her arms with a smug grin. "No. Because we're going to finger their collars."

"We're going to what?" Stein shot her a look of bewilderment.

"It's a British idiom – means arrest someone. Is that what we're going to do?"

"Yes. As soon as the middle man leaves with the painting, we either follow or surround the gang and take them back to Hamburg for interrogation."

Beatrice watched the scenery flicker by, although her mind was already in a blacked-out surveillance vehicle filled with screens, consoles and tension.

"Presumably the Dutch force will grab the middle man on the other side of the border? Or wait till he gets back to base?"

"We'll track him and see what happens. We hope he'll go directly to the industrial estate in The Hague, where he'll be arrested and the painting placed in the hands of professionals. We're just not sure if there might be one or two more switches of vehicles to misdirect the police."

"Yes, they can be extremely slippery, these types. What's our role, Herr Stein? I assume Tomas and Herr Meyer are running the show."

"I don't know yet. Briefing at eighteen-hundred hours. I estimate our arrival in Hamburg at twelve-thirty and then we must go to bed."

She bit her lip, amused. "If you insist."

"You need your sleep, DI Stubbs. It's going to be another long night." His stern tone was undercut by the crinkling of his eyes.

They were both quiet until Stein parked in the queue for the car train. He made a call in German, very clipped and professional sounding, while Beatrice peered through the windscreen. The weather was foul, sleet hitting the windscreen in irregular furious bursts. When he rang off, she leaned back in her seat to look at him.

"I still haven't said thank you. For driving me all this way, giving up a decent night's sleep, being so kind and reassuring all the time and not once losing patience with this wild goat's chase. I really am most grateful."

He twisted his torso to face her. His cleft chin and sculpted jaw impressed her all over again but the real danger was in those deep brown eyes. She blinked to break the hypnotic pull.

"I told you. I was pleased to help. Adrian seems like a nice man." He rubbed behind his ear, still gazing at her. "Do you think it was a... how do you say that in English? A trick to make someone pay attention?"

"A ruse? No, I wouldn't think so. Why would he want *my* attention anyway?"

"Not yours. Didn't you say Holger is his ex-boyfriend?"

"Yes. But the split was amicable. They're friends."

"People sometimes change their minds. Maybe Adrian wants him back."

Beatrice blinked, surprised to hear hypothetical gossip from someone who looked like he'd just stepped out of a razor commercial.

"In which case, why would he stay on the island?" she asked. "Holger all but begged him to come back to Hamburg. If he wanted Holger, why opt for a Danish bloke and his dog instead?"

"To make Holger jealous?"

Beatrice's laughter died in her throat.

Stein started the engine. "Here we go." He drove onto the car train with typical precise caution, while Beatrice thought about his words.

What if it was the other way around? What if Holger had engineered this whole charade to restart their relationship?

Adrian might not love him, but he could certainly be forced into needing him. Her mind turned over the issue of the CCTV and she realised she had no idea why Holger had popped up four hours from his home when Adrian was at his most vulnerable. The situation preoccupied her all the way to Hamburg.

She woke at quarter to five after a succession of frustrating, alarming dreams with a head like tar. She showered, took her medication and tried to assess whether this distance from reality was due to exhaustion or withdrawal. Focus, she ordered herself. She checked her emails, trying to shake off the thick black fug between her ears. Admin from Scotland Yard, updates from the Hamburg operation, but nothing Stein hadn't told her. A gentle query from Matthew and two hellos from friends in London, including Dawn Whittaker, apparently loving her new role. Beatrice smiled. A note from Hamilton, thanking her for dinner but with a classic dig at the end. *Your company much appreciated, at least for two courses*. Nothing from Adrian, but she'd received two text messages on the journey enthusing about Daan's beachfront shack and assuring her of Mink's continuing recovery.

Time was getting on so she dressed in practical stakeout gear – dark layers – and spent several minutes choosing a snack from room service. With the possibility of being stuck in an enclosed space with members of Hamburg's police force for hours on end, she did not want her body to betray her. She opted for a cheese salad with a high energy drink. A combination which would have appalled Matthew, no doubt.

While she waited, she called him, just on the off chance. He picked up.

"Professor Bailey?"

"It's me."

"Hello stranger. Are you having fun?"

With a sudden rush of longing, Beatrice wanted to be there, to crawl under a duvet with him, tell him everything that had happened, share her concerns and quite simply offload. So much had altered since they last spoke that the sheer volume of things she had to tell him choked her.

"Fun? Other words leap sooner to mind. It's been rather more hectic than I'd like. Never mind that, because I can't go into detail anyway. Tell me what's happening in Brampford Speke."

"Very well. Mince pie failure, early carol singers, tree decorating with a three-year-old, mulled wine spice spilt on the carpet, wrapping paper coming out of my ears and I can't find the sellotape. Half my Christmas card list is either dead or divorced. Can one apply to be excused from the festive season, do you know?"

"Oh you Scrooge. I'm rather enjoying the Germanic take on Christmas. Their Glühwein and markets make Oxford Street look tacky."

"There is nothing on this earth that does *not* make Christmas on Oxford Street look tacky. When will you be back? The way things are going, I'm fearful of even preparing the pud without your guidance. Leave alone the roasted parsnips."

"Monday. I need to smooth Hamilton's feathers so I'll have to put in a full week. Office party on the eighteenth, so what say I come down on the Saturday? Stay for the whole holiday fortnight."

Matthew's smile could be heard in his voice. "If you bring authentic German goodies, I could probably put up with you for that long."

A knock came at the door. "That'll be room service. I must dash. Shall I call you when I'm back in London?"

"Yes, please do. Give my very best to Adrian. Take care, Old Thing."

She replaced the receiver, her mind on roasted parsnips and that wonderful man. Matthew could never advertise grooming products. Which was precisely why she loved him.

Considering this was a five-way operation involving the BKA, three German police forces and a Dutch one, Beatrice expected to be sidelined, perhaps attached to Tomas Schäffer. He would direct operations from the Hamburg base, using intercepted communications to guide his decisions. The most useful thing Beatrice could do, especially as she wouldn't be able to follow the language, would be making tea. Three sites were the focus of attention. The house in Bremen from which the Grosz would be stolen, the hypermarket car park where the gang would hand over the painting and the final destination, assumed to be The Hague, where the Dutch intelligence service would be poised to make the arrest.

So she was surprised and delighted to discover that she was to accompany Herr Stein and his team to Osnabrück, in order to assist in making the initial arrests. Right slap bang in the middle of action, just the way she liked it.

Stein's briefing was meticulous. Safety was paramount as the gang were likely to be armed and had proved themselves violent. Bulletproof vests, protective helmets and weapons for the arresting officers, roadblocks prepared in detail and GPS slap-and-track devices tested and ready. One of the blonds, Kurt, was tasked with attaching the devices to the vehicles. This meant using a launcher, hence a distraction was required. Two younger officers were briefed on their roles as boy racers using the car park to test their souped-up saloons. They wore baseball caps and saggy jeans and looked as if they'd yet to learn to shave. Margrit's shrill cackle at her colleagues' appearance drew a frosty look from Stein.

Finally, Beatrice received her own instructions. While Stein, Margrit and Rudi moved in to arrest the gang, she was to record the whole operation on camera. She fixed her attention on the map, listening to Stein's explanation of who, what and where, her sense of anticipation wobbling on the brink of nerves. Briefing over, Margrit accompanied Beatrice and Tomas back to the glass-walled room to demonstrate how to use the police video camera.

"There's also a zoom function on top. It makes more noise,

but you're only capturing pictures tonight. We'll need detailed close-ups of everything. Not just faces and number plates, but shoes, watches, hair, everything."

Beatrice practised using both functions by filming Tomas, who looked as shifty as any criminal. "Right, got it. Thanks Margrit."

"You're welcome. Oh, I've got something for you." She pulled out a folded sheet of paper from her back pocket and handed it over. "That convent you asked me to check out. You said you didn't want anything overly religious, right? This is a translation of their homepage. I'll let you decide." She boggled her eyes in an expression of exaggerated alarm as she left the room. Beatrice read.

> Here at Kloster St Ursula, we are at war.
>
> Christianity is under siege. Today children learn that there are no values, there is no right, no wrong, no God.
>
> We wage war on a number of different fronts. On protecting the church and Christian principle according to the teachings of the Bible. On making the womb a place of safety, by protecting life from the moment of conception. On resisting all earthly claims such as family bonds, as our ultimate allegiance is focused on the imminent return of Jesus. On defending the erosion of the only true marriage, between a man and a woman.
>
> We use every means at our disposal and all the strength that God supplies to fight this war, including negotiations with the earthly whilst

```
always staying mindful of the powers
in the unseen realm.

Here at Kloster St Ursula we are
committed to a Biblical worldview,
where Creator and created are sepa-
rate, and where the marriage supper
of the Lamb is distinctly between the
Redeemer and those redeemed through
the blood of Jesus.

-Sister Immaculata
```

"Good God."

Tomas looked up from his screen. "What's the matter?"

"Nothing." Beatrice shook her head. "People can be very strange."

"I know exactly what you mean."

Stein opened the door. "Time to go."

Butterflies started their nonsense in her stomach again as she wished Tomas good luck and followed the police unit down to the car park. A sudden seriousness permeated the atmosphere. The team piled into a van, but Stein gave a murmured instruction she should ride with him in the unmarked Mercedes. The clock showed 19.00 on the dot as they belted themselves in for the two-hour journey to Osnabrück.

Stein flicked on the wipers to clear the screen of snowflakes. "The theft is due to occur at half past eleven. It will take the gang around ninety minutes to reach Osnabrück. Which means we have six hours to prepare the trap and conceal ourselves. Are you ready?"

Wide-awake and eager, Beatrice gave a decisive nod. "Let's go."

Kurt stood in police combat gear apart from his helmet, holding something like a cannon in his arms. His blond hair shone white in the moonlight while the matt-black weapon reflected nothing. He looked like Rutger Hauer in *Blade Runner*. The team had concealed themselves at the furthermost points of the car park: in a thicket of trees, behind the recycling bins, in the neighbouring lot. Everyone found their positions, waiting for the opportunity for a cautious rehearsal. The hypermarket was still open and Friday evening shoppers hauled trolleys across the tarmac, full of pre-packaged Christmas-in-a-box. Beatrice thought back to Matthew's query. '*Can one apply to be excused from the festive season, do you know?*'

In the shadow of the police van, Kurt took aim at tree trunks without pulling the trigger.

Stein spoke at Beatrice's shoulder. "It shoots fake bullets which embed themselves in the vehicle body. They contain GPS trackers so we can follow, but the problem is the sound when they hit. This is why we need the distraction. If the 'racers' can make enough noise, Kurt can attach trackers to the Dutch vehicle without raising alarm. The only risk is attracting their attention. Kurt's timing is crucial."

Beatrice whispered, despite the strains of the supermarket's piped *Der Tannenbaum* drifting across the night air. "What if he does attract their attention?"

"We have to make the arrests immediately. Right here. We cannot lose the middle man, with or without the painting. If he suspects we're in pursuit, he'll change tactics and hide. He won't lead us to HQ and then all we'll have is a stolen painting and a bunch of goons playing dumb." His tone was patient even as his keen eyes ranged over the area.

A tannoy released a series of warning bleeps, followed by an announcement. The shop was closing for the night. Stein made a brief gesture, as if turning a key to his lips. The team gave varying signs of assent and retreated to their positions.

She followed Stein into the surveillance van, clunked the door shut and settled into position. "Radio contact only in an emergency, I assume. What about the roadblock people?"

"Radio contact will be essential, but any movement or

conversation outside the vehicles should be kept to a minimum. We expect our visitors in approximately three hours. I want total silence and stillness for at least two hours before that. Just in case our friends from the Low Countries arrive early. Any 'natural needs' should be managed now."

She shook her head. "My natural needs are under control. What about you?"

To her surprise, Stein laughed. Quietly and with more shaking shoulders than sound.

"Yes," he said, on an intake of breath. "Mine too."

Chapter 25

Everything had gone exactly to plan, right up until someone else had natural needs. Via radio, Tomas assured them the operation in Bremen met all their expectations. A security guard had admitted a Mercedes-Benz Viano with blacked out windows at 11.15. Three men entered the house, removed the Grosz painting, covered it in protective wrapping and took it to the van. While they were inside, a police officer had attached a tracking device to the vehicle, out of sight of the getaway driver in the cab.

Once the Mercedes had left, the guard let exactly thirty minutes pass before calling the police, claiming he had just managed to untie himself after an aggravated burglary. The van's movements were visible on the GPS screen, heading directly for Osnabrück. Contrary to expectations, the wait passed quickly. Only fifteen minutes to the van's estimated time of arrival remained when a Hummer cruised into view and parked behind the shopping trolley shelter.

The atmosphere in the van, already charged, changed into something deeper, the feel of gears engaging.

"Commence filming," said Stein. The camera's position was almost perfect, just a few degrees left. Beatrice adjusted the angle, twiddled with the focus and sat forward, observing the dark, silent, tank-like lump. More of a hippo than a Hummer. Activity buzzed behind her and she turned to watch. Margrit fed the number plate detail back to HQ and Stein was giving sharp instructions into the radio as he pulled on his combat gear.

Margrit gave her a quick smile. "He's talking to the racers. They must be visible to the gang but not too noisy or someone might report them to the police!" She pulled a quizzical face.

Beatrice returned her smile, her expression far more relaxed than her mental state. Her nerves grew more taut with each click of buckle and metal. She ran over the plan once again.

The thieves would arrive any minute now. They would hand over the painting to the man, or men, in the Hummer. Under the cover of backfiring exhausts, Kurt would shoot GPS trackers at the Hummer. Both vehicles would depart. If all went according to plan, the Mercedes would run into a roadblock. What then?

Existing evidence presumed the van contained four men, but could they be sure? Such a brutal, professional crew would do anything to resist arrest. Up to now, her main concern had been how to arrest the gang without giving them time to warn the Dutch middleman. Now, faced with the blank armour of the squat vehicle less than thirty metres away, her fears slipped into the cracks between certainties.

Headlights swept across her face and she froze before reminding herself she could not be seen. The Mercedes Viano circled the car park, in no hurry. It passed horribly close to their concealed spot behind the trees and she sent a silent thank you to the cloud cover. Finally, it parked alongside the Hummer and switched off its lights. For a few seconds, nothing happened and it seemed the entire empty expanse was holding its breath. Then an interior light came on as the door opened.

This was her moment. She zoomed in on the vehicles, watching silhouetted figures emerge. Faces, features, expressions, narrowed eyes, a lit cigarette; everything came sharply into focus.

"Four men out of the Merc. One looking around the car park, two gone round the back, one leaning down to talk to... aha, the Hummer window is down. Can't see a face. They've opened the side door of the Mercedes. A man just got out of the back seat of the Hummer. He's going inside the van."

Stein listened and muttered something into the radio. Seconds later, a jarring screech of tyres ripped across the car park and Beatrice saw all three men guarding the Mercedes reach inside their jackets and withdraw handguns. The driver of the Hummer got out and beckoned to his colleague inside the van.

"Three men are armed and have their weapons ready."

Two absurdly customised VW Golfs shot across the forecourt to the hypermarket, revving and changing gears with such a racket Beatrice worried they might be overdoing it. At some invisible signal, both drivers hit the accelerator, so that the cars emitted startling bangs and flashes from their exhausts. They screamed around the car park, engines whining and exhausts popping, setting Beatrice's teeth on edge.

The men in her viewfinder watched the spectacle, their heads following the trajectory until the two cars burst out of the car park and back onto the street. A moment of stillness passed, until every echo of the intrusion had faded. Then the Hummer's driver opened the back door and a large padded package was transferred carefully from the interior of the Mercedes.

Stein's radio scratched into life. He replied and Margrit gave Beatrice a thumbs-up. Kurt had hit his target. She looked back to her screen and saw the occupants of the Hummer close the door, get back inside and wind up the windows. When the vehicle's lights came on, Stein spoke into his radio, his voice calm but urgent. The Hummer peeled away, steady and slow, out of the car park and onto the street.

Margrit got behind the steering wheel and Beatrice braced herself for the moment they would pursue the Mercedes van. Yet nothing happened. One man was still smoking and the other three stood around, apparently shooting the breeze. Taking advantage of the close formation, Beatrice zoomed in, making sure she got each face on film. Then one man broke from the group and started walking straight towards her.

"Herr Stein!" she said, her eyes fixed on the approaching

figure. In direct contradiction to her sudden alarm, the other three men burst into laughter and shouted something after their friend. He bent into a crouch and waddled a few steps, eliciting more laughter.

"*Scheisse!*" spat Margrit.

Stein leaned over Beatrice to watch as the figure grew steadily larger. "*Scheisse* is the right word. It seems our friend has some 'natural needs' that cannot be relieved in the car park. So he is coming into the trees to..."

Beatrice was horrified. "He's coming over here to take a shit?"

Stein's eyes darted around the interior. "We'll have to move now. If he sees us and raises the alarm... we can't risk it. No, we snatch him here and surprise the others immediately. It's too late to wait for back-up."

He spoke into his radio, his voice guttural and harsh, nodding to Margrit as he did so. She waited till he'd finished, then cocked her gun and slid open the panel door before melting into the darkness. Stein pointed at the camera and followed Margrit, closing the door behind him.

Beatrice's fingers shook as she put her hands back on the camera. The looming man had moved out of her sightline so she trained the focus on the trio by the van. Her peripheral vision picked up shadows scuttling across the car park. The three men, sheltered by the van on one side and the trolley station on the other, continued smoking and chatting, oblivious of the tightening noose.

Several things happened at once. A volley of yells ricocheted across the tarmac, headlights from concealed police vehicles threw the scene into harsh illumination and the boy racers squealed back through the entrance. The three men scrabbled for guns or phones, but at the clicks of readied weaponry, they lifted their arms in the air, hands visible. She watched as Rudi, Kurt and Stein arrested the men, removed their weapons and eased them into waiting Polizei vehicles. Margrit came into the picture from Beatrice's left, marching a handcuffed man ahead of her. Only when the patrol cars left with the suspects did she switch the camera off.

The side panel swung back and Stein stooped to enter. He was sweating, but had an air of triumph. He threw her a crooked grin before picking up his radio and relaying the successful result. Beatrice clambered out to stretch her trembling legs. Margrit and Kurt came over to shake her hand, as if she'd done something useful. She just managed to express her admiration of their slick professionalism when the atmosphere changed. Stein stood with his hands on his hips until everyone gathered into a semi-circle around him.

He addressed the team in German, but Margrit whispered a translation for Beatrice's benefit. "Suspects taken to Hamburg... BKA officers interrogating... our team stands down... good job, no shots fired... debrief tomorrow at fourteen hundred... congratulations... get some sleep." She grinned at Beatrice. "He's pleased, I can tell. I'm going to have a couple of beers with the boys when we get back. Surplus energy, you know? You'd be welcome to join us."

"Thanks Margrit, that's very thoughtful. But wild horses couldn't keep me from my bed tonight. Enjoy your beers, you deserve it."

Margrit held out her hand. "Another time. Goodnight."

Beatrice shook it with a warm smile and made her way back to the van, in weary anticipation of another two hour drive.

"DI Stubbs!" Margrit hissed, running after her.

"What is it?" Beatrice's heart began the adrenalin pump all over again.

Margrit's smile lifted her cheeks into crab-apples. "The guy who started all this, the one who came into the trees? Guess what his name is?"

Beatrice stared at her, lost for words.

"He's called Anton Baer," said Margrit, barely suppressing her amusement.

"I don't..."

Margrit leaned forward to whisper. "You have an English expression I learned. Do Baers shit in the woods?" Laughter escaped and she covered her mouth.

Beatrice's eyes widened and a bubble of mirth rose from her stomach. "I don't suppose this bear...?" Her voice wavered as she tried to control her giggles.

Margrit shook her head, squeezing her eyes shut. "He didn't have time."

Beatrice bit her lips and sang in a stage whisper, "If you go down to the woods today, you're sure of a big surprise..."

Margrit clutched her arm and they doubled up in the shared laughter of relief and complicity, drawing puzzled stares from their colleagues.

Chapter 26

Six hours of dreamless sleep. She couldn't believe it. The alarm was set for midday but Beatrice awoke, bright-eyed and smiling, at half past eleven. Serene and rested, she ordered brunch, had a shower, caught up with emails and almost enjoyed her brisk stroll through the crisp salty air to the police station.

The atmosphere inside was equally upbeat. Margrit and Kurt, both on their phones, lifted hands in greeting as she made her way through the open-plan section. She waved back with a happy grin. Stein was in the glass office, peering over Tomas's shoulder with a coffee cup in his left hand. Even from this distance, Beatrice could tell they'd both been here for hours.

Stein spotted her and beckoned. Clean shaven he might be, but tell-tale grey skin shadowed his eyes. Part of her was relieved. Even Mr Perfect had off days. Tomas looked up briefly and offered an unusually broad smile. Stein opened the door for her.

"Good news, DI Stubbs! In addition to our four arrests, the Dutch police followed the middle men to The Hague and caught the gang in the act of receiving the stolen painting. Six men were arrested at four o'clock this morning and another ten individuals are being questioned."

"Ten? This thing is bigger than we thought!"

Stein exhaled a short laugh. "You have no idea. Come."

He led her back through the building to a small cubbyhole

with several screens and a console. He gestured to the seat and fiddled with the controls while she settled herself.

"Obviously most interviews were in Dutch or German, which I'm having translated for you. One man they arrested is a New Zealander. This is significant for two reasons. Firstly, they interviewed him in English. Second, he agreed to cooperate if the threat of deportation was removed. He has a partner and children in Amsterdam. There's a lot more to the case than his testimony, but it will give you an idea of what we're dealing with. Press this button to play and this one to pause. The good bit is at around fifteen minutes in. I'll get you some coffee."

She pressed play as the door closed and focused on the picture in front of her. A police interview room with stark overhead lighting which made the faces on screen look more chilly and tired than they probably were. An interviewee sat opposite two police detectives, leaning his forearms on the table and yawning as the interview commenced. They spent some time establishing his identity and the events of the evening. Beatrice twigged he was the driver of the Hummer.

She listened to the initial questions and stonewall response. Then his attitude changed. The insolent folded arms and closed mouth changed as the Dutch detective laid down his offer. In exchange for cooperation, he would not be charged and would be permitted to remain in the Netherlands with his pregnant partner and child. She watched as the sullen posture altered and a decision was made. He asked for it in writing and agreed to tell them what he knew. Beatrice wrinkled her nose. Snitches were solid gold from the police perspective, but it didn't stop her despising them as self-interested cowards. After a few more minutes, she attuned to his curious habit of accenting his statements as questions. She could see he was telling the truth. She speeded up the film to fifteen minutes into the interview.

The detective asked another question and the man hunched his shoulders, tucking his hands into his armpits.

"Like an agency, we deal with buyers and sellers. Look mate, it works like this. People send a request for a particular painting, or a kind of painting. We find out where it is and by that I mean exactly? Not just the house, but the room, the alarm system, the exits and what condition it's in? We instruct our people to take it. Gently. Like with all the care of museum curators? We have perfect storage conditions for even the most delicate artwork. Our team are professionals. The important thing is that the artwork is not damaged. We keep it safe until the noise dies down and then we do what the client tells us. Offer it to the insurance company, ransom it to the owner, hand it over to another dealer or collector, whatever they want us to do, hey?"

One of the detectives flicked through a file and spoke. "The artworks themselves may not be damaged, but several people were seriously hurt during these aggravated robberies. A cleaning woman in London is still recovering from a head injury. A householder in Hamburg spent six months in hospital."

The New Zealander rubbed his nose with the palm of his hand, a casual gesture of weariness and lack of concern which Beatrice suspected indicated the opposite.

"Outsourcing. What can you do? Their methods aren't our concern. All we ask is to get the right piece at the right time and in pristine condition? You can chuck the book at us for receiving stolen goods, but we can't be implicated in bodily harm. It was up to him to clear the place. He knew when the boys were coming. That's not my problem, mate."

"Sorry. *Who* knew when the boys were coming?"

"Waring. He commissioned us. A private collector bought the Dix piece and Waring wanted the insurance on top? No worries, we're happy to help. We take it, hand it over to the collector, Waring claims the insurance and everybody's a winner."

"To be clear, the man who commissioned the Otto Dix *Salon II* theft was its owner, Mr Chet Waring?"

"Yep. We only ask one question – can you afford us? That's all we need to know. In fact, it's easier when you work with the owner? Precision intel, you know?"

The door opened and Stein returned with two coffees. He handed one to Beatrice and stood behind her, watching the screen for a couple of minutes. The interviewer asked if any of the other thefts under the scope of the Interpol investigation were committed with the knowledge of their legal owners.

The lanky Antipodean bent over the table to look at the images the officer had drawn from the file. "No. Nope. We've had a request for that Schad with the boar, but security is way too tight. Aha, now you're talking! That was one of ours."

"Can you please indicate which picture you're identifying for the tape?"

"Sure. Max Beckmann's *Exile*. We had orders from de Vries to move that one fast. Stolen, secured and off the continent before the theft was reported? These were all for the same collector but we only ever dealt with intermediaries. Yeah, I recognise several others. This one, *Nina in Camera*, we should have lifted last week until we heard you guys were watching."

"*Nina in Camera?* Did your instructions to steal that piece come from Herr Walter?"

For the first time, the Kiwi looked uncomfortable. "Nah, not him. His son. The collector got hold of some stuff on the kid, I don't know the details, but he blackmailed him into fixing things. He's only nineteen with more bollocks than brains."

"And the painting you took last night. The Grosz from Bremen? Was that theft also arranged by the owner?" asked the interrogator, voicing Beatrice's next question.

"Yeah, Frau Birmensdorfer was ready to sell fifteen years ago. That Grosz featured in our private catalogue. No one bid. Now, with the Schad under police surveillance, we managed to persuade her to drop the price? In under six hours, we got confirmation the money was in escrow, to be released when the painting was delivered to the collector."

The interviewer raised his head. "*The* collector. All these pieces were destined for the same person?"

"Yeah. Whether they were for him or he was a dealer selling

them on, I don't know. But this guy knew exactly what he wanted."

Stein leaned forward to press pause. His thigh brushed Beatrice's and she found herself acutely aware of the confined space.

"As far as our case goes, four thefts were either commissioned or inside jobs. Waring, de Vries, Walter Junior and Frau Birmensdorfer."

Beatrice shook her head. "So Tomas was right all along. Despite Herr Meyer's insistence the anonymous collector is nothing more than a myth. Someone, somewhere is coveting Expressionist eyes. You know, that bloody slimy git Waring said as much when I interviewed him. 'Some wealthy oligarch is amassing German Expressionist art from the 1920s and needed a Dix for his collection.' He was so cooperative and pleasant, after I'd been warned he was difficult. I should have realised. A classic criminal tactic."

"Classic, I agree. Tell a partial truth with a sin of omission – the fact that the wealthy oligarch had a willing seller. No surprise he was pleased to see you. A police report equals insurance claim. He never expected your investigation to get this far."

"Nor did I, to be honest. Did that bloke give us much more?" Beatrice jabbed a finger at the screen.

"Enough detail to implicate another ten people and a whole network of leads and connections. But we won't find him." Stein's shoulders slumped.

"Who?"

"The collector. Even if we had the time and resources to follow up every last lead, we'd get no closer. Whoever he is, he's made sure there are no direct connections to him."

Beatrice narrowed her eyes. "You can't know that. Sounds to me as if you're settling for a consolation prize."

"I'm not settling for anything. This is an Interpol operation. They call the shots. They've fulfilled their mission and arrested a gang of fine art thieves. Meyer's already writing a concluding report."

"What? This is nowhere near concluded! What about all the complicit owners? Surely they will be charged with aiding and abetting, and fraud, and acting as an accessory?"

Stein switched off the monitor and leaned back against the desk, facing Beatrice with a sad smile. "Yes, they'll be charged. Their legal teams are already rubbing their hands in the sure knowledge they will be acquitted, or in the unlikely event they are found guilty of some charges, it will be a minor matter of paying fines they can afford and restoring reputations. We plugged a leak, DI Stubbs. Just one hole in the dam. While we prepare the paperwork to dismantle this ring, another will quietly take its place. The collector will continue to collect and those paintings will never be recovered. At least not in our lifetimes."

His voice carried a cynicism and defeat she recognised from the howls of her own black dogs. She had learned to manage hers but to hear that same tone in one so young and decent seemed heart-breaking.

She met his eyes and he shrugged with his eyebrows. "We did our job," he said. "And if we finish the paperwork today, you can return home tomorrow. Or do you plan to go back to Sylt?"

Beatrice released a huge sigh. "I have absolutely no idea."

The rest of the team, as well they should be, were demob happy. As Beatrice was packing the last of her paperwork, Rudi tapped on the door of the glass office to invite her for a drink with them all. She opened her mouth to offer an excuse but caught sight of Tomas hovering a few paces behind with an expression of concern. Further back still, she saw Stein feigning jovial high spirits with Margrit, but he too was watching for her reaction.

"I think we deserve it," she smiled at Rudi, giving him an unnecessary and uncharacteristic double thumbs up. Out in the open plan area, three faces broke into a smile.

Margrit yelled across the room. "No one can resist Rudi!"

Beatrice laughed and allowed the large blond to take her suitcase. She would make sure she sat next to Tomas.

An hour later, the party was getting into full swing. Everyone had been toasted for their role in the operation, Tomas twice. His discomfited delight was apparent to all, but the banter was good-natured and inclusive. Several times she caught Stein's eye and exchanged an almost parentally proud smile.

After the second beer, Beatrice judged it an opportune moment to take her leave. She shook hands with everyone, thanked them repeatedly, wished them all a good festive season and then Stein stood. She assumed he would only escort her to the door, but he made a few rapid-fire wisecracks in German and gave a mock-salute to the team before picking up Beatrice's case and guiding her to the door.

"I hope you're not leaving on my account, Herr Stein? I'm perfectly capable of getting back to my hotel alone, you know."

He shook his head and led her outside through a curtain of snowflakes to his car. He opened her door and went to the boot to stash her case. Only when they pulled into the flow of Saturday evening traffic did he speak.

"Do you want to go to your hotel or can I take you somewhere else?"

A wash of weariness overtook her. A younger, livelier, better-rested Beatrice would have invited him for dinner, but she needed time to herself and space to think.

"That's very kind of you. Lack of sleep and two powerful beers have left me running on empty. So if you wouldn't mind, the hotel sounds the best option."

"Of course. It's been a heavy week."

They drove in silence, Beatrice gazing out the window at the Christmas scenes, humming a vague tune even she didn't recognise. In a few minutes, she realised they were passing the station and only moments from her hotel. She remembered her manners.

"Herr Stein, it's been a real pleasure to work with you. You've been extraordinarily kind, not to mention tolerant. I hope we meet again one of these days."

He smiled at her while they waited at the traffic lights. "Yes, I'd like that. It was an interesting experience meeting you. Maybe in future, we could use first names? Mine is Jan."

"Good idea. Please feel free to call me Beatrice..."

The lights turned green and Stein pulled away slowly only to hit the brake as a last pedestrian dashed across the road.

"Bloody fool!"

Beatrice glared at the idiot whose impatience could easily have got him killed as he continued running towards the station.

"Beatrice Bloody Fool? If you insist." Stein grinned.

The figure disappeared into the crowd and Beatrice squinted. That was when a familiar figure crossed her line of sight.

"Did you see that man in the puffy jacket just then?"

"Sorry, I was watching the road. What about him?"

"I could have sworn that was Holger."

"Possibly it was. He does live in Hamburg."

"But why would he be heading to the train station at ten to seven?"

"No idea. Did you speak to Adrian today?"

"That's my number one priority as soon as I get in."

Stein slid the car into the forecourt, stepped out and retrieved Beatrice's suitcase. He offered his hand.

"Goodbye Beatrice. Safe journey and it was a pleasure to meet you."

"You too, Jan. You're an impressive leader and a very decent person. We could do with more like you. All the best."

He squeezed her hand. "I meant what I said. I would like to see you again. Call me if you need anything."

"I will. Goodnight and Merry Christmas."

"Goodnight. Same to you."

Beatrice waited on the pavement to wave him off. As soon as his car turned the corner, she asked the doorman to take her bag inside, then hurried across the road and back towards the station.

Chapter 27

Only a dog could recover from such an ordeal without a backward glance. Just before the sun set, Daan fed Mink some cold rice with chicken pieces and peas. She devoured the lot in seconds, checked the bowl ten more times and scratched at the door.

Adrian laughed as he slipped his feet into his boots, harried by the dog. Mink was eager to get outside, bunting Daan's legs and Adrian's hands, her tail a constant happy pendulum. They strolled down to the beach, grinning at Mink's antics with lumps of driftwood, relaxing into the expanse of sand and sky in silence. Neither spoke, content to observe the rhythm of the waves and the darkening sky as the sun slipped below the horizon. Tangy scents of seaweed mixed with the ocean spray, encouraging hearty breaths.

Daan stopped and looked out to sea. "There she is," he said.

Adrian followed his sight line to a small fishing boat. "That's yours?"

"Yes. I spent two years getting her seaworthy. Inside isn't luxurious but comfortable enough. You should come back in the summer. We can do an island tour from the sea. Less traffic."

"I'm not much of a sailor, but I'd give it a go."

Daan bent to tug at the stick Mink had brought him but she wouldn't let go, throwing all her weight backwards with her jaw clamped firmly on the wood. With a twist, he succeeded in wresting it from her and threw it in a long boomeranging arc down towards the sea. She took off after it, her white scut like a leader's flag.

"As if last night never happened," said Adrian.

Daan nodded, his eyes watching the dog, the fondness in his face evident. "She's a tough one." His expression changed, a frown tensing his brow. "The thing I don't understand is why someone would do that. The farmer swears he didn't lock her in there and I believe him. She doesn't trust many people. She likes you. She likes Holger. But you're the exceptions. So why did she follow whoever it was?"

The mention of Holger gave Adrian an internal twinge he chose to ignore. "Maybe she didn't. If they left food in there, they could have waited till she went in then locked the door."

"But why? Who would be hanging around with a lump of meat on a deserted beach at midnight?" Daan kicked a pebble which tumbled ahead of them.

"I wish she could talk. I don't suppose we'll ever find out what really happened."

They walked further along the dunes, Adrian lifting his collar against the bitter blasts of sea air. The lights of a distant ship glittered on the far horizon. Daan was unusually silent as they both gazed it.

"Daan, you know it wasn't me who shut Mink in there, don't you?"

Daan stopped in amazement. "Of course I do! You were as worried as I was. Shit, I know it wasn't you and it wasn't Holger."

Adrian sighed, a mixture of relief and a surge of concern. He'd heard nothing from Holger, or from Beatrice, and kept his promise to say nothing about the CCTV anomaly.

"Thank you."

"Let's turn back now. It's freezing. Don't forget it's your turn to cook tonight. Mink, *komm jetzt*! *Fuss!*"

Mink bounded towards them, her face sandy from digging. During the walk, the night had assumed control, bringing a vicious, skin-flaying wind. Both men bent their heads and Adrian walked the last stretch with his gloved hands over his perished ears. The glowing windows of Daan's ramshackle house acted as a beacon. Unlike Holger's place, which had the reassuring twinkling lights of distant neighbours and the nearby town of List to remind you of civilisation, Daan's boatyard was the only sign of life along this stretch of coast.

Outside the house sat a red and white *Strandkorb*, the beach basket chairs everywhere on the island. Daan lifted a corner. "Spare key under here, in case you get locked out."

"Thanks Daan. It's really good of you to let me stay."

As they took off their boots, Daan looked at his expression. "Don't worry about Holger. He'll get over that scene this morning. He's just very proud. Typical Bavarian."

"You reckon? I just want to speak to him. Do you mind if I try him again now? And then call Beatrice about flying back together tomorrow?"

"OK, but be quick. You need to start dinner because I'm already getting hungry. What are you going to make for us?"

Adrian's mood lifted. "Typical British."

Daan's eyes lit up. "Cornish pasties?"

"No, not pasties. Fish and chips."

Hundreds of people swarmed around Hamburg Hauptbahnhof, all in a hurry to get somewhere. A disproportionate number appeared to be tall, blond men in padded black jackets. The chances of finding Holger in this melee were zero   a weevil in a haystack. Unless, of course, one knew where he was going. Beatrice scanned the departures board for trains to Westerland and found the 19.16 was due to depart from platform 11. She had four minutes.

She speed-walked the length of the concourse and slipped onto platform 11, already crowded with noisy groups of youngsters. For fear of being spotted, she hid behind taller folk, which wasn't difficult. Around a third of the way along, she saw the one she wanted. His stillness gave him away. Everyone else was shifting, reading, fidgeting in impatience, pressing buttons on phones, staring at screens or laughing with their friends. Holger stood in silence, his gaze remote. Beatrice assessed her options. The most sensible, not to mention appealing, course of action was to go back to the hotel, phone Adrian and casually mention Holger was on his way to Sylt. Just to warn him. Warn him of what? She had no reason to mistrust Holger, other than the CCTV issue. He could well be heading back to build bridges with his friends.

The huge bulk of the Deutsche Bahn engine cruised into the station. A four-hour train journey was the last thing she needed. She'd be far better off going back to her room for some dinner, packing and sleep. Even if she got on this train, how could she ensure Holger wouldn't see her? It would be a busy journey, people wandering up and down looking for seats. The answer presented itself as the train eased to a halt. A door opened right in front of her and a few passengers disembarked. The sign on the window said First Class Dining Salon. An obvious invitation. She boarded the train.

She had her choice of seats in the first class carriage so selected a rear-facing seat in the Quiet Zone. It was plush and hushed and suited her mood perfectly. She switched her phone to silent and shoved it back in her bag, intending to call Adrian from the toilets once she had decided what to say. Then she left her coat on her seat and went in search of the conductor and the dining-car.

After a fruitless half hour trying to get a signal on his phone, Adrian used Daan's landline to leave a message for Beatrice, but couldn't reach Holger. He gave up, went into the kitchen and started peeling potatoes. There would be various possibilities for flight times to London. He'd book as soon as he spoke to Beatrice. It would be much nicer if they could travel together. A lovely warm airport taxi on police expenses was infinitely preferable to trains or Tube. Despite himself, he mentally planned his route from London City to Boot Street and experienced an unexpected pang of homesickness. He made up his mind to leave first thing in the morning whether he'd heard from Beatrice or not. Facing fears could be done anywhere. In fact, he should never have run in the first place. It was time to go home.

Outside in the shed, Daan whistled as he hacked blocks of wood into fireplace shapes. Mink had opted to stay indoors, in the warmth of Daan's rough and rustic kitchen and in pole position when it came to the chances of food.

The domestic comfort of the situation could not be further removed from the solitary terrors of the previous night. Adrian chopped up the potatoes into wedges and mixed the beer batter, his mind calming with the ritual gestures of food preparation. He was just skinning the fish when his phone beeped. He washed his hands and checked.

A message from number he didn't recognise. He opened it and recoiled as if he'd been slapped.

YOUR NO SINNER
A SINNER CAN REPENT.
THE DEVIL MUST BE DESTROYED.

Then the phone vibrated in his hand, emitting its shrill song. It gave him such a shock that this time he dropped it onto the fishy work surface. He snatched it up immediately and saw Beatrice's name on Caller Display.

"Beatrice! Finally!"

"Yes, sorry I missed your calls. My phone was on silent for a while. Is everything all right?"

"It was till about ten seconds ago. I think I just got a death threat."

"What do you mean? Another note?"

"No, a text message. Unknown number." He read the words and the number to her, aware of Daan talking to Mink in the living room. "Should I call the police?"

"Hmm. Not sure. We could make a strong case for harassment or stalking, but it's a bit oblique for a death threat. I mean, it doesn't mention you specifically. If I were you, I'd report this to the police in the morning. Don't delete it but don't let it unnerve you."

"So do nothing tonight?"

"Where are you?" She raised her voice over the sound of a loud rattling in the background.

"At Daan's place. I'm making fish and chips for us. Where are you? It sounds very noisy."

"Fish and chips? I'm in a restaurant, just about to order and you've just helped me make up my mind. Is Daan there?"

"Yes. He's laying a fire."

"Do you think I could have a quick word?"

Adrian was offended. "To discuss my paranoia? That text message is right here in front of me. I can show him."

"Adrian, the only paranoia here is your suspicion of my motives. In point of fact, I'm following up one of my theories on who's trying to scare you as we speak."His offence dissolved into curiosity. "Are you? Which one?"

"Not over the phone. I'll tell you when I see you. Will you put Daan on now?"

"Hang on, what time are we flying back tomorrow?"

"Not sure yet. I'll talk to you later."

Adrian sighed, took the mobile to the living-room and handed it to Daan. He stood in the doorway while Daan listened intently and answered a series of questions. He gave her his full name, his address, a few mysterious yes and no replies then bid her goodnight. He handed the phone back.

"Show me this message," he demanded.

Adrian showed him.

Daan screwed up his face in distaste. "What the hell is that supposed to mean? You know what I think? This is some religious freak. A closet case himself, deep down he's attracted to you and blames you for it."

The theory made a perverted kind of sense to Adrian. "I'll tell Beatrice. Why did she need all that info about you?"

"Paperwork, she said. Has to get the facts right for her report. How's dinner coming on?" Daan went into the kitchen to wash his hands.

"It's on its way. But even if this is a stalker, what kind of weirdo would follow me from London to Hamburg to Sylt to try and freak me out?"

"Food first, talk later. I'll heat the oil. And before you do anything else, wash your phone. It stinks of fish."

Train travel was so refined, so classic, Beatrice sensed she'd been born for it. Each table bore its own lamp, casting a pool of intimate light over the linen, glassware and silvery cutlery. Other diners were few and all better dressed than Beatrice.

She chose sea bass with a lemon sorrel sauce on olive oil mash, her tastes swayed by Adrian's menu. Dawdling over the wine list, she polished off all the mini seeded rolls with their chilled pat of butter before selecting a glass of Spatlese. When the dapper little waiter brought her wine, she sat back to absorb the genteel ambience. Matthew would love this. Perhaps next year, when her retirement released them from time pressures, they could finally fulfil their dream of the Orient Express.

But she'd not yet retired and had work to do. She dragged her notebook from her bag and prepared a variety of scenarios:

A: It's not real:

1. Adrian - under stress, over-sensitive and a little paranoid connected unrelated incidents in London and invented those in Germany to gain sympathy. From??? Me? Holger?

2. Holger - London events weren't connected but Adrian's vulnerability gave Holger an opportunity to act as protector. Isolated him in a place he knew well and tampered with the video footage.

3. Daan – amused by Adrian's fears, plays practical jokes to add to the alarm, returning to "find" his own dog. In which case, Adrian is not in the best place but at least not likely to suffer physical harm.

B: It is real:

4. An ex-boyfriend – perhaps unable to deal with rejection, own sexuality, collision of faith and love sets out to punish his former lover. Holger dressing as a nun?

5. An admirer – perspective or circumstances make him resent the temptation and act as avenger.

6. A nun – taking the hard line against homosexuality decides to pick a gay man at random to terrorise.

The Kloster, or convent of St Ursula, had plenty of hard lines, but she hadn't found any connection to Holger or Adrian.

Her food arrived. A delicate citrus aroma met her nostrils and the artful presentation displayed the dish at its most appetising, rather than hiding a miserly portion with pretentious flair. The dish, the wine and muted ambience of the carriage brought a smile to her lips. The kind of moment which tempted one into a selfie. *Look at me!* She dismissed the idea with a snort and tucked into the mash.

After her meal, she returned once again to the toilets to make a call, this time to a taxi service in Westerland. She spelled her name and gave them Daan's address. By the time she returned to her seat, there were just under two hours of the journey remaining. She switched her phone to silent, but put it in her jacket so vibrations would wake her, and settled down for a post-prandial nap. It was essential to be one of the first off the train.

The smell of frying still filled the house. Adrian opened the kitchen window while rinsing the plates in the sink but the blast of minus-five wind soon changed his mind. Daan made coffee and they sat in front of the fire in the same desultory gloom which had hung over the meal.

"That was a great dinner," said Daan, again.

"Yeah, you said. I couldn't really taste it."

Daan nodded. "It was good, trust me. Adrian, there is nothing more you can do. Beatrice is right. Someone is trying to scare you. Meanwhile you're safe here with me and Mink. Tomorrow you can join Beatrice in Hamburg to fly back to London. First job in the morning is to visit the police station to discuss that SMS."

"Also known as death threat."

"Also known as Stupid Message Shit. Come on. What do you want to do? Sit here shivering in fear and let this freak achieve his aim, or carry on with life and ignore him?"

A sharp report like a bursting balloon came from the direction of Mink's back end. She whipped her head around to the source of the sound. Both men laughed.

"Fish as well as bones?" asked Adrian.

"Bones, fish, peas, everything makes Mink fart. Talking of digestion, I want a drink to help me sleep. Have one with me."

"Akvavit? I don't think so."

Daan leapt to his feet and rummaged in a cupboard. "Not akvavit. This is different. Bliss in a glass. Stay there."

He clattered about in the kitchen as Adrian checked his phone. Nothing. He brought up the message again. YOUR NO SINNER. A SINNER CAN REPENT. THE DEVIL MUST BE DESTROYED. 'Your' no sinner. Not 'You're'. A rushed typo or an error? A non-native speaker of English? An anti-grammar troll? He recalled the graffiti on his shop – HERE SODOMY. Something unnatural about the syntax, something mere millimetres off...

"Daan's Dangerous Liaison!" Daan burst into the room with such energy, Mink jumped to her feet, her tail wagging. "*Nichts für dich.* You can't have any. Well, maybe some milk."

"Milk? We're having hot chocolate?" Adrian asked.

"No. My version of a Dangerous Liaison is Cointreau and chocolate milk with a dash of cinnamon. You will love it."

"Sounds revolting. Surely it will curdle?"

"Wait and see." He poured a healthy measure of Cointreau into two scratched glass tumblers, shook the bottle of chocolate milk and filled them to the brim. Then added a sprinkle of cinnamon.

"Taste it."

Adrian bent to take a sip. "That *is* nice. Dangerously innocent."

"Exactly. A Dangerous Liaison to send you to bed happy. *Prost*!"

"*Prost*!" The warmth of the orange liqueur permeated the silky sweetness of the milk and comforting spice. Adrian wondered why he'd never discovered this before.

Daan settled back with a smile. "Jochi introduced me to the idea of a Dangerous Liaison. It should have Kahlua and other ingredients but we adapted it to use what we had. We were camping in Zealand and this was the only luxurious thing we experienced in two weeks."

"You were in New Zealand?" Adrian asked.

"Old Zealand. We travelled all over Denmark and Germany trying to get laid. Then our first weekend in Sweden, we both lost our cherries. That country will always have a special place in my heart."

Adrian laughed at Daan's wistful expression. "Who's Jochi?"

"Joachim, Holger's brother! I showed you the photo. He must have told you about Joachim. Those two... I love them both like family. We were all born in the same year and they're the closest thing to brothers I ever had."

Mink sat up and stared into Daan's face. She dropped her nose but kept her eyes on him, as if she were looking over a pair of spectacles.

"*Was willst du*?" he said. He hauled himself out of the chair and poured a glug of milk into the dog's bowl. She waited till he had finished and began to drink.

"She's got you well trained," Adrian observed with a yawn.

Daan nodded. "It's the eyes. She hexes me and I have no choice but to obey." He topped up Adrian's glass. "One more Dangerous Liaison before bed. It will help us sleep. Yes, summers on Sylt were always Holger, Joachim and Daan the Dane. Every year we had a project, got in trouble, broke bones, made discoveries and grew up a little. My parents only saw me at bedtime. Right after breakfast, I cycled across to the Waldmann house." His face in the firelight radiated happy summer memories.

The Cointreau was working its magic. Laughter bubbled up from Adrian's stomach. A sleepy relaxation lulled him into an almost horizontal position on the sofa as he pictured the two blond boys and their dark Danish friend growing, experimenting and bonding. For the first time, he regretted being an only child.

"What does Joachim do for a living?"

"He's a master carpenter. Teaches apprentices how to make furniture. He and Holger have a way of encouraging people to learn. Holger with his instruments, Joachim with his furniture. It's funny if you think about it. All three of us grew up to work with wood."

"And their sister?"

"God knows." He laughed, throwing his head back. "Actually, God is the only one who does know. She's a bride of Christ."

"A what?"

"She took holy orders. That's why she won't accept Holger's sexuality. It's against the scriptures so he must confess his sins, repent and be pardoned or cast out forever. I tell you, the language she uses, it's mediaeval."

Adrian sat up, all warmth and comfort draining from him. "Holy orders? You mean to tell me she's a..."

"Nun? Oh yes." His laughter died in his throat as he caught Adrian's expression. "Oh shit."

A gentle hand shook Beatrice's shoulder and she opened her eyes. An elderly woman pointed to the window. "Westerland. *Endstation*."

Beatrice jerked upright. The carriage was empty, her back was stiff and her eyes gummy. She'd slept through their arrival. Passengers had departed and had it not been for this kindly lady, she'd still be snoring.

"*Danke*," she said, gathered her things and scrambled to her feet. Holger would be long gone. All she could hope for was the cab driver would still be waiting. She stumbled onto the platform, still not fully awake and followed the sign for the taxi rank. As she turned the corner, yawning and cold, she collided with someone coming in the other direction. The impact knocked her sideways and she fell onto her side, dropping her handbag. Pain pulsed through her hip and elbow as a hand reached down to help her up.

"Beatrice?"

"Holger!"

He pulled her upright and retrieved her handbag, his expression both solicitous and surprised. The temperature drop after just waking up was cruel, so Beatrice brushed herself off and dragged her coat on, trying to gather her thoughts.

"What are you doing here?" he asked, handing over her bag.

"Protecting Adrian. And you?" Her tone was aggressive, partly because she'd been caught out, partly because she'd just woken up.

"The same." He shook his head. "No, not only that. I want to stop a person I love doing something stupid, but it's the same thing. We must get to Daan's place as soon as we can. The next bus isn't due for twenty minutes. That's why I came running back this way to see if there were any taxis."

"I booked one earlier but he might have given up on me."

Thankfully, the cab was still waiting and after Holger confirmed their destination, the driver took them off in the direction of the west coast.

Holger glanced at his watch. "We'll be there in half an hour."

"So will you please tell me what the hell is going on?"

His eyes rested on hers for a second then stared beyond her head, out into the freezing night.

"Holger? Talk to me. If you know anything about what's been happening to Adrian, you'd better tell me now."

"It is not me, Beatrice. I am not the person trying to scare him. I'm another victim. Earlier this year, I had a very similar experience. My way of dealing with it was to ignore it and hope it would go away. Not cowardice but a specific strategy. If these people get no reaction, they move on to the next target. This person is imbalanced and delusional, but not dangerous."

"You know who it is?"

"Yes. It's my sister."

Chapter 28

By the time Adrian had told Daan the whole story, from his first sighting of the nun opposite his shop to the crucifix wedged in the door, the fire had died to nothing and the chocolate milk was empty. Daan was horrified at the level of fear Adrian had undergone while he'd taken such a casual attitude.

"Shit, I'm sorry. I showed more concern for the dog. Holger said to keep an eye on you, that's all. No one told me what was going on."

Adrian shook his head, his gaze absorbed by the embers in the grate. "No one knew what was going on. I'm still not sure myself. If it's really Holger's sister and she's trying to frighten me off, how does she know so much? My shop, my flat, my mobile number. How did she know I was here? Who's helping her?"

The room fell silent as both men considered the implications.

Daan spoke. "At least we know she's not dangerous. Patti is sly and sneaky and very good at mind games. But the worst she can do is make you afraid. Tomorrow we'll report her to the police and make her stop this bullshit."

Adrian closed his eyes and took a huge breath, exhaling with immense weariness. "The funny thing is, for an inveterate drama queen, this is not my style. Ask Beatrice. I hate being tense and freaked out and nervy. All I want is to go home to my own little rat run, drink good wine, cook lovely food and sleep with gorgeous men. I don't judge other people's choices. Well, apart from clothes, soft furnishings and tastes in music. Whoever she is and whatever her beliefs, she has no right to judge me. Seriously, I am sick and tired of being scared."

Daan heaved himself across the sofa, looped an arm around Adrian's shoulders and pulled him into a sideways hug. His beard bristled against Adrian's temple.

"I'm giving you the night off. Tonight, you will not be scared. I was going to make up a bed for you on the couch, but I changed my mind. You will sleep in with me and Mink. With me and her either side, you'll be safe as houses. Apart from the farts and the snoring, it'll be the best night's sleep you ever had."

Adrian relaxed into laughter and Mink wedged her nose between them, eager for her share of affection.

After they cleared up the kitchen, Daan locked the doors while Adrian got ready for bed. The wind rattling at the bathroom windows didn't bother him as he cleaned his teeth, so mellow did he feel. His face in the mirror looked a bit more than mellow, if he was being honest. Certainly soft around the edges, thanks to the Cointreau. In the living-room, Daan clattered around raking the ashes of the fire, locking the doors and speaking unintelligible words to Mink. The bedroom was cold in comparison to the fireside sofa, so Adrian dived under the layers: a duvet, a pleated quilt and a sheepskin. He curled up to fend off the chills, wishing he'd kept his socks on as well as his T-shirt and boxers. The bottom edge of the bed bounced and Mink landed beside his feet. She circled the same spot a few times, scratching the sheepskin into shape before settling with a heavy sigh on Adrian's feet. He smiled at her but the blue eyes had closed.

Daan yawned and scratched himself as he emerged from the bathroom. "Be warned. She sleeps down there for about half an hour, then she gets cold and comes up here to get as close as she can and shares my pillow. If you wake up and find you can't move, you've been Minked." He got into bed and switched off the lamp.

"She's the best hot water bottle ever. Goodnight Daan. And thanks for everything."

"Sleep well. We've got a busy day tomorrow. Goodnight."

The taxi rolled along the coast road, its headlights swooping across the dunes, reminding Beatrice of Ingmar Bergman landscapes.

"I don't understand. Why on earth is your sister terrorising Adrian? And how long have you known about it?"

"I suspected that evening after the zoo. When he told us the details of what was happening, too many elements pointed to her. She joined a convent years ago and has very strong views on sin. In her weird way of looking at the world, Adrian is to blame for my sexuality. When I told my family, she did the same kind of thing to me. Sending me leaflets about the church's view on homosexuality, offering to pray for me, asking me to repent, generally freaking me out. Then I found out she was in Hamburg. You see, I have a wall in my studio where I pin pictures, photos and so on."

Beatrice said nothing, glad of the darkness to hide her blush.

"After a while, I noticed certain things were going missing. Usually postcards from Adrian. Or pictures of the two of us together. I kept replacing them, they kept disappearing. She can be very determined."

"Why didn't you tell him?"

"I had to speak to her first. To be sure. That's why I suggested Adrian get out of the line of fire while I dealt with her. Unfortunately, when I went to the convent, they told me she'd been asked to leave over two months ago. Her behaviour, they said, was not suited to a place of prayer and contemplation. I had no idea where she was, so I contacted her via her blog."

"She has a blog?"

"Her withdrawal from the secular world did not include the virtual. She used to run the convent's website until she became too extreme. Now she posts weekly updates or rants against every aspect of modern life. I sent her an email asking her to leave Adrian alone and explaining he did not 'turn me gay'. I told her she could spend the rest of her life chasing away any man that came near me, but it wouldn't change who I am." He slipped a hand into his padded jacket and pulled out a folded sheet of paper. "Today, I got a reply."

"And?"

"It's in German so I'll paraphrase. She accuses me of unnatural sins and offers me redemption. If I renounce evil and embrace Christ, I can be forgiven. But for the devil that turned me from the path of righteousness, there can be nothing but destruction. He must burn in hell forever."

"Good Lord. What kind of woman is she?"

Holger gave a helpless shrug. "I don't really know her any more. Even before I came out, we didn't get along. My brother and I were closer to Daan than to her. Then when she got obsessed with the church, it got worse. I don't have a problem with religion, unless she tries to pressure me to 'find Jesus' and 'save myself from earthly torment.' I cannot have that kind of conversation."

"Rhetoric of drama. Extremists love it," Beatrice huffed.

Holger looked at his watch again. "She's certainly an extremist. I feel many things for my sister: pity, incomprehension, sadness and even occasionally, loss. But before now, I never felt fear."

"You think it was her at the house on Thursday night?"

Holger gave her a level look. "It was someone with a key, who removed family photos and replaced them with a crucifix. I checked all the security camera footage. No sign of her, or anyone else. But she knows that system better than all of us, because she was the one who had it installed. We used to call her Paranoid Patti."

"When was the last time she was at the house?" asked Beatrice.

"In November, I think. I didn't know she used it any more.

My grandparents say she has never asked their permission, but a neighbour saw her last month. She must have stayed up there when she got kicked out of the convent. She has a key. We all do."

"Holger, if you think she's dangerous, perhaps we should call the local police. Do you really think she is capable of doing more than scaring people? Would she hurt you?" She reached for her phone.

"I don't think so. But she's still here, on Sylt, watching." He lifted the paper in his hand. "She rages at me for allowing 'that pervert' into our grandparents' house and talks about purging the place of his sin. What worries me is that she must have seen Adrian with Daan."

Beatrice snapped her head round to stare at him. "She hates Daan too?"

"No, that's the problem." Holger exhaled and shook his head. "He was her first love. But he couldn't stand her. We were all young and stupid, thoughtless teenagers. Patti took rejection badly and became very bitter. That's why I came back to talk to them. I don't want to alarm anyone, but they need to be aware that she's here. She's irrational and angry and I just don't know how her mind works. I have no idea what she's planning to do." His eyes were as bleak as the coastline.

"Holger, I'm sorry, but I would feel better if you called the police."

Beatrice saw defeat in the angle of his head. "All right. We can't handle this on our own."

She squeezed his shoulder and handed him her phone.

The bed was bouncing. Not like an earthquake kind of judder, more an irregular bumping as if someone was trying to heave it over. Adrian opened his eyes and tried to shake off sleep. Something feathery brushed his face in the darkness. He flinched. A muffled grunt to his right reacted to the next bounce. All he could make out was a weight on the bed and a strange snuffling. His breath quickened.

"Daan?"

The sounds stopped, the mattress beside him sank and something cold and moist touched his face. He squealed and brought up a hand to defend himself. A familiar shove pushed into his palm. Mink's muzzle. She prodded again, less playfully, and Adrian protested. Then she barked, right in his ear.

He inhaled sharply in fright. That was when he smelt it.

Gas.

He wrestled his way out of the covers and shook Daan. It was like rousing a black bear. Mink leapt to the floor, her claws clattering on the wood.

"Daan! Daan! Come on!" The smell was stronger now he was upright.

"DAAN! Wake up now!"

"*Was ist?*"

Adrian sensed him turn and roll towards the lamp. "NO! I can smell gas. Do not turn on the light! We have to get out. Please move!"

The bed seemed to heave upwards as Daan sat up.

"*Scheisse!* Out the back door. Mink, *wo bist du*? Grab a blanket, let's go."

They fumbled out of the bedroom and into the passage, where enough faint moonlight shone to indicate the door. The smell was thick and noxious. Mink whined and scratched until Daan found the key. Adrian's panic rose as the fumes filled his nose. He couldn't remember if you should get lower or higher with gas. His shoulder brushed against a rail of jackets and he scooped up an armful, his head beginning to throb.

Mink whipped her way through the door before it was fully ajar. Adrian and Daan ran after her, leaving the door wide open, and raced over coarse grass and shingle until they stumbled down the beach side of a dune. Panting and shaking, they collapsed into the sand. The heat of exertion and adrenalin in an outside temperature of minus seven degrees evaporated faster than it took for their breathing to return to normal. Without speaking, they shared out the coats, wearing some, sitting on others. Daan searched the pockets of each garment while Adrian lured Mink closer by patting a spot next to him. She gave in, but sat bolt upright, still tense.

"Are you OK?" Daan asked.

"Yeah. Shaken. You?"

Daan sat back. "One hell of a headache."

"What do we do now?"

"Get away from the house, keep warm, call for help. We have no phones or shoes. That's bad. But we have winter coats and I found a torch, gloves, a couple of lighters, a bunch of tissues and some chocolate."

"Should we go up to the road and flag down a passing car?"

"There's no traffic at this time of night and the nearest neighbours are around two kilometres away. The quickest way to get help is the radio on the boat."

"How are we going to get out there? You don't seriously want us to get in the sea?"

"Not us, just me. I don't want to either, but I have no choice as the dinghy is back at the house. It's too dangerous for you and Mink. I can't look after you two as well as wade out there in bare feet. You stay on the beach and light a fire. Not here, we're still too close. Let's move."

Adrian's feet were stiff with cold. He scrambled upright and gathered the coats, with a glance back at the top of the dune.

"Adrian, come on! The house could blow at any second with the amount of gas in there. The only reason it hasn't gone up yet is because we left the back door open. As soon as the generator kicks in or any other thing sparks, it's toast. I have no idea how far a gas explosion will throw debris. We must get farther away. Mink! *Fuss!*"

He snapped his fingers and Mink trotted to his heel, her tail tucked between her legs. The three trudged down the beach, each cowed against the fear of what was behind them.

The taxi driver was unhappy about the pot-holed track so dropped them at the top of the lane. Cold pierced Beatrice's coat the minute she exited the warm interior of the cab. Her mother's voice returned. *If you don't take it off indoors, you won't feel the benefit.* She surveyed their semi-visible surroundings. The moon played searchlight tricks, offering teasing glimpses of the landscape before clouds concealed everything like a magician's cloak.

Daan's boatyard bore no advertising, not even a sign, just a rough track leading to a hollow. You couldn't even see the house from the road. The red tail-lights of the taxi faded into the distance and Beatrice switched on her Maglite. She crunched across the stony, pot-holed ground beside Holger, illuminating the path ahead in steady sweeps. Despite his confident step down the track, Holger maintained a tense silence.

In a break between the clouds, the house hove into view along with a scrubby yard rather than a garden. A large shape to the right seemed to be a breeze-block garage, although Daan's Jeep was parked right in front of the house. The wind lashed Beatrice's face, whipping strands of hair into her eyes and strafing her skin. With a grudging sense of relief, she saw that up ahead wooden steps facilitated access on foot. Rough, mismatched planks, but infinitely preferable to the pitted track.

She glanced upwards to see the cloudbank moving north, taking the wind with it to leave a starlit sky and the promise of frost. The moon added an eerie wash to the spotlight of her torch.

Down in the hollow, not a single window was lit in Daan's squat shack. If they weren't home, where were they? It was barely midnight. As they started down the steps, Holger placed a hand on her arm. He pointed. Away to the right, far down the beach near the sea, a small fire was burning.

"There they are!" Holger's smile was audible. "I bet they're drinking beer on the beach. In December! Poor Adrian. This is a typical Daan rite of passage." He cupped his hands to his mouth and yelled. "HAAALLLOOOO!"

Bitter cold, exhaustion, stupidly dangerous male rituals and the downright foolhardy nature of the entire enterprise blew a fuse in Beatrice's patience.

"Holger, don't be ridiculous! They won't hear you from this distance. I'll call Adrian's mobile. Can we get in the house?"

Holger seemed oblivious to her sharp tone. "Sure. I know where he keeps a spare key. But I'm not sure your mobile will work down there. Daan always has problems with the signal at his place."

"Fine, I'll try from up here or flash the torch to attract their attention."

"Yes and I'll go inside and use the house phone." His boots sounded solid on the wood as he followed the steps towards the house.

She yelled after him. "Put the kettle on!"

He gave her the thumbs up.

The cold bit at her fingers as soon as she took off her gloves. She wedged the torch under her arm to reach for her phone and pushed her damp hair from her face. The Maglite beam shone against the back of Daan's garage. In the pool of light was a disembodied female face, staring back at her with saucer eyes. Beatrice jolted in fright and the torch fell to the ground. She scrabbled to pick it up and directed it back at the same spot, her breath short. A black-clad figure raced out from the shadow of the garage away from her and towards the house. An unearthly scream ripped through the air, sending a primal shiver through her scalp and spine. She froze and heard a thud, a scuffle and a peculiar hiss. She swept her light across the hollow below but the vehicle obscured her view. She hurried down the steps, her skin prickling with fear, crept along the wall of the garage and listened.

"Holger?"

The next second, an almighty bang followed by a white blast punched her backwards, lifting her off her feet and slamming her onto the ground. Her torch somersaulted off into the sky.

All the air left her chest and around her there was nothing but silence. Seconds passed before she managed to haul in a breath. She curled instinctively into a ball, her lungs heaving, her nostrils full of singeing heat and the stench of burning hair. Liquid ran into her eyes and beyond the echoing ring in her ears, she heard the crackle and spit of flames.

Chapter 29

The fire was starting to take. Adrian pushed another piece of driftwood into the pile and leaned forward to feel the warmth. Mink's attention remained on the sea, at the precise spot where Daan had gone into the waves. She had sat and stayed, as per his instructions, but didn't take her eyes off the huge black bear of a man as he waded out, swearing at the freezing water. For the hundredth time, Adrian switched his gaze between three points. The boat; still no lights. The house; dark and silent. The fire; damp wood burning and giving off more a sense of comfort than actual heat. He stood, straining his eyes for any hint of Daan, but the shifting midnight ocean camouflaged him perfectly.

He glanced back at the house and did an immediate double take. A shaft of light was coming down the track. He checked out to sea, where the boat bobbed on the tide, its cabin still unlit. Had Daan managed to radio for help already? The moon came out, turning the beach grey and shedding enough light for Adrian to pick out two figures making their way down to Daan's house. They stopped and Adrian caught a noise, as if someone had yelled. For the first time, Mink's ears twitched and she looked back up over the dunes, a low growl in her throat.

"Stay, Mink. Sit."

Whoever it was, they shouldn't go any closer to the house. Adrian waved his arms, feeling futile and helpless. He put two fingers in his mouth and whistled. Pathetic. The torch wobbled about and one figure moved out of sight. They must have heard him! One of them was coming down to the beach. Adrian looked out at the boat and with a wash of relief saw the cabin lights on. He couldn't see Daan at this distance but knew he must have made it.

"He's safe, Mink! Help is on the way." He selected a few more sticks and was just dropping them on the fire when a horrible screech reached his ears. His whole body seemed to drop several degrees in temperature. He reassured himself. It was an owl. A seagull. Some kind of predator killing a rodent. Then he saw Mink's ears flat against her head, her hackles in spiky ridges along her back, staring up at the house and his mouth went dry.

At that moment, the night exploded. A shocking boom echoed across the beach and a ball of flame erupted above the dunes. A wave of heat washed over him and strange splatting sounds began hitting the sand. He grabbed Mink's collar and they ran, away from the shower of objects and into the sea. The icy water was brutal but Adrian pulled Mink further until he was thigh-deep in the sea and she was swimming. He stopped, clutching the dog to his chest as her feet kept paddling. While missiles hissed into the shallower water, his focus was on the fire blazing above the dunes. He waited till he could hear no more falling debris and carried Mink back onto the beach, his teeth chattering and legs numb. She shook herself, spattering him with wet drops he could barely feel. Adrian peered out at the boat. Still no sign of Daan but the boat's headlights came on, adding to the illumination of the beach. He could stand it no longer.

"Mink, come with me. *Fuss*!" He turned to the dunes and broke into a run.

Adrenalin and nerves charged his veins as he approached the scene and the cold no longer seemed to matter. He pushed up the sandy bank in the direction of the garage, Mink hard on his heels. Close up, the damage was shocking. Over half the house had gone. The back section, where he'd been asleep less than an hour ago, was still standing, but judging by the ferocity of the fire, it wouldn't be for long. He recalled Daan's voice. '*You sleep with me and Mink... you'll be safe as houses.*'

Thick black clouds of smoke rolled inland and the Jeep lay on its side, its windows blown out. He kept away from the heat, creeping around the back of the garage, his hand on Mink's collar. A series of small explosions stopped him in his tracks and he heard the sound of broken glass shattering. Mink balked, so he gave her a reassuring stroke. But she stiffened and sniffed, the tension in her body tangible. Adrian's own hairs rose. There was something there, lying on the ground.

It moved and Mink leapt backwards like a spooked cat. Whatever it was let out an odd moan, like an elderly person does when getting to their feet. Not agony, but discomfort. Adrian despaired, faced with the idea of administering first aid, in German, in pitch darkness while trying to control an unnerved dog.

"Umm, hello? *Guten Tag*? Are you OK?"

"Adrian?"

He started in disbelief and reached out a tentative hand. "Beatrice? What in the name of... ?" He touched something warm and heard her suck in air through her teeth.

"Sorry, sorry. Are you hurt?"

"Adrian, listen to me. Holger's down there. Much nearer to the house. Call emergency services. Don't you go any closer."

"I don't have my phone, but Daan's radioing for help. Are you hurt?"

She shifted and drew a ragged breath.

"Beatrice! What is it?"

"Phone... my jacket. Help him! Help Holger!"

Her voice cracked in desperation. Adrian ran his hands along her coat and located a lump in her pocket. He'd just withdrawn the device when he sensed Mink bound away, back down the beach. Out of the shadow of the garage, moonlight shone on the figure of Daan, powering up the dune, wearing a wetsuit. Sirens grew louder, overcoming the noise of the burning house and Adrian watched five vehicles approach.

"They're already here, Beatrice."

She didn't respond.

"Beatrice, talk to me." His cold hands fumbled for hers, trying to find her pulse. A fire engine came down the track, its headlights penetrating the shadows. Adrian gasped when he saw Beatrice's face. Her eyes were closed and a tributary pattern spread from her forehead, like Leigh Bowery face paint. Except this was not makeup.

Chapter 30

The Westerland Klinik, quiet during the winter, was having an unexpectedly busy night. Adrian received a full check-up and a cup of coffee. The nurse answered all his questions with great patience. Beatrice was still in surgery. No, she couldn't say how long it would take. Daan was fine and waiting for him in reception. She had no information on Holger, because he was not being treated at this hospital.

When Adrian was given the all-clear, he returned to reception to find Daan. But the only person in the waiting area was Herr Rieder, the same police officer who had come to the Waldmann house. He stood up.

"Hello again, Mr Harvey. Is everything in order?"

"I'm fine, apart from being worried sick about the others. Where's Daan?"

"He's at the police station, helping Herr Weiss understand what happened. He's the detective in charge and he would like to talk to you too."

"First I need to make sure Beatrice is OK. I want to wait till she's out of theatre. Do you know where they've taken Holger? He's not being treated here, they said."

Herr Rieder dropped his eyes. "Herr Weiss can give you more information. I can tell you the dog is also at the police station."

Adrian gripped his arm. "Please tell me. Is Holger...?" The word stuck in his throat. He swallowed.

"Two people were airlifted to Hamburg with severe injuries. I have no further updates, but if you come to the station, they can tell you more."

A headache loomed with the remorseless progress of a steamroller. Tension, exhaustion and the knowledge that things were far from over made him want to cry. He closed his eyes, imagined lying down on a cream-coloured sofa, covering his head with a pillow and just drifting off on a cloud of cinnamon.

"Mr Harvey?" A doctor approached, with overnight beard growth and a white coat over jeans and trainers. "You're waiting for news of Ms Stubbs?"

Adrian jerked to his feet. "Yes! Is she OK?"

"It seems so. She suffered a fractured bone in her forearm, which required setting. There are several skull contusions resulting in concussion. In addition, various abrasions and some bruising. We'll monitor her over the next few hours and do further tests. But my opinion is that with care and rest, she will make a good recovery." He looked at his watch. "Come back this afternoon and you will have the possibility to see her."

Adrian thanked him and drew on the last reserves of his energy to accompany Herr Rieder to the police station. At least this time he was not under suspicion.

Morning broke, sunlight forcing its way into the interview room. An officer brought a new pot of coffee, more bottles of water and this time, warm breakfast rolls. Daan immediately tore into one and asked for some butter. A sour caffeine bitterness in Adrian's stomach made him refuse until the smell of fresh bread proved irresistible.

Once the separate interview sessions had been completed, the atmosphere was collegial and workmanlike. Somehow, the normality of morning took the edge off the weary piecing together of events. Although the two detectives and Rieder joined in with the impromptu breakfast, the questions kept coming. The same questions already answered, alone in other rooms. What time was it when they left the house? How long did it take Daan to get to the boat? How many people could Adrian see coming down the track? Who had a key to Daan's house? Where is the gas tank? How is it possible the emergency call was made before the house blew up? Adrian and Daan answered all the questions again, only foundering when it came to the whys.

Why would Beatrice Stubbs and Holger Waldmann travel to Daan's house at midnight without warning them of their arrival? Why was Patricia Waldmann at the scene? Why would anyone want to poison them with carbon monoxide? Why had she attacked her own brother? Why had the house exploded?

They didn't know.

After the long lonely silence of the night, the station had woken up. Three times, an officer knocked at the door with a message for one or the other detectives. Each time, Adrian held his breath, willing it to be news of Holger. Eventually, it was.

Herr Rieder showed the message to the two detectives, both of whom scanned the words with impassive expressions. Then he cleared his throat.

"I'm sorry to say it is bad news."

Daan gripped Adrian's hand but kept his focus on the police officer.

"Patricia Waldmann was pronounced dead at six-twenty this morning. Internal injuries caused a fatal haemorrhage."

"What about Holger?" Adrian asked, his voice constricted and high-pitched.

Rieder glanced back at the printout. "Holger Waldmann – third degree burns on 10% of his body. Condition stable. Next of kin notified."

Daan shoved back his chair and got to his feet. "We must go. We've done all we can here. Please bring me my dog. We're leaving."

Adrian couldn't leave Beatrice, Daan couldn't leave Mink. So they compromised. Daan left for Hamburg while Adrian stayed the night in the hospital's accommodation for relatives, sharing a narrow single bed with the flatulent husky. Other than walking the dog, he spent his time at Beatrice's bedside, arguing.

In spite of the stitches down her forehead, half her head obscured by a bandage and her arm in a cast, her stubborn defiance did not waver. She refused to let him talk to Matthew.

"If I was him, I'd want to know," Adrian insisted.

"No. He can't do anything from Devon and God knows I don't want him travelling all the way up here. I'm fine. I'll be out tomorrow or the next day. This looks worse than it is."

"Well, it looks terrible."

"Thank you. Adrian, please let me deal with this my way. I promise I'll talk to Matthew. But I'm going to play this down and you may not contradict me, do you hear? Go and visit Holger then get back to London. Once they've done the scan, I'll follow you. I want to see Holger myself and apologise in person."

"Me too."

Daan returned on Monday afternoon with positive news about Holger's condition and they switched places. Adrian prepared to depart for Hamburg, leaving Daan in charge of his obstreperous neighbour who insisted on getting out of bed and trundling around the hospital at every opportunity.

It was a strange farewell. In such a short time, this huge hairy man and his beautiful dog had become his close friends. On the station platform, he dug his fingers into the thick ruff of hair around Mink's neck and scratched. She leaned into him, her back leg kicking. With one last stroke of her muzzle and a look into her trusting china blue eyes, he said goodbye.

Daan had obviously spotted the welling tears and saved them both embarrassment by opening his arms for a hug.

"Come back in the summer. We're going to rebuild the house. Me, Holger and Joachim. Another pair of hands would be very welcome. Plus I never did give you the island tour."

"I will. I don't need asking twice. In fact, I'm already looking forward to it."

Daan released him and looked down at Mink. "She's going to miss you. So am I. Look after yourself, OK?"

"You too. Take care of Beatrice for me."

"Don't worry, you can trust me. See you in the summer! And Adrian?"

"What?"

"When you come back, can you bring me a Cornish pasty?"

As the train pulled away, Adrian strained to catch the very last glimpse of the hairy pair on the platform. Daan was still waving.

Chapter 31

How to look hot when seeing the most handsome man in the world? Head partially shaved with cumbersome bandage, stitches down forehead, left arm in sling and burnt-off eyelashes. In the grand cinematic tradition, set in the monochrome romance of a German railway station, Beatrice imagined Clark Gable meeting the Bride of Frankenstein.

Unlike all the other passengers on the train, Jan Stein didn't flinch when he saw her. He was waiting at the end of the platform, looking chiselled and elegant in a long grey coat. When he spotted her, he smiled and came to take her suitcase. He didn't even attempt a greeting over the constant noise of the Hauptbahnhof and simply guided her outside to his car. Once the door closed, he turned to look at her, his stare unreadable.

"Last time we spoke, you asked me to call you Beatrice Bloody Fool. Then you left for Sylt, alone and without back-up, to walk straight into a life-threatening situation which left one person dead and another seriously injured. Every single judgement call you made earns you the name Beatrice Bloody Fool ten times over."

Beatrice lay back against the headrest, too tired even for sarcasm. "You're right and I'm sorry. You can call me all the names you want and I'll accept every one. Thank you for meeting me."

"You're welcome. How's your head?"

She touched her bandage. “Bit of a mess.”

“Inside or out?”

“Both. Can I go and see Holger now?”

He drove through the city with no questions, no probing glances, no more comments on her behaviour. The silence acted as an unguent, soothing and healing.

She was the first to speak. “I don’t suppose there’s any news of the art collector?”

Stein gave her a sideways smile.

“There is?”

“Yes, there is. Tomas never gives up. Dutch police analysed all the communications logged by the art theft ‘agency’. The collector was using various re-routing IP addresses to hide his tracks. One was in St Petersburg, and another in Amsterdam.”

Beatrice snapped her head up and wished she hadn’t. “De Vries!”

“You’re spoiling my story. Tomas remembered what you said in your report about de Vries and his business interests in Russia. He passed the information on to Meyer. This time, Meyer took him seriously. The BKA followed up that line of enquiry and Dutch intelligence forces made an arrest early this morning. Geert de Vries is an art dealer in more ways than one. He has a private gallery filled with stolen artwork on his country estate in Amersfoort. Some but not all of the paintings have been recovered.”

“What an absolute swine! Getting his own paintings stolen, claiming insurance and then selfishly depriving anyone else of the pleasure. His greed beggars belief. Will the Köbels get their picture back?”

“I don’t know yet. I have no information on which paintings they seized. But I hope so.”

“So do I.” Beatrice wondered if that sweet woman’s blank face might react to seeing her favourite picture again.

Stein continued. “Not only that, but Waring has agreed to a plea bargain and given a full statement, implicating seven other high-profile businessmen in arranging to have their own artworks stolen. It seems we lifted the lid on an international operation. Red faces from here to Washington."

"But bloody Waring weasels his way out of a jail sentence by squealing on everyone else?"

"He'll serve a few months, I expect. Somewhere comfortable."

Beatrice snorted and looked out at the city streets, the sparkling shop windows, Christmas lights and shoppers. For the first time since her arrival, she missed the familiarity of London, of Matthew, even of Hamilton.

She spoke. "Human nature still surprises me."

"Me too. Which is why we need people like Tomas, Margrit and Rudi. They still have a lust for justice."

Beatrice studied his fixed expression and accepted the confidence without question. She thought of DS Pearce and his intellect, Dawn and her sympathy, Ranga and his open mind, all battling the endless effluent of London's underground.

As if reading her mind, Stein spoke. "I booked you on the 16.40 flight to London City. I can take you to the airport when you've finished at the hospital."

"That's kind of you. But a detective has better things to do with his time than ferry me around. I'll call a cab when I'm ready."

He didn't speak for several minutes. "Do you want to tell me what happened at Daan's house, or would you rather not talk about it?"

"We don't have the whole story yet," she sighed. "Current theory is Patricia Waldmann got into the house via Daan's not-so-secret key and switched on the gas rings in the kitchen while Adrian and Daan were asleep. Whether she intended to cause carbon monoxide poisoning or create an explosion, we don't know. The dog woke them and they got out the back door. They ran down to the beach and Daan called the emergency services from his boat. A taxi dropped Holger and me at the end of the lane and we saw a fire on the beach. We assumed it was them and I stopped at the top of the steps to call Adrian. I sent..." she clenched her teeth and swallowed. "I sent Holger down to the house. Patricia was hiding behind the garage. I actually saw her face. Frightened the life out of me. Then she attacked Holger. The gas ignited and the house exploded, burning Holger, injuring me and killing Patricia."

Stein shook his head. "Why did she want to kill Daan and Adrian?"

Beatrice sighed more deeply. "God only knows."

The Mercedes finally peeled out of the traffic and into the hospital drive. Stein reversed into a parking bay and switched off the engine. "I'm happy to wait. I'd like to make sure..."

"... I leave the country? I promise I'll go this time. Thank you, really, but a taxi will be fine."

He came round to open her door and helped her heave herself gracelessly out. She extended her right hand.

"Thank you. For everything."

He took her hand and reached for her shoulder, his fingers squeezing gently yet with a particular pressure. "Please take good care of yourself, Beatrice. We need to keep you." Leaning closer, he brushed his lips against both her cheeks. "Goodbye. Or better, *Auf Wiedersehen*. Till we see each other again?"

He held her gaze and the magnetic pull of those eyes might have drawn her closer, had she not caught sight of her reflection in the glass doors of the hospital behind him.

"Yes, *Auf Wiedersehen* sounds about right." She dragged herself and her suitcase away.

She'd expected worse. A tent lay over Holger's legs and gauze bandages covered the lower parts of his arms. Tubes snaked under the sheets and he appeared to be hooked up to an extraordinary number of monitors. One ear and the left side of his face looked raw and painful but his eyes and smile were as genuine as ever.

She couldn't speak at first, pressing her fingers to her mouth, holding back tears which were both inconvenient and painful.

"I want to hug you," she said. "But I can't see a safe place to touch."

His voice was hoarse and breathless. "There isn't one. Virtual hug?" Holger raised his arms and shoulders a few millimetres but she could see it cost him considerable effort.

She embraced the air in front of her. "I can't tell you how relieved I am to see you. We were all so worried."

He indicated his throat and pointed to a thin tablet computer on a side table. She passed it to him and watched him use one finger to type. When he'd finished, he turned the screen to her.

The specialist says I will be fine. It is going to take some time and I don't want to think about what I would do without morphine. My worst fear was that I had permanently damaged my hands, which is not the case. There will be some scar tissue but I will be able to use them and that is the important thing. What about you?

Beatrice sat on the visitor's chair and pointed to her bandage. "Fifteen stitches and a fractured ulna, plus a few other bangs and scrapes. Good news is it gets me off work for a week. I should have been back in the office this morning."

He typed some more, his eyes reddening.

Beatrice, I am so sorry. I want to apologise to you, Adrian and Daan for this whole stupid, ugly mess.

"This mess is not your fault. You can't blame yourself. Your sister is not your responsibility. For her own twisted reasons she wanted to destroy you all, so she alone bears the guilt."

He shook his head and spoke. "She tried to save me."

"Holger, she attacked you!"

He shook his head again and typed. In a way she was glad of the enforced wait for a reply. It gave her time to control her temper.

No. She stopped me from going into the house. When she screamed, I turned around. She was dressed in black so all I saw was a white face coming at me. I stepped backwards and fell over.

She helped me up and pushed me behind the Jeep. All the time she was hissing at me to get away. When the blast came, her body took most of the impact. That's why I'm still here and she is not.

Beatrice chose not to argue. Painkillers could do funny things to the brain and even if the woman was an attempted murderer, she was still his sister. Her own speech, apologising for mistrusting him, now seemed surplus to requirements.

"You've seen Daan and Adrian, I gather? How was that?"

Half his face smiled.

Emotional! My family visited too. They said Daan and Mink should live in our place on Sylt over the winter. After I get out of hospital, I am going there to recover. My brother and I are going to help Daan build a new house, in spring, when the weather improves. Adrian plans to take a holiday and join us. I think the four of us could make a good team.

He'd added a smiley at the end. Beatrice touched a finger to his unburnt cheek, the only gesture of affection which would not cause him pain.

"Four men and a dog. Sounds wonderful. Will you invite me to the house-warming? Sorry, poor choice of phrase. How about a Phoenix Party?"

He lifted a hand in a gesture of triumph and rasped, "You can be Guest of Honour."

Chapter 32

The taxi driver who took her the final leg of the journey, from London City Airport home to Boot Street, was a wellspring of advice. The best thing for bruising was to drink pineapple juice. He should know. Twice he'd been beaten up while working nights and the last time, he tried pineapple juice. Bruises faded almost overnight. Like a charm. Beatrice should try it. She promised she would.

As she paid him and waited for her receipt, she noticed with surprise and disappointment Adrian's windows were unlit. He'd sent her a text last night to assure her of his safe arrival, so there was no call for alarm, but she'd been looking forward to a debrief and a hot dinner. He was probably still catching up at the shop. It was not yet seven o'clock. She asked the driver to leave her case in the hallway, exhausted at the thought of trying to heave it upstairs one-handed. She tipped him and trudged up to her flat.

Bless Adrian. He'd collected all her post, put the heating on and watered the plants. She opened the fridge. And to crown it all, he'd bought milk. She made a cup of tea and sat back on the sofa, savouring the sense of peace and sanctuary. Her head and neck throbbed so she lifted the weight of the sling from her shoulders and rested her cast in her lap. Just for this evening, she would ignore the pile of letters, overlook the blinking light on the answer phone and forget her promise to Dawn to phone as soon as she got home. All of it could wait till tomorrow.

Everything except Matthew. She reached for the landline, grateful it was not her right arm in plaster, about to press speed dial 1.

From the dining-table, her mobile rang. *Great minds think alike.* She got to her feet in anticipation, but the caller display showed Rangarajan Jalan. She answered.

"Hello, Ranga."

"Beatrice, I heard about your accident. How are you?"

"Could be worse. Bashed about a bit and totally shattered but glad to be home in my own flat."

"You're home already? I wasn't sure if you were fit to travel. Did your neighbour come home with you?"

"Adrian flew back yesterday."

"I mean is he with you now? Is someone there to take care of you?"

"No, but I'm fine, Ranga, really. I'm relieved to be alone and enjoying my own company."

There was a pause. "The reason for my concern is that I have some bad news and despite the awkward timing, I wanted to let you know personally."

"What do you mean, bad news?" Beatrice's mind seemed to seize up entirely, incapable of even fearing the worst.

"Superintendent Hamilton passed away this weekend."

She sat down with a thump, jolting her arm. "Hamilton is dead?"

"A terrible shock for us all, I know."

"He told me he was seriously ill, but I had no idea it would be so soon."

"None of us did, except for him. Beatrice, he chose the timing. Hamilton ended his life at a clinic in Switzerland on Friday."

Beatrice's skin cooled. "Friday? So he came to say goodbye," she whispered.

"Sorry?"

Tears stung her eyes and her face grew hot and swollen. "He came to Hamburg on Thursday. We had dinner. He told me about his illness and mentioned taking some time out. I assumed it was a holiday."

"Beatrice, are you sure you're OK?"

She swallowed. "I should have realised. It's classic Hamilton, controlling to the last. Literally." Her voice lacked any bass tones.

"Everyone said the same thing. Myself included. I only wish he'd given us the opportunity to say goodbye. At least to say thank you. But you're right, this is classic Hamilton. As always, he did things his own way."

She sniffed and dug in her pocket for a tissue. "What happens now?"

"Chief Super asked me to act up over Christmas and the board will make some decisions in January. Beatrice?"

"What?"

"Both our names are on the table as replacements. Can we talk about it, just between us, before the end of the year?"

She held the receiver away while she blew her nose.

"Of course. I think that's best. Thing is, I'll be in Devon over the Christmas holidays but let's ring-fence a breakfast meeting on the first Monday back to work."

"Perfect. Thank you. Listen, I don't know when you plan to leave for Devon, but there's a memorial service for Hamilton on Friday. Eleven o'clock. Sharp."

She released a snort of tearful laughter at Ranga's use of Hamilton-speak. "I'll be there. Thanks for letting me know, Ranga. Goodnight."

The desire for solitude instantly transformed itself into the opposite. Beatrice became a communicator. She made a series of calls.

Reassuring Matthew she was well.

"*Ready whenever you are and already steeling myself. Worse or better than the incident in Vitoria?*"

"Worse, I'm afraid. Fractured ulna. You'll have to peel all the parsnips."

"So long as you are here with me and supervising the Christmas pud, I'm sure we'll muddle along. I miss you, Old Thing."

Exchanging shocked exclamations with Dawn.

"Nope, not a bloody clue. Board must have known as he'd helped them choose a successor. Cooper's talking about organising a wreath from the whole team – want to contribute?"

"Of course I do. I'm officially on sick leave, but can we have lunch on Wednesday?"

"Deffo. I want to see your bruises. Can you drink wine?"

Checking on Adrian's whereabouts.

"Happy Hour somewhere on Dean Street. You will not believe who's at the bar right now ordering me a cocktail!"

"You're on a date?"

"Hell yeah! Detective Sergeant Quinn! The one who interviewed me after the allegations. He popped into the shop this morning to ask me out! Looks like my luck is changing! God, I so love the police."

She launched into her emails, tackling everything urgent and ditching the rest.

After more tea and a painkiller, she ran a bath. In an uncomfortable position, shower cap protecting her head wound, the cast resting on the soap shelf in the steam, grazes stinging in the warm water, she recalled every conversation she'd ever had with Hamilton, including the last one. She closed her eyes and bid him goodbye. Salty moisture – sweat or tears, she wasn't sure – slipped past her bruises into the bathwater and dissolved.

At ten to ten, she got into her pyjamas, made herself a hot chocolate and switched on the TV, ready to watch the news. While waiting for Huw Edwards, she flicked through the post, sifting it into three piles: Christmas cards, bills and junk. Some items didn't fit. A postcard from an old friend in Spain. An appointment reminder from James. A letter with a Swiss stamp on hotel stationery in familiar handwriting. With an unsteady hand, she opened the envelope and sat down to read.

Dear Beatrice

Please excuse familiarity of address.

Our conversation last night was curtailed sooner than I might have wished or there would be no need for this letter.

As you will know by now, I have taken my leave. The outcome would have been the same had I let the disease take its course, incurring pain and indignity for myself as well as inconvenience and expense for others.

This is not a decision taken heedlessly. I spent some considerable time putting my affairs in order and setting the record straight. One element of the latter required my coming to Hamburg to talk to you. However, as often happens when Beatrice Stubbs is involved, things did not go to plan. (By the way, I hope your friend is safe and well.)

I came to Hamburg firstly to apologise. For fifteen years, I have patronised, goaded and bullied you, rarely giving you the credit you deserve and worse still, never admitting the reason why. Allow me to state now that you are one of the finest detectives I have ever known and for every cowardly, selfish time I vented my frustrations on you, I suffered twice.

There is a second reason I had to speak. Fifteen years ago, one Monday morning, you joined my team. My fate was sealed. You were happily not-married to another man. I was your boss. Most of our colleagues believed I was either celibate or homosexual. Our personalities clashed and we fought like cat and dog. Nevertheless, I fell in love. For me, no other woman could ever come close to Beatrice Stubbs. When you tried to end your life, I wanted to follow. Yet as luck would have it, I go first.

You have been, for better and worse, the most powerful force in my life. From the moment we met, I loved you. If there is such a thing as a soul, I always will.

I wish you well.
Paul Hamilton

Acknowledgements

For information, advice and opinions, my gratitude to Liza Perrat, Jane Dixon-Smith, Gillian Hamer, Catriona Troth and Barbara Scott Emmett of Triskele Books. This book owes a great deal to Florian Bielmann, The Goethe Institut, Rohan Quine, Julie Lewis, Nicholas M. O'Donnell, James Lane, Perry Iles, The Tate Modern and Kunsthaus Zürich. For original inspiration, thanks to Jo Cottrell.

Also by JJ Marsh

Behind Closed Doors

"Beatrice Stubbs is a fascinating character, and a welcome addition to crime literature, in a literary and thought-provoking novel. I heartily recommend this as an exciting and intelligent read for fans of crime fiction." – Sarah Richardson, of Judging Covers

"Behind Closed Doors crackles with human interest, intrigue and atmosphere... author JJ Marsh does more than justice to the intelligent heroine who leads this exciting and absorbing chase." – Libris Reviews

"Hooked from the start and couldn't put this down. Superb, accomplished and intelligent writing. Ingenious plotting paying as much attention to detail as the killer must. Beatrice and her team are well-drawn, all individuals, involving and credible." – Book Reviews Plus

Raw Material

"I loved JJ Marsh's debut novel Behind Closed Doors, but her second, Raw Material, is even better... the final chapters are heart-stoppingly moving and exciting." Chris Curran, Amazon reviewer.

"Some rather realistic human exchanges reveal honest personal struggles concerning life's bigger questions; the abstruse clues resonate with the covert detective in me; and the suspense is enough to cause me to miss my stop." – Vince Rockston, author

Tread Softly

"The novel oozes atmosphere and JJ Marsh captures the sights, sounds and richness of Spain in all its glory. I literally salivated as I read the descriptions of food and wine. JJ Marsh is an extremely talented author and this is a wonderful novel." – Sheila Bugler, author of *Hunting Shadows*

"There are moments of farce and irony, there are scenes of friendship, tenderness and total exasperation - and underlying it all a story of corruption, brutality, manipulation and oppression with all the elements you'd expect to find in a good thriller, including a truly chilling villain. Highly recommended". – Lorna Fergusson, *FictionFire*

Cold Pressed

Editor's Choice – The Bookseller

This is J J Marsh's fourth, snappily written crime mystery featuring the feisty but vulnerable Stubbs, a most appealing character. It's all highly diverting, and an ideal read for those who like their crime with a lighter, less gruesome touch. – Caroline Sanderson, The Bookseller

Thank you for reading a Triskele Book

If you loved this book and you'd like to help other readers find Triskele Books, please write a short review on the website where you bought the book. Your help in spreading the word is much appreciated and reviews make a huge difference to helping new readers find good books.

Why not try books by other Triskele authors?
Choose a complimentary ebook when you sign up
to our free newsletter at

www.triskelebooks.co.uk/signup

If you are a writer and would like more information on writing and publishing, visit http://www.triskelebooks.blogspot.com and http://www.wordswithjam.co.uk, which are packed with author and industry professional interviews, links to articles on writing, reading, libraries, the publishing industry and indie-publishing.

Connect with us:
Email admin@triskelebooks.co.uk
Twitter @triskelebooks
Facebook www.facebook.com/triskelebooks

CPSIA information can be obtained
at www.ICGtesting.com
Printed in the USA
LVHW032322190319
611230LV00001B/156

9 783952 425862